NAKED DESIRE . . .

"I'm going for a run," Dylan said, taking off toward the woods. His people had wronged Sophie. He was convinced of that now. And still she had come home to him, of her own free will—for their son.

His wolf clawed at his spine for release. Its fury, its need, its desire for the woman who'd had the courage to return for their child was no longer controllable.

The wolf wanted out.

Having her near and within reach was akin to pain.

Perhaps it was a good thing Sophie hadn't invited him to stay, Dylan thought as he entered the forest, ripping off clothes as he walked. For if she had, he wasn't sure if he could have controlled his hunger.

It had been too long . . .

Celtic Moon

JAN DeLIMA

ACE BOOKS, NEW YORK

THE BERKLEY PUBLISHING GROUP
Published by the Penguin Group
Penguin Group (USA) LLC
375 Hudson Street, New York, New York 10014, USA

USA I Canada I UK I Ireland I Australia I New Zealand I India I South Africa I China

Penguin Books Ltd., Registered Offices: 80 Strand, London WC2R 0RL, England
For more information about the Penguin Group, visit penguin.com.

CELTIC MOON

An Ace Book / published by arrangement with the author

Ace Books are published by The Berkley Publishing Group.
ACE and the "A" design are trademarks of Penguin Group (USA) LLC.

For information, address: The Berkley Publishing Group,
a division of Penguin Group (USA) LLC,
375 Hudson Street, New York, New York 10014.

ISBN: 978-0-425-26620-5

PUBLISHING HISTORY
Ace mass-market edition / October 2013

PRINTED IN THE UNITED STATES OF AMERICA

10 9 8 7 6 5 4 3 2 1

Cover illustration by Gordon Crabb; Celtic symbols © Santi0103 & Leshik / Shutterstock.
Cover design by Diana Kolsky.
Interior text design by Kelly Lipovich.
Interior art by Jan DeLima.

This is a work of fiction. Names, characters, places, and incidents either are the product
of the author's imagination or are used fictitiously, and any resemblance to actual persons,
living or dead, business establishments, events, or locales is entirely coincidental.
The publisher does not have any control over and does not assume any responsibility for
author or third-party websites or their content.

ALWAYS LEARNING   PEARSON

To my husband

Acknowledgments

I feel very fortunate to have friends and family who have supported me throughout my writing journey. To all of you, and you know who you are, I am forever grateful to have you in my life.

There are a few who helped directly with this project whom I must mention by name, an amazing group of women I am honored to call my friends: Ann Marie, whose advice on firearms and self-defense from a woman's perspective was invaluable; Sue, an expat Brit, classicist and teacher, who is as generous with her time as she is with her knowledge; Kathy, a coworker (and cohort in crime), who always encouraged my writing; Wendy, a prolific reader with a keen eye for small details; Janet, for her sound and gentle guidance; Patricia Allen, an intelligent woman of many talents, who proofread my manuscript every time I asked. You're awesome, Patty!

Thanks also to Michelle Vega, my editor, for believing in my story, and to Grace Morgan, my literary agent, for her continual supply of patience and wisdom.

Lastly, I must acknowledge the scholars and translators throughout history who undertook the monumental endeavor of transcribing *The Mabinogion*, or *The Mabinogi*, into English. Because of their insight and dedication, the magical tales from primarily two medieval Welsh manuscripts, *The White Book of Rhydderch* and *The Red Book of Hergest*, have inspired many authors over the years. Hence, the tradition of storytelling continues . . .

I shall be until the day of doom on the face of the earth.

—Taliesin
From *The Mabinogion*
Lady Charlotte Guest Translation

One

Rhuddin Village, Maine, USA
Present Day

> *Described in a recent travel guide as, "A quiet town tucked into the base of Mount Katahdin at the end of the Appalachian Trail."*

ANOTHER WAR WAS INEVITABLE.

Dylan felt this with utter certainty. The Katahdin territory, *his* territory, had remained unspoiled over the years by human progress—due to his calculated precautions. Nature thrived in untouched glory, raw and powerful, a precious achievement during these modern times.

An achievement his enemies coveted.

"It's a message," Dylan said with deliberate calm as he watched his brother stalk across the kitchen.

"No shit," Luc snapped, throwing a crumpled ball of linen in Dylan's direction. Dressed only in a pair of faded jeans, with wild black hair tangled about bare shoulders, Luc looked just as much a predator now as he did in wolf form. His skin was absent of tattoos, indicating that he had shifted in haste, a warning to those who knew him well to tread lightly.

Dylan snatched the offending item in midair and smoothed it out on the wooden island. It was blue linen with a gold stag embroidered across the top, circled by a horned snake. The royal banner of the *Gwarchodwyr Unfed*, the Originals of their kind. *The Guardians.* Vicious, powerful, and without conscience. Self-appointed protectors of their race.

Inbred assholes, the lot of them.

He traced the hand-hewn embroidery of the banner. "Where was it found?"

"On the north ridge." A dangerous light sparked in Luc's silver eyes, promising vengeance. "Tied to the Great Oak."

The tree stood a short distance from the north entrance to their territory. Not a direct challenge. *Not yet.* But the message was clear: *We are watching you.*

"It seems"—Dylan brushed the banner to the side, his inner battle carefully masked by a calm exterior—"that the Guardians are restless."

"We must respond."

"I know," Dylan growled. The walls of his control began to fracture. His wolf didn't understand politics or passivity. It wanted the blood of the idiot who dared challenge his dominance.

He walked over to the sink, shoved open the window, and breathed in the fresh spring air. The scent of his forest, pine and wet earth, soothed the animal within.

Luc stilled, watching, waiting, utterly quiet—a pose unnatural to a wolf just as dominant, just as powerful as Dylan.

"We will respond," Dylan continued after a few moments, arriving at a dangerous decision. "But not in the expected way. I'm going forward with the plan as discussed. It's time to gather with other leaders who have valued territories."

Leaders without loyalties to the Guardians.

Luc stayed silent for several moments, and then gave a sharp nod. "I just wonder who'll have the balls to come."

"All of them," Dylan surmised. "Either out of curiosity or need."

"Or deceit."

"That too."

"But they are Celts." Luc sounded more persuaded by that simple fact.

Celts protected their people.

They were also suspicious, stubborn bastards, unwilling to follow any form of leadership other than their own. Add a little wolf blood to the mix and any gathering had the potential to be downright volatile, as history had proven countless times.

"So be it." A malicious smile of anticipation spread across Luc's face. "The time is ripe for a gathering."

Dylan ignored his brother's comment as he looked out the kitchen window. Spring was quite possibly the *worst* time of year for a gathering of their kind.

Orange hues from the setting sun filtered through bare branches, forming dark silhouettes against the horizon. His forest looked dormant, with brown fields and patches of snow lingering in sunless areas. However, Dylan knew the truth, as did his brother, as would anyone with wolf blood running through his or her veins. Underneath the shroud of a waning winter, plants grew, buds formed, animals ended their hibernation. Life awakened. Its energy hummed along his skin like a thousand fingers, whispering promises of power. "We must watch our sister closely."

"Elen can take care of herself."

Dylan braced his arms on the counter, letting his head fall forward. "That's what concerns me."

Luc chuckled, a sound more sardonic than amused. "It may be time we revealed our strength."

"If our enemies push us," Dylan said, looking over his shoulder to meet his brother's gaze, "they will learn soon enough."

Luc crossed his arms and leaned against the center island, his relaxed stance a controlled deception. "I suggest
we call everyone in from the cities."

"Agreed." A few of their people lived amongst pure humans, secret ambassadors of sorts, as was necessary to influence the laws of an accelerating world. "Let's bring all our
people home."

SOPHIE THIBODEAU STOOD OUTSIDE THE PROVIDENCE
Public Library trying to decide who was more insane, the
homeless man practicing a colorful sermon on a milk crate,
or her as she punched in Dylan's number on her shiny new
disposable prepaid phone.

There was a strong possibility that she may have won the
crazy contest, considering the man she was about to call
had been hunting her for over fifteen years.

Sophie hugged her jacket closed as a chill shuddered
down her spine. She had traveled into the city specifically
to activate the phone using a public computer at the library.
Her location needed to be as untraceable as possible. Was
she being a tad paranoid? *Hell, yes.* Hiding from a man who
wasn't exactly human had taught her a few lessons.

Her heart pounded as she stared down at the phone.
Questions flooded her thoughts, weakening her resolve.
What if Dylan wasn't there? What if the number had been
changed? What if he refused to accept the call, deciding
instead to contact her on *his* terms? To hunt her down and
trap her.

Calm down, she coached herself, taking a deep breath.
And just push the little green button.

For Joshua.

The transient paused in his sermon, adjusting a rainbow-
colored beret over matted brown and gray hair. A cool
breeze carried his stench: mildew, unwashed skin, and alcohol. Sophie thought he had paused for dramatic effect,
but then large brown eyes met hers.

"Are you okay, child?"

Child? For the love of God, she was thirty-six years old. *And* pathetic, if a drunken homeless man was asking *her* if she needed help.

"I'm fine," she answered back with a tight smile, simply because her mother had taught her never to be rude. Her mother had also taught her not to be a coward. The man didn't look too convinced. No surprise there; neither was she.

Sophie turned her back on him and walked a short distance down the sidewalk. The streetlights flickered on, mingling with headlights from passing traffic. Either she was going to make the call or brave Providence traffic during rush hour.

She pushed the button and held the receiver to her ear.

Six rings, then a terse, "Hello."

Male, but not Dylan.

Her breath whooshed out. But the rush of relief lasted only moments until reality forced her to form coherent words. "Is Dylan available?"

"No." The tone was dismissive. "Are you wanting to leave a message?"

Porter, she guessed. *One of Dylan's guard dogs*—a tattooed skinhead on steroids. The prick had locked her in Dylan's room once. She had escaped under his watch. That thought gave her some satisfaction. She cleared her throat, gaining courage. "This is Sophie."

Silence.

Is it a sin to gain pleasure at someone else's discomfort? Probably. A small part of her enjoyed it anyway. "I will be at this number for another hour. If Dylan wants to talk to me, have him return my call." Three heartbeats later she added, "It concerns his son."

No answer.

"Are you still there?" she asked.

"Yes." The single clipped word screamed, *Bitch*.

She gave Porter the number and hung up, tucking the phone into her coat pocket. To keep busy, she grabbed her

purse, found twenty dollars, and walked over to the homeless man.

He reached out a gloved hand but paused when a passerby
snapped, "He'll only drink it away."

Sophie turned to the middle-aged woman, dressed in a
casual coat and jeans. "Maybe that's what he needs to survive this world."

The woman shrugged and kept walking.

"God bless you, child." The transient snatched the money.
"I'll pray for you."

"Thank you, sir." Sophie fingered the phone in her
pocket. "I need all the prayers I can get."

She searched the area for a secluded place to wait and
headed toward a vacant park across the street. There was
no grass in this section of the city, just brick and pavement,
marble-colored benches, and tall slabs of granite.

As she dashed across the busy street, her left thigh began
to ache, a tingling numbness rather than true pain, where
nerve endings had been severed in a long slash from hip to
calf by a red wolf with golden eyes. *A female wolf.*

The scars bothered Sophie most when it rained, an annoying reminder of the night she ran away from her son's
father, the night she learned that the monsters in legends did
indeed exist.

Two

DYLAN ESCAPED TO HIS SECOND-FLOOR STUDY TO CLEAR his head. He poured himself a glass of scotch, leaned back in his perfectly worn leather recliner, and took a large gulp, savoring the smooth heat as it spread down his throat. Logs and paper had been stacked neatly in the fireplace, ready to be lit when necessary. Porter's work, no doubt, even though he'd been told on countless occasions not to do menial tasks.

Loud voices and laughter filtered up from the main floor. Rhuddin Hall had always been open to the people of his territory. On most nights he enjoyed the sound of their contentment. On this night, however, he was on edge for many reasons.

Only a select few had been told of recent events, guards and defenders, all of them powerful, most of them shifters. The rest remained uninformed for one more night. A village meeting had been scheduled for the morning.

But, *unfortunately*, thoughts of his people were not his main cause for distraction. Oh, no—he took another sip of scotch—his restless conscience was all due to *her*. Always her. For reasons he was unaware of and could not control, Sophie was heavy on his mind this night.

Like poison that refused to be purged, anger and fear churned in his gut. Worst of all was the fear. And the not knowing. Where were they? Was his child well? Were they hungry? Were they safe? Cold? Scared?

Alive?

A soft knock jarred Dylan away from his self-destructive thoughts. Elen leaned into the doorjamb, with her Birks in one hand and a glass of red wine in the other. She wore black slacks and a plain white shirt, simple as always in a world that cherished the extravagant.

She took a sip from her glass. "Luc said you wanted to see me."

"Come." He waved her in with a purpose.

Elen set her glass on the butler's table, settled into the sofa, and loosened the tie in her hair. She groaned as golden waves fell around her shoulders. Very few saw his sister like this. Relaxed. Unguarded. Most only knew the doctor. Although some, he was well aware, remembered the child who had been tortured by their mother in an effort to force transformation.

At one time, the Guardians wrongly believed that survival instincts might call the wolf.

Not so for Elen, no matter how brutal the sessions. And since a shift never occurred, two thin scars remained on either side of her lower spine. The torture had been administered *under* the surface to produce the maximum amount of pain with the least damage. Their mother, if anything, was prudent. Merin would not have threatened her daughter's beauty. Beauty had value. Sanity, not so much.

Elen looked up, and then frowned. "You think of Merin."

Dylan forced a smile. "Do you read minds now too?"

"No need." Sadness settled into her soft blue eyes. "You always get that distant look on your face when you think of our mother."

"I'll always regret leaving you with her." Very rarely did either of them speak of that time. Why, he wondered, did he choose this moment to breach such a forbidden subject? Weariness, perhaps.

Her eyes widened.

Had he never apologized?

No, he supposed not. Apologies were for the weak.

Elen swallowed hard and then took a deep breath, gathering courage to voice difficult memories. "Please don't regret what cannot be changed. Everything happens for a reason. You were only thirteen, and Luc needed you more. Merin would have killed our brother but not me." Her voice softened to a whisper. "Besides, you came back for me."

Her words didn't lessen the guilt. Dylan suspected they never would. Over sixteen hundred years had passed and he still remembered the night of his brother's birth with regret.

It had been close to dawn when Aunt Cady barged into his roundhouse, covered in blood. Wild-eyed and hysterical, she handed him a wolf cub and said, "Run. Run or watch your brother die."

He had been forced to choose a sibling, and he chose Luc—the first of their clan born in wolf form. Dumbfounded, Dylan had ogled the black ball of fur mewling in his arms.

"Go to the high grounds of Gwynedd," Cady had whispered as she tucked a wool cloak around the cub Dylan held. "There are others like your brother. Families. They will help you."

His disappearance, Dylan knew, had harmed his sister more deeply than the metal spikes shoved under her skin.

"Justice has come full circle," Elen whispered.

Dylan looked up, slogging his way out of old memories. "How so?"

"We were chased from our homeland and forced to settle here, across the ocean, far away from the rest of our kind." A thread of melancholy weaved through her voice, despite her harsh words.

"Has it been so bad?" he asked softly. It had taken a long

time for her and many others to accept that Cymru, now known as Wales, was no longer their home.

The Guardians had claimed Cymru, like maggots within a rotting carcass. Descendants with mixed lineage, or others considered beneath them, were forced to become servants or slaves. *Or killed*, if judged too feeble in power, unworthy of procreation, dangerous to a weakening race losing its ability to call the wolf with each new generation.

A few powerful shifters had rejected the Guardians' demands. Some, like Dylan, had been unwilling to watch their loved ones suffer and escaped to new lands.

A gathering with those other leaders was long overdue.

"Of course not," she chided. "And you're missing the point. In our absence Cymru has become barren of wolves, overrun with sheep and empty hills, while we thrive. Our forest is rich with life. We have taken the precautions necessary to make sure that our land is protected against development. For some of us, wolves run through the trees once again. We are blessed."

"Yes," Dylan agreed. "Perhaps a little too blessed. It will not be long before we are challenged."

"I know. I feel it too." She sighed, as if the weight of their conversation was a tangible substance. "Luc showed me the banner. Our time of peace has ended. Forgive me if I'm not so eager."

"I'm not eager," he argued. "But I *will not* bow down to Guardian threats."

"Like I would ever expect you to." Elen gave him a sad smile. "Because of me you have become the leader of the unwanted. And you will defend our home at all costs." She lowered her voice. "Even when your sacrifice is the greatest."

Dylan purposely ignored her last comment. The sacrifice she referred to was not a place he chose to dwell. "No one is unwanted here."

Over the years many had come for sanctuary, those in danger of Guardian judgment for either being too human or too wolf. Most stayed—*for a price.* Anyone who lived on his land, under his protection, must cut all ties to their old life.

Full loyalty or else they must leave.

No exceptions.

Not even for the one woman who had deserved leniency. A human, no less. An innocent in his dangerous world.

Sophie.

Again, her name whispered through his mind, muddling his thoughts with poisonous emotions. Anger. Temptation. Betrayal. Hatred.

Need.

He got up and poured himself another glass of scotch.

"You will find them," Elen offered as solace. "She can't hide forever."

Dylan turned and frowned at his sister, more annoyed than angry at her insight. "When have I become so easy to read?"

"Only to me." Her eyes fell to his glass. "I know what your loyalty to our people has cost you. Others don't see. Or choose not to." She shrugged. "Too many count on your protection."

He shook his head, uncomfortable with her words. "Our numbers only make us stronger."

Elen sighed, but allowed him to veer away from his painful memories, switching to hers instead. "That is not how the Guardians view me. Or others like me. To them, if we cannot shift then we are weak. *Forsaken.* To them, we will always be . . ." She whispered a word in the old tongue, *"Drwgddyddwg."*

Evil Bringer. A vile name created out of fear by ignorant leaders.

Dylan growled. *"Never* use that name in my house."

Her profile did not conceal the mordant smile. "I've earned the right."

Annoyance made his tone harsh. "We will be hosting a small gathering of leaders who have fertile land. Potential allies against the Guardians, those without loyalties to the old ways." He gave her a moment to process that information, knowing that the news would unsettle her. And with good reason. "In numbers, our strength would be unmatched."

She hissed, snapping to face him. "If word reaches Cymru that we're even discussing this—"

"You think I have not considered those consequences?"

"Does Luc know of your idea?"

"Yes."

Elen waited in reserved silence. Finally, with obvious hesitation, she asked, "Who are you thinking?"

Dylan had considered territories first—the ones that had the most to lose under Guardian rule. "New York, Montana, Idaho, Virginia, Ontario, Alaska and Minnesota."

Elen counted off the leaders of each of the territories on her fingers. "Nia, Madoc, Ryder, Drystan, Daron, Kalem and Isabeau." She held up her hands. "Seven. What about Llara? She will join us. I know it."

"Yes, I don't doubt that Llara will stand with us, but she has her own battle at hand. Her territory is *inconvenient*." The humans in Russia were too observant of their surroundings, or perhaps more open-minded about old superstitions. When the Soviets were in power they almost eradicated the wolf population—and not all of them just wolves.

Elen frowned. "We should give her the choice. And the Himalayas? Both Mabon and Sioni will join our cause."

"Let's start closer to home. If all goes well, we can proceed from there."

With a jerky nod, Elen picked up her glass, rolling it in her hands. Potential disasters raced behind keen blue eyes. "When are you planning to hold this meeting?"

"Five days from now. Messages have already been sent. I will call tomorrow to confirm. I don't want to give them too much time to think."

She let out a deep breath. "But enough time to respond."

Dylan studied her face. "There will be powerful wolves around us, some who'll remember."

She met his eyes, unflinchingly direct. "I'm stronger than I once was."

"I know that. *They* don't."

Her lips tilted upward, mocking. "Are you asking me to behave?"

"Do I need to?"

"No," she clipped.

"Good."

"And I don't want you *or Luc* hovering around me either."

"You're our healer. We need you safe."

She rolled her eyes. "That excuse has become tiresome. I can do more."

Dylan shrugged, unapologetic. "Then prepare the clinic for what will come if this gathering proves ineffective."

Her chin lifted. "I'm always prepared for the worst."

"Of course."

"We may need to add more beds in the future," she conceded.

"I will defer to your judgment. Order anything you think necessary."

A muffled ring came from her pocket. She smiled an apology, leaning to the side to retrieve her cell.

The unnatural sound was like acid on his nerves. "I wish you wouldn't carry that thing."

"You're so paranoid," she teased. "Porter keeps me protected. And this *thing* has freed me from living at the clinic. The convenience far outweighs the risk." She looked down at the incoming number and raised her eyebrows. "Porter."

Dylan stilled, his instincts on alert. Porter never wasted words—*or* his time. If he called, there was a valid reason.

"Hello. Yes. He's here with me." Elen met Dylan's stare, her eyes intense. "Okay. We're upstairs in the study. Do you want to talk to him?" She blinked, staring down at the phone, then back to Dylan. "Porter just hung up on me."

Three

PORTER BARGED INTO THE STUDY, HIS BREATHING UN-even. His raven-dark brows narrowed over fierce blue eyes as he glared at Dylan with obvious annoyance. A tattoo of a Celtic cross covered his bare cranium. He always kept his head shaved bald, flaunting his Irish mother's symbol. The personal insult the Christian emblem represented to the Guardians was just an added perk.

He marched over, brandishing a cell phone. "If you will not carry your damn phone"––he took in a large gulp of air, his nostrils flaring—"I'm wondering why you bother having it."

Dylan accepted the phone and placed it on the mantel. "What's wrong?"

"You had a call on the main line." Porter crossed thick arms, his chin raised. He wasn't an overly tall man, barely six feet, if that. But what he lacked in height was more than compensated for by width. He was vicious in battle, fearless—his inability to shift irrelevant.

"And—"

"It was that woman."

A fist wrapped around Dylan's gut and squeezed. There was only one person Porter called *that woman*. "Excuse me?"

"You heard me."

Elen inhaled sharply, edging to the side of the sofa. "Sophie? Are you sure?"

Porter shot her a disgusted glare before handing Dylan a piece of paper with a number. "She gave you an hour to call." He checked his watch. "And I wasted fifteen minutes trying to find you." The censure in his voice eased into respect. "She was wanting me to tell you that it concerns your son."

"A son," Elen whispered.

Dylan stared down at the number, immobile. All thoughts of the Guardians, Cymru, his people, the gathering—*gone*. Until that moment he hadn't known the sex of his child. He turned his back to the room, facing the fireplace, not wanting his weakness observed.

"Watch yourself," Porter warned. "That woman has more cunning than a mother fox."

Dylan hadn't needed the warning. He'd underestimated Sophie once, on the night she ran. Four months pregnant and he still hadn't been able to track her. Then she erased her life. Completely. Everything except her father's grave. Desecration, it seemed, was where her line of betrayal ended.

Porter cleared his throat, giving his form of consolation. "You almost had her in California."

"Four years ago," Dylan snapped, unappeased. "And she cleared out just before we got there."

Five times he'd almost caught Sophie, but not once had he gotten a glimpse of his child. Every time she had eluded him as if an unseen force had warned her. A ridiculous notion, he knew . . . because Sophie was only human.

Dylan felt a delicate hand on his shoulder and shrugged it off. "I want to be alone for this call."

Elen's footsteps retreated to Porter's side of the room. "We'll wait for you outside then."

"Use the house phone," Porter added. "I'll be tracing the call."

*　*　*

SOPHIE SAT ON A GRANITE BENCH AS MOISTURE SEEPED into her jeans. She almost stood, but slumped back instead, figuring a wet ass was the least of her worries.

The waiting was brutal.

She checked her watch for the hundredth time, almost convinced Dylan wasn't going to call, when the phone lit up, its unfamiliar ring causing every muscle in her body to tense.

With shaking hands, she brought the receiver to her ear. "Hello."

"Sophie?" Deep and calm, but with an underlying edge of controlled anger.

She had rehearsed this conversation a thousand times, but the reality of hearing his voice erased all rational thought. "I'm sorry," she whispered. "This was a bad idea—"

"Don't you dare hang up on me, or—"

"Or what?" The hairs on the back of her neck stood on end. His arrogant tone flooded her with unpleasant memories. "You'll hunt me down like a rabid animal? Been there. Done that."

"You've held on to your anger well, Sophie, yet I'm the one who's never seen my son's face."

She swallowed hard, clutching the phone with both hands. "You gave me no other choice."

"Not true." His tone dropped dangerously low. "You could have stayed."

"As a prisoner."

"No," he growled. *"As my wife."*

"Is there a difference?"

Silence filled their tenuous connection, thick and vile, poisoned by mutual betrayals.

A muffled sound followed, as if Dylan had pressed the receiver into something soft to hide his reaction.

"I'm sorry," she whispered. "I didn't call you for this."

"What's my son's name?"

Her breath caught in her throat. Such a simple question . . . and yet it held agonizing impact. "Joshua."

"Joshua," he repeated in a low tone. "A good name. Is he well?"

"He's beautiful," she said with a heavy heart. "He's the reason I called. I need to ask you something."

A slight hesitation. "What's wrong?"

"Josh has been," Sophie chose her words carefully, "acting *odd* lately. And not the normal teenager odd."

"What are you suggesting?"

"I'm suggesting that he may have inherited more of his father than I had hoped."

A long pause. "Are you talking from a cell line?"

She understood his concern. "I can call you from another phone."

"No," he snapped, and then softened his tone. "You need to bring my son home. If what you're suggesting is true, it's a dangerous time for him."

She felt dizzy, nauseated, panic edging to the surface. "How dangerous?"

"He could die."

Her heart clenched with the worst kind of pain. It was what she had feared most. "What can I do?"

"Come home," Dylan coaxed. "I can help him . . . before it's too late."

An overwhelming apprehension drove her to make an unplanned offer. "We can meet you somewhere."

He didn't answer immediately, the predator having sensed her fear—using it well to sway her decision. "He needs to be around his own kind now. Are you willing to risk his life because of your hatred for me?"

"You're so clueless," she snapped, letting all her painful memories fill those few words.

"Then enlighten me."

"It's irrelevant now." She closed her eyes, weighing her options. Her son's welfare, as always, influenced her decisions. However, Sophie had a distinct advantage over the last time she'd been in Rhuddin Village; she was not the same naïve woman that Dylan once knew. She was older now, wiser, and had learned how to defend herself and those she loved.

Quite well, in fact. "Is the lake house still available?"

"It can be."

"I need a few days to clear things up."

"You must come now," he said, his voice firm. "A few days may be too late."

"I'll be there tomorrow," she conceded, not liking the fact that it revealed a hint to her proximity. She had others to protect. "We'll be there in the evening." She calculated the travel time in her head and added six hours. "Probably around eight. I'll call you on this phone when we reach Maine."

"Hold on . . ." His voice trailed off and then returned. "Let me give you my cell number."

An unexpected laugh erupted from her, or more like an involuntary release of pent-up nerves. "You have a cell?"

"You find that amusing?"

"Maybe a little," she admitted.

"The world's changing. Sometimes we're forced to adapt."

"Yes," she agreed. "Sometimes we are."

The easy banter opened a door of mutual awareness. "If I asked you where my son is now, would you tell me?"

She sighed. "We're coming to you. Let that be enough."

"And if something happened to you, how would he know where to find me?"

Sophie wasn't offended by the question because she had prepared for that possibility. "Your son has always known where you are."

There was a muffled sound, as if, again, Dylan pulled the phone away to hide his reaction. When the line cleared, he spoke low, his voice strained. "How much does he know about me?"

"Everything I know," she answered honestly, then ended

the call before Dylan asked more questions she wasn't prepared to answer.

THEN HE KNOWS NOTHING.

Dylan shoved the phone away and ran his hands over his face. He hadn't been prepared for the sound of her voice. He wanted to throttle her. He wanted to lock her in a room and destroy the damn key.

He wanted . . .

Dylan stood abruptly, scraping back his chair and making his way down to the media room. As he walked past the kitchen, Elen hurried after him, her face expectant. He held up his hand, a silent message to wait. She pursed her lips, unhappy but compliant.

Porter sat at his desk, focused on his equipment, his shiny head bobbing to the heavy metal sounds of "Crazy Train." For a former Jacobite, born late sixteen hundreds, he had an unnatural obsession with modern technology. Several computer monitors lined the far wall. Two flat-screen TVs broadcasted national and local news.

Porter looked up, acknowledged Dylan with a sharp nod, and lowered the stereo volume via universal remote. "I'm having a hard time identifying the source. That woman used a disposable phone, recently registered under a suspicious account." Respect mingled with frustration as his fingers danced across a keyboard. "That's all I've got so far."

"Keep trying."

Elen stood in front of Dylan, blocking his view, refusing to be ignored any longer. Questions spilled out in random succession. "What happened? What did Sophie say? What did she want?"

Porter added his own comment. "The timing is curious, don't you think?"

Dylan didn't like the implication. "She called because of my son." He looked to his sister. "His name is Joshua."

"Joshua," Elen repeated with a soft smile. "And he's healthy?"

Dylan hesitated. "I'm not sure. Sophie believes he might be . . . *changing*."

Her eyes narrowed. "You know that's not possible. A shifter hasn't been born in over three hundred years."

"I'm aware of that." He met his sister's gaze. "But Sophie isn't."

Elen frowned, tilting her head to one side. "What did you tell her?"

"That he's in danger—that he'll die without my help."

She gave a heavy sigh, tinged more with regret than censure. "More lies, Dylan?"

"He's my son. I will use any means necessary to get him home. And whatever's happening to him, it's got Sophie spooked enough to call me. She's agreed to come."

Elen looked doubtful. "I hope so."

"I've always known my wife to be completely candid about her intentions," Dylan reflected bitterly.

If you don't let me go to my father's funeral, she had screamed during their last and most explosive disagreement, *I will leave you.*

And she did.

"I'll have the north rooms prepared for the boy." Porter made the assumption Sophie would be staying in the master suite.

The north rooms were the most protected and easiest to guard.

Dylan stilled as an inner battle raged. Sophie's angry accusations buzzed fresh in his mind, like an annoying swarm of hornets. And much like the flying insects, forced confinement just pissed her off.

You could have stayed.

As a prisoner.

He shook his head, making a decision that defied all natural instincts. "She asked for the lake house. That's where she'll stay. At least for a few days until our guests arrive."

Elen crossed her arms and regarded Dylan with somber eyes. "In light of Sophie's return, you might consider postponing the gathering."

"Why? Her arrival changes nothing." Dylan frowned down at her, realizing he had been too soft earlier if she questioned his timing now, regardless of personal interruptions. "We're being watched by the Guardians. Should I just sit back and wait for more messages? Consider their demands?"

Porter grunted, a crude sound that confirmed his view on the subject.

"Of course not," she snapped, offended. "But what of Sophie and your son? How will she react once she's learned what you've lured her back into?"

"They are safest with me regardless." Dylan began to pace, annoyed by his sister's insight. "My son is without training—helpless in a fight. Weak like a human. Without me, he's vulnerable and ignorant. Alone and unprotected." Fear merged with disgust. "Besides, it's imperative the gathering remain unnoticed. If all goes well, Sophie won't even know they're here."

"And if all doesn't go well?"

A valid possibility with seven dominant leaders in unfamiliar territory.

"Then she'll learn the reality of my world. I kept her too protected before. She accused me of making her a prisoner—"

"You *did* make her a prisoner," Elen pointed out, her sensitivity toward that particular subject well known.

"Well, then." Dylan growled, his patience with this conversation finished. "Maybe it's time she understood why."

Elen walked toward him and placed a gentle hand on his arm, stilling his motions and calming his anger. "Just don't choose our safety over your own happiness." She lowered her voice. "I'll not allow that a second time."

Four

Balancing two grocery bags in one arm and her keys in the other, Sophie shoved her way through the front door of their cottage. She set the bags down on the counter, and hung her coat and keys on the hallway hook.

"Hello," she called out. "I'm home. Sorry I'm so late." Due to traffic, the drive from Providence to Newport had taken over two hours, plus she had stopped at the grocery store to get a few things for their trip in the morning. She checked the clock. Almost eight. Joshua must be starving.

Tucker, a Great Dane mix, trotted into the kitchen. He nudged her arm and waited for her usual greeting. Sophie bent down and kissed him on top of his head. "Have you behaved yourself today, Tuck?"

The dog huffed, as if bored with her petty demands of proper conduct, and then turned away, snout up, with obvious dismissal.

"Hey, Mom," Joshua yelled from the hallway. He bounced

into the kitchen a second later, like a plow truck fueled by pure adrenaline. At fifteen, Josh had the body of a man with the energy of a two-year-old, awkward and lanky, as if his limbs hadn't yet adjusted to his ever growing height.

"What have you been up to?" She yanked off her boots, dropping them by the door, mulling over the best way to break the news to her son.

He grinned, wagging his eyebrows. His dark eyes, so like his father's, twinkled with mischief. "Ask me why I'm awesome."

Sophie groaned, yet, unable to resist her son's antics, she played along. "Okay . . . why are you so awesome?"

He yanked up his T-shirt with one hand, showing off his midriff. "Look at this six-pack."

The muscle tone was there, *barely*. "Oh, God . . . put your shirt down. You're going to traumatize your mother for life."

He laughed, letting the shirt drop. His confidence at fifteen boggled the mind, something else he had inherited from his father.

"What's for dinner?" Joshua hovered over her, crowding the kitchen.

"Did you find the subs I left you?"

"Yeah." He grinned. "Thanks. I had those for a snack."

Sophie thought of food in the fridge that needed to be used. "How about a meat loaf?"

"That takes too long." The deep timbre of his changing voice contradicted the whine of an adolescent. "How 'bout chicken Alfredo?"

"The chicken's frozen. Do you want a BLT?" She worked around him, organizing food on the counter. Not an easy task considering he was a half foot taller than her and twice as solid.

And hungry.

"Come on, Mom. I'm starving. BLTs are, like, *hello*, a lunch. I need real food. Cheese. Pasta. Chicken. I'm wasting away here."

"Ravaging locusts eat less than you do, I swear." She

searched the fridge for Parmesan cheese and cream. "I don't know where you put it all."

"I'm a growing boy." Again with the grin. "That's why you should make me chicken Alfredo."

"Okay," Sophie conceded, putting four chicken breasts in the microwave to defrost.

"Thank you, Mama."

"Mama" was his latest term of endearment when she caved on something he wanted. She tended to give in a lot.

How could she not? He was, it seemed, her only weakness. She had done the unthinkable to keep him close. And she would do so much more if necessary.

"Where's your grandmother?" Sophie chopped garlic for the Alfredo and set it aside. She then pulled frozen basil from the freezer, along with cream, wine, cheese, and butter from the fridge to start the sauce.

Joshua leaned his head out of the snack cupboard, his hand in a bag of Oreos. "Huh?"

"Your grandmother?" she repeated. "Where is she?"

"Playing chess with Mr. Ayres," Joshua mumbled around a mouthful of cookies.

"We need to talk," Sophie said calmly, even though her insides heaved in protest.

Joshua stilled, eyeing her warily. "You're using your serious voice."

Sophie waited until she had added the wine to the pan, and then set the sauce to simmer. She turned to face her son, searching for the right words, and decided on blunt honesty. "I called your father today."

His reaction was physical, a slight shifting of skin and an unnatural narrowing of the skull, hardly visible and gone in a second.

The changes were so minute a regular person might not even have noticed. But she wasn't a regular person. She was his mother.

She knew her child.

Just as she knew the shifts caused him considerable pain,

although he tried to hide that fact. They had begun three weeks ago, each one more pronounced than the last.

He could die.

Her stomach clenched with the sickening reminder of those words, and she reached out to her son. The instant her hand touched his arm, gooseflesh formed on her skin as if kissed by lightning.

An unusual scent filled the air, like rain on hot sand, elements colliding. Nature manipulated. The scent was sharp and distinct and forever ingrained in her memory. It took her back to the only time she had witnessed Dylan become the wolf . . .

Leaves and pine needles crunched under her sneakers, crisp from rain starting to freeze. Evening clouds obscured a waning moon, masking their journey with darkness. Dylan held her firm, dragging her by one arm down a cleared path as Luc, Porter, and five other guards walked ahead and behind, blocking all escapes.

They were far from the house now, deep in the forest, surrounded by trees going dormant for winter, with leaves shaded red, orange, and yellow, happy colors muddied by night that didn't soothe her racing heart.

Sophie shivered, more from disbelief than fear. "Where are you taking me? Why are you doing this? I don't understand . . ."

Dylan pulled her farther into the woods, his grip unyielding, bruising her pride more than anything else. He spoke for the first time since their argument. "There is much about my world you don't know or understand."

She yanked at her arm, numb to the wrenching pain as she fought for freedom. He always spoke in vague references, alluding to some great secret, as if she were a child too naïve to comprehend his adult reality. "You can't keep me here against my will."

"Yes, I can." And his voice held complete conviction in

his ability to do just that. "And I will . . . as long as you carry my child. If you choose to leave after the birth, I will not interfere, but if you do leave . . . the child will remain with me."

Sophie felt a tear slide down her cheek, disgusted by her own weakness but unable to stop the rush of emotion. She wrapped her free arm around the small bulge of her belly. Protective. Instinctive. Possessive.

Hers.

He let her go suddenly, almost as if he felt her intentions. She stumbled forward into a glen sheltered from the rain by an arching oak tree.

Dylan walked before her, his blond hair plastered against his face and neck, streaks of rain trailing down his rigid jaw. There was no warmth in his expression, no emotion other than harsh resolve. The passion they had once shared as lovers had turned to anger months ago. Once he'd become aware of their child, everything had changed.

He changed.

His eyes met hers, black as death in the distance, holding her rooted to that spot in the glen, even though every instinct in her being screamed, Run!

"Now you will know why I keep you guarded, Sophie. Why you must forget your old life."

He methodically began to remove his clothing until he stood before her naked. The lure to watch was potent. Shadows danced across the hard planes of his chest and stomach, like a gypsy's dance teasing a potential lover.

Even in anger, she was drawn to him.

Undaunted by their audience, he stood before her confident and glorious, his wide shoulders squared under her inspection, his thick legs braced a foot apart, his stance unconsciously dominant, innately beautiful.

His sex hung dark and heavy against his thigh.

Luc and two other guards surrounded him, like warriors falling in behind their leader. Dylan opened his arms wide, tilted his somber face to the sky—and the forest wept.

The scent of elements filled the air, rain and earth and heat churned by the wind. Nature combined, melded together into one constituent of furious power. Leaves fell around her feet like snow in a blizzard, night creatures stilled, and the earth went silent in one hushed moment before reality as she knew it irrevocably changed.

She watched in stunned horror as the father of her unborn child melted into a mound of distorted flesh. Bones snapped and reformed, fur covered skin, human moans turned animalistic, and then there was no sound at all as the black eyes of a golden wolf returned her stare.

And she ran.

She ran out of fear, yes, but also for other reasons, intuitive reasons. As her mind struggled to accept the impossible, she was certain of only one thing: Dylan would never let her leave now that his unearthly secret had been revealed.

His earlier comments were spoken only to pacify her into compliance. She would be guarded forever by people-wolves—these things *that despised her*. And eventually, if she stayed, so too might her child one day follow their example.

Or worse, be taken from her.

They were slow to react, or perhaps too sure of their ability and her limitations. It gave her an edge, a slight advantage.

But soon, too soon, the breath of wolves and the shouts of guards closed in fast at her back. Frenzied, her stomach cramping, she stumbled off the trail and crawled into the husk of a rotting tree. There she willed her body into stillness and prayed in silence, forgotten prayers from childhood Sundays, desperate prayers of need and promises.

God answered, she supposed, in His own way. A nest of skunks didn't appreciate company in their cozy home—and, ultimately, blessedly masked her scent.

Or, more likely, disabled the wolves' keenest hunting ability.

Except for one.

Siân.

The female wolf had watched Dylan's little demonstration from the woods, silent in the shadows, waiting until all the others had gone to search the roads and all human exits from their territory, unaware their prey had never left . . .

SOPHIE TOOK A DEEP BREATH AND SHOVED THOSE UN-wanted memories to the back of her mind. Hysteria, she had learned a long time ago, was a useless reaction.

"Joshua . . . can you hear me?" She shook his arm.

He frowned down at her as if she'd lost her mind. Not that she could blame him, having thought the exact same thing on countless occasions since that night in the woods.

"Ah . . . *yeah*, Mom. You're like a foot away from my face."

She laughed, her heart thudding in her chest to hear the normalcy of his voice. "We're going to Rhuddin Village."

The bag of Oreos fell from his grasp, forgotten. "When?"

"Tomorrow."

Big dark eyes widened with unease. "Was he mad?"

The childlike question broke her heart. "The only reaction your father had was concern for you." She masked her fear, keeping her voice decisive. "The time has come for you to meet him."

He nodded slowly, accepting her decision. "How long are we going to stay?"

His lack of argument was both a worry and a relief. The worry lingered longer. "As long as we need."

He gave a jerky nod, absorbing that information. A hint of a smile touched his lips, more, she knew, for her benefit. "I'm going to miss my last quarter of school."

"I'm telling your teachers you have mono. There's a good chance you'll have to make up your classes this summer."

A false hope, she knew. But did it matter where they were

this summer, or the next, or the one after, as long as Joshua was there to experience them?

No. Losing him was the *only* thing she could not handle.

She gently tucked a strand of light brown hair away from his face, the one trait he had inherited from her. Everything else was Dylan. "I love you more than life itself, Joshua."

"Love you too, Mom," he said automatically.

"Are you ready for a new adventure?" It was the question she always asked just before a major change, usually a move. They had moved too much in his short lifetime. The cottage was their longest stay in one place, almost four years now, thanks to a generous employer.

"Yeah," he said, and for the first time not complaining. "Is Grandma coming too?"

"Not this time." That saddened Sophie to no end, but it was too much to ask of her mother, especially without disclosing all the facts, and Sophie didn't intend to do that anytime soon. Her last attempt had been rewarded with a lecture on drug use.

"Does she know?"

"Not yet."

He snorted. "Good luck with that."

A BITING WIND RUSHED THROUGH THE AYRES COURTYARD, carrying the scent of salt air and turbulence. Red streaks appeared along the horizon, tempering the blue shadows of dawn, as if nature forewarned a difficult journey.

"Mom, we have a problem." Joshua's voice echoed across the brick driveway where Sophie stood with Matthew Ayres.

Shooting her boss an apologetic smile, she called back, "What is it?"

"Grandma won't give me the keys."

"Don't think for a second, Sophie Marie, that you're going anywhere without me." Waves crashed in the distance, mingling with the sound of her mother's adamant message.

Matthew cocked his head to one side, golden curls

whipping about wide shoulders. He wore the blue sweater and plaid pajama bottoms Sophie had given him for his birthday, looking more like a surfer forced to wake before noon than the heir to a massive fortune.

A slight grin tugged at his perfectly sculpted lips. "I think you might have a dilemma."

"I'll be there in a minute," she yelled to her son, then turned back to Matthew. "I'm sorry for the short notice."

Aqua blue eyes focused in on her. "Tucker's going to be heartbroken. I think he's forgotten that I'm his owner."

She nodded, finding it unusually difficult to say her farewells. Matthew valued his privacy, maybe even more so than she valued hers, but a friendship had developed regardless. As his personal cook and housekeeper, a certain amount of intimacy had been unavoidable. He had no surviving relatives that she knew of.

And for whatever reason, it felt wrong to leave him alone. "You have a week's worth of meals in the freezer. The cooking instructions are taped to the top."

"I'll be fine, Sophie."

"I should only be two weeks."

"Okay." He smiled as if somehow he knew she wouldn't be coming back.

"Good-bye, Matthew." On impulse, Sophie leaned forward and kissed him on his cheek. They had never touched before and the gesture became more personal than intended.

He covered the spot she had kissed with his hand and then turned away as if to leave. "Wait here a moment." Reluctance darkened his request. "I have something for you."

Sophie frowned as she watched him walk back up to the main house. Out of the corner of her eye she saw her mother dragging a duffel bag down the walkway, clothes spilling out.

"Oh, come on, Mum," she hollered over, frustration making her voice harsh. "We discussed this last night."

Francine straightened, glaring back at her daughter, yesterday's mascara smudged under her eyes. Her dyed brown hair, cockeyed from sleep, added to the impact of her displeasure.

Her mother *never* left the house without makeup. Sophie had intended not to wake her; the plan hadn't worked out so well.

"Do you honestly think I'm going to let you go there alone?" Francine straightened to her full height, barely five feet, hands on hips. *Tyrant position in place.* "I'll lay in front of that car first." Her brown eyes snapped with defiance. Even at fifty-eight, bedraggled and furious, her mother was a stunning woman. She lifted her chin. "You know I will."

Nerves raw from lack of sleep and concern for her son, Sophie threw her hands up. "Fine, Mum, you can come. But remember—*I warned you not to.*"

Francine gave a smug smile. "Joshua, you heard your mother. Come help Grandma put this bag in the trunk."

At the sound of a soft chuckle, Sophie turned back toward the house. Matthew had returned holding a brown paper grocery bag rolled closed at the top.

She eyed the no-frills packaging and couldn't help but smile. "What is it?"

"Just a little something," he teased.

"Thank you." She felt guilty accepting the gift. The weight of it surprised her. "What's in this thing? Rocks?"

"Hardly," he said dryly.

Curious now, she started to unroll the top.

He gently covered her hands with his, stopping her motions. "Open it when you reach your destination."

"Mom, we're ready." Joshua headed over. "The car's all packed. I stacked the coolers so Grandma can have the front seat. And I locked up the cottage."

"Good luck on your trip, Josh," Matthew said, holding up his right hand, knuckles forward. "Remember our lessons. And listen to your mother."

Her son answered with a butting fist. "I will, Mr. Ayres."

Francine followed, pulling Matthew down for a motherly hug. She always coddled the man as if he were a child, although he never seemed to mind. "Behave yourself while we're gone."

Matthew didn't release her immediately, prolonging the embrace. "I will miss our chess games, Franni."

"Now cut that out." She stepped back and shooed him away. "We'll be back before you know it."

Sadness hung heavy in the air.

"Okay then," Sophie interrupted, hating good-byes. She gave her little cottage one last wistful glance. "Time to go."

ive

LUC CIRCLED THE TRAINING YARD IN A DEFENSIVE CROUCH that demonstrated perfect balance and control. A group of young faces, ages ranging from four years to twelve, stood in a half-moon, absorbing his instruction.

Dylan watched with a heavy heart. Eight children total, eight precious gifts for a dying race—all unable to shift form.

Under Guardian rule they would not survive.

Luc held no weapon, only his hands. He wore sweatpants and sneakers, leaving his chest bare. A new tattoo of a brown owl with outstretched wings covered his torso from collarbone to navel. A cool breeze carried the faint stench of fear. The children had been warned what might be coming.

A few faces turned and noticed their leader, then instantly looked down out of respect.

Luc pivoted to meet Dylan's stare, his silver eyes piercing the distance. They shared a silent message of sadness.

Too soon. Too innocent. *Too weak.*

It brought Dylan back to another time, to his homeland, to a place where the forsaken cowered in forbidden forests or suffered under Guardian rule . . .

* * *

THE WANING MONTHS OF WINTER WERE GRAVE TIMES FOR THE *outcasts who hid within the northern forests of Cymru, when the earth held no succor, nor color, nor even the shelter of leaves to help conceal their dwellings from the Guardians. Thus when a shout rang out within their camp, alerting of an approaching visitor, Dylan had good cause for concern.*

The visitor drew closer; a woman, but barely so—more like a girl. She stumbled into their camp clutching a swaddled infant to her chest.

Dylan stepped into a clearing to draw the girl's attention away from where their young were kept. Others followed, both in human and wolf form, as curiosity overcame caution. Or perhaps, like Dylan, they sensed another victim of a Guardian's cruel hand.

Dirt and mire caked the girl's naked form. The scent of blood clung to her skin, along with more offensive odors. Hair the color of harvest wine hung in ragged clumps to her frail waist. He could only wonder at its true splendor, if it displayed such a color under filth.

"What is your name, child?" Dylan searched indigo eyes for a response and found none. They were too calm, like the great sea after a violent storm when monsters continued to swim within the murky depths.

"Her name is Isabeau." Elen skirted around the crowd and approached the girl. "Get back," she ordered, shooing everyone away, but only a few listened. "Her family serves the Guardian Rhun. Last I knew, Isabeau's mother had been with child."

Too little time had passed from when Dylan had removed Elen from Merin's influence. She had recent knowledge of the families who were forced to serve the Guardians— families with daughters and sons and siblings who were unable to draw power from the forest.

With soothing whispers, Elen eased the bundle from

Isabeau's embrace, gently unraveling the woolen cloth. "A wolf," Elen said softly. "A Bleidd." Somber blue eyes met Dylan's and he knew before she confirmed, "'Tis dead."

Isabeau crumbled to the ground, as if hearing the truth spoken aloud stole her strength, or more aptly—it was the final violation of her will. "They are all dead," she whispered on a broken sob.

Dylan removed his outer cloak and wrapped it around the girl, but made no further attempt to console her, sensing she would recoil from his touch. "Who is dead, Isabeau?"

"My mother, my brothers . . ." The stench of fear and anguish filled the air, more vile than the other odors that clung to her skin, especially when coming from someone this young. "Rhun killed them all . . . Because of the Bleidd." But another scent rose above the others. It hinted of vengeance, of power, and of hatred.

She'd been allowed to live, Dylan knew full well, because of the wolf he sensed within her. Had the Guardians not claimed her innocence before, they had done so this night; if not from her body—than from her soul.

"PRACTICE WHAT I'VE TAUGHT YOU," LUC ANNOUNCED, snapping Dylan back to the present. His brother dismissed the students. "We'll meet the same time tomorrow." After the sound of young voices lessened in the distance, he strode over to Dylan. "Any word yet from your woman?"

Thankful for the distraction, Dylan opened the window of his cell phone then snapped it shut. "No."

"I could smell the fear of our people this morning." The disgust in his voice referred to the village meeting, *not* the children.

"These modern times have made us complacent. It's why an alliance is necessary." Dylan folded his arms and looked across the landscape of his territory. "I've made the calls. All leaders have agreed to come, except Nia and Kalem, who'll be sending representatives."

"Did any of them reveal if the Guardians marked their territories?"

Dylan shook his head. "Our conversations were guarded. No confirmations were given over the phone." He was not the only leader distrustful of modern technology. "We'll learn more on Friday, when we talk in person. Until then, we need to prepare. Have you done as I asked?"

Luc gave a sharp nod. "Ceri and Gabriel will take the area directly around the lake house. Teyrnon is set to guard the north ridge. Malsum and John will supervise a crew within the forest. Sarah has the east range. Porter and Caleb will cover the main house with Taran at the entrance gate."

The strongest had been assigned to protect their most vulnerable points, the lake house being their highest priority.

"I've asked the leaders not to draw attention as they arrive, and to keep their guards to a minimum." It was the second request that concerned Dylan most. More than one leader had been reluctant to concede, Isabeau especially. "Some may send scouts," he warned. "If so, we must capture—*not* harm."

Luc snorted.

Dylan pressed his point. "Keep Taran with you."

"No." He shook his head. "I want her at the entrance gate."

Pressure built along Dylan's spine in an all too familiar ache. The refusal of a direct command annoyed his beast. Two dominants in one territory had always been a tentative balance, managed only by loyalties stronger than the instinct of the wolf.

He took a deep breath. The human, *the brother*, must remain in control at all times. "Explain your reasoning."

Luc stayed calm, recognizing Dylan's battle, respecting it without challenge. "Our visitors should be greeted with strength. Taran has earned her place in our guard."

"Fine," Dylan grudgingly agreed, irritated that his distrust was based on personal misjudgments of his past. "But make sure she knows to stay away from Sophie. I fear Siân has clouded her sister's judgment." Ultimately, Taran's loyalty would lean toward her own family and not his, and as Siân's younger sister, her judgment toward Sophie might be compromised. "I don't trust either wolf around my wife, *especially* Siân. Her mind has become . . . *disturbed*." And because of him, her hatred toward Sophie was justified. "I want her watched."

Luc gave a sharp nod. "I'll take care of it."

"Send Michael," Dylan added. Of all the guards, Michael had been the first to notice Siân's odd behavior, and one of the few who had not succumbed to her enticements.

"Michael's a good choice. Sarah can help cover his watch."

Somewhat appeased, Dylan fingered his cell, flipped the window open and checked the time, and then pushed a button, making sure the thing worked. When a green number appeared on the small screen, he snapped it closed.

Luc's eyes followed Dylan's motions. "Nervous, brother?"

"Bugger off."

He chuckled, a rare sound of genuine amusement. "Ah, it's a good day if I can get a rise out of you." His tone lowered, although his grin remained. "I'm anxious to meet my nephew."

Dylan turned to the only person allowed to see his concern. "I pray he's well."

Luc's smile faded as he placed a hand on Dylan's shoulder and squeezed. "He'll be thin. Sophie won't have had the knowledge to keep him sustained through his growth period. He may even be stunted."

"I know." The heaviness in his chest refused to subside. Even as a latent, the metabolism of two animals in one being needed an enormous amount of nutrition to achieve normal growth. "I'll take him in any condition."

"We'll make him strong."

"I should have listened to you that night." Dylan voiced his regret aloud for the first time, wondering with some disdain at his recent lapses into personal reflection. "Sophie wasn't ready to see my wolf. I thought . . ." He shrugged. "I thought it would help her understand. Koko handled it much better."

A shadow passed over Luc's face with the mention of his

dead wife's name. "Koko came from a different people." *A better people,* his tone suggested of Koko's family, a band of traveling gypsies. Like many in the late 1800s, they had come to America for the opportunity to wield their trades. "She understood the power of the earth. Her mind was open, not closed like these modern races."

There was pain in his voice when he spoke of her, even now after sixty years of mourning.

"But," Luc continued, "I don't think revealing the wolf was your greatest mistake."

Only his brother would dare to make such a comment, the exact reason, Dylan supposed, he had chosen him for this. "And what do you think was my greatest mistake?"

"Voicing aloud your intentions to keep your child. I remember that night well. I didn't sense real fear from Sophie until that moment." Luc shrugged. "You should have just kept your mouth shut and done what was necessary when the time came."

Dylan didn't respond. Luc wouldn't understand because he had never truly been mated, but only an ass or an idiot would remind him of that fact. Luc honored Koko as his mate of choice; their union, sadly, had been childless.

Once the wolf intervened and a child was conceived, *choice* was just a pretty word for bards and philosophers. The human heart can be reserved, even controlled, but the animal only knew want and need.

He had felt Sophie's intentions that night, *and her hatred.* Nothing in the world, or Otherworld for that matter, could have kept him silent.

The shrill ring of his phone made him tense, a shot of nightshade tonic preferable to the unnatural sound. "Yes."

"Hi, it's me . . . Sophie." As if she had needed to identify herself.

"I know." A tacit snarl of satisfaction spread through his limbs. That wanting never receded, regardless of the other mate's betrayals.

"Um . . . I promised to call you when we reached Maine. We're in Saco. We should be in Rhuddin Village around four."

Earlier than expected. "The lake house is ready for you."

"Thank you. And just so you know . . ." She paused, her voice dropping to a whisper. "My mother's with me."

"Your mother?" Dylan frowned, turning his back to Luc's raised eyebrow. "How much does she know?"

"Not much." Her voice took on an odd tone, high-pitched. "Nothing of significance."

"Do you think it wise to bring her now?"

"No," she admitted.

"Then why do it?" The last thing Dylan needed at this time was another human in his territory, and Sophie's mother no less.

"You don't know my mother."

RHUDDIN VILLAGE HAD THE APPEARANCE OF A NORMAL town, with a post office, clinic, homes and stores, its secrets well hidden from unsuspecting visitors, as Sophie had learned all too well.

Her heart raced as she drove past the brick church that marked the entrance to the wilderness reserve, where sidewalks ended and asphalt became gravel, where forest and lakes remained forever wild in a valley under a snowcapped mountain—and where Dylan waited not too far away.

"How much longer?" her mother asked for the twentieth time in the last half hour. "I need to go to the bathroom."

Sophie kept her eyes on the winding dirt road pitted with puddles. "We're almost there."

"You said that an hour ago."

"You didn't have to come," Sophie reminded her, immediately regretting her impatience.

Joshua groaned from the backseat, recognizing his mother's error.

"I'm tired of hearing that tone from you," Francine snapped, her voice like boiling water over thin ice, a warning that Sophie had stepped too far and was about to fall in. "When you came to me just after your father died, hurt and pregnant . . . and you told me that . . . *that man* wanted to take the baby from you, what did I do? When you told me that I either had to come with you or go into hiding and forget you—*what did I do?*"

"You're right, Mum. I'm sorry." Sophie tried to defuse the lecture that she knew had only just begun.

"I completely relocated my life, that's what. Without question. To be with you and my grandchild. I changed my name to *Brown*, for the love of God. Do you think I'll walk away now that you've decided to face whatever demons you need to face?"

"I said I was sorry." She ground her teeth. "And Joshua doesn't need to hear this right now."

Francine sniffed, her posture going rigid. "Then don't bring it up again."

"I won't."

"We're a team." It seemed she wasn't quite done yet. "Don't ever forget that. And if *that man* even tries to keep me away from my grandson, then he'll know what it's like to face the wrath of two Thibodeau women at once." She blew out a breath of air, fanning herself. "Now look what you've gone and done . . . My blood pressure's all upset." She gave a low laugh, starting to calm down. "I must admit, it felt good to say my real name again."

Sophie patted her mother's arm. She almost felt sorry for Dylan. *Almost.* "Did you take your pills this morning?"

"Yes, at the rest stop."

Sophie nodded, recognizing the last turn up ahead. "This is it. We're here." She braced herself as the car bounced over roots and holes in a driveway of sorts, protected by a canopy of tall pine trees. She parked her Ford Taurus alongside a black Chevy Avalanche.

Her heart pounded so hard she felt physically ill.

The truck, no doubt, belonged to Dylan.

Sophie forced herself to get out of the car; the scent of pine and forest assaulted her senses and her memories. She tried to calm her emotions, tried to keep those memories at bay, but in the end, her pitiful attempt to shut out the past crumbled under the weight of a simple sound. The soft rush of Wajo Stream could be heard in the distance, the water high from melting snow, bubbling over rocks and fallen trees, taking her back to the last time she'd been in these woods . . .

THE STENCH OF SKUNK SURROUNDED HER, MAKING HER EYES *water and her lungs burn. Sophie pressed her cheek against the rotting walls of her narrow shelter. How long had it been? Minutes? Hours? It was quiet, too quiet, as if some-one,* or something, *had silenced the forest.*

She dared not move, dared not breathe.

The soft padded steps of a four-legged beast soon closed in, circled around her—and then paused.

Sophie was trapped, unable to move; her hiding place became her prison. She tried to scramble out but her position was awkward, and the wolf had anticipated her move; the log crumpled just before a sharp pain ran down her side.

Her breath lodged in her throat, stunned as nerve end-ings screamed. Her vision blurred as she plunged forward onto the wet forest floor. Pine needles and leaves stuck to her face, the cold earth keeping her lucid, reminding her to fight and not give up. She rolled onto her uninjured side, using her good leg to scoot backward against a tree, holding her belly and sucking in deep breaths of air as she lifted her eyes to her attacker.

And a red wolf stared back, eye level to Sophie's sitting position, smaller than Dylan, with softer lines and golden eyes filled with hatred, too much hatred for mercy.

Sophie recognized her death in those golden eyes, and in a moment of calm clarity, her brain adjusted to her pre-dicament. These were wolves. They did not show compas-sion. They did not respect fear; prey showed fear.

They understood dominance.

Sophie lowered her chin and leveled a glare at the female wolf. "If you harm me . . . you harm Dylan's child."

In response, the wolf lifted her head to the sky. Sophie sensed the air thickening, as if the earth stilled to give its breath, its very life force, to another. And again, in a surreal show of melted fur and broken bone, a being changed its form, this time from a wolf into a woman.

Sophie, unfortunately, recognized that woman.

Siân unfolded into a standing position, naked and un-ashamed, tall and lithe like an athlete. Wet strands of dark red hair trailed over pale skin as she glared down at Sophie.

"Look at you," Siân sneered. "So weak. So . . . human." Full lips peeled back over small white teeth, wolf's behavior despite the human form. "I don't believe that child you carry was fathered by Dylan."

Sophie was about to dispute the vile accusation, but something in Siân's voice stopped her, something desperate and a little . . . unstable.

Sophie stood, slowly; her wounded leg threatened to crumple but eventually held her weight. She stole a quick glance at her shredded jeans covered in blood. Just a flesh wound, she prayed, because she needed the ability to run.

She wanted freedom, not death; she wanted her baby to live, and a lie was such an easy price to pay for what Sophie wanted.

"You're right." Somehow she sensed those words were her key to freedom. "My baby isn't Dylan's."

A triumphant smile touched Siân's lips. "Then you don't belong here."

"No, I don't." Sophie almost laughed at how much she agreed with those words.

"You're not worthy of Dylan. You're not strong enough to lead by his side. You're not strong enough to protect us."

Sensing victory, she kept her voice calm. "Let me leave and someone more deserving can have him."

A predatory light entered Siân's golden eyes. A different plan danced within those eerie depths that the wolf within found more appealing.

"Dylan believes my child is his," Sophie reminded her.

"*Even now, he may smell my blood on your hands. What would your punishment be, I wonder, if he thought you had harmed his child?*"

Doubt filled Siân's expression, and then fear as she dumbly stared down at her hands, where blood remained even after changing forms, damning streaks of burgundy against pale skin. "*So fragile . . .*" Her voice was breathless, almost in awe. "*Like a newborn lamb.*"

"If you let me leave," Sophie continued, weaving threats and planting ideas, knowing her only defense was ingenuity and not physical strength, "you'll have time to clean up, to go home. He'll never know . . ."

Siân frowned then, as if weighing her options. "Yes," she whispered finally, "that would be for the best. Your only chance is to keep to the water. You don't have much time. The guards have separated but they'll circle back soon. Go south along the stream. Stay in the water. It will hide your stench."

"I know the way." Adrenaline rushed over her, fueling her resolve. She headed straight for the stream, refusing to look back, the pain of her wounded leg dulled by the promise of freedom.

Laughter whispered through the trees.

"*Run, human. Run far away and never return . . . because if you do, I'll kill you and that bastard child you carry in your womb.*"

Sophie didn't run, couldn't run—her injured leg barely supported weight—but she managed to hobble over fallen limbs and narrow trails until the sound of rushing water reached her ears. She waded in shallow water for hours, staying close to the shore and off the more slippery rocks with deeper currents, hoping she'd gone far enough to obscure her trail. The burning in her leg had disappeared long ago, numbed by the frigid water.

Fearing hypothermia, she crawled onto the bank of the stream and listened for footsteps, or voices, or the warning of a too silent forest, but instead heard chickadees in the trees and moving cars in the distance.

The interstate was just up ahead.

It was then, with the sound of freedom within her reach, that Sophie paused and her heart cried out. Because her heart, despite everything, belonged to Dylan. No matter what he was, no matter what he'd done, she loved him.

She would always love him.

And for a moment, just a moment, she wondered if she could conform to his will, to this magical world that hated her humanity. To live in a mansion of stone. To sleep in Dylan's bed.

Was such a prison so bad?

She wrapped her arms around her belly and cried, hating the emotional weakness that Dylan, or perhaps pregnancy, brought on. Hot trails streamed down her frozen cheeks and her heart felt the loss to her very core. But in the end, no man was worth her soul.

No man was worth living in fear for her child.

Her decision made, she wiped away her wretched tears and crawled toward the sound of freedom . . .

A CAR DOOR SLAMMED SHUT, SNAPPING SOPHIE BACK TO the present, and the sound of rushing water faded in the distance.

The lake house loomed above her, rectangular like a colonial, constructed with fieldstone and mortar and large pine beams. It still had its original movable shutters, painted black to match the front paneled door. Ivy branches snaked their way up the front porch, dormant still, even though the calendar had already proclaimed spring.

It had been built on an angle, facing the mountain. The afternoon sun cast a deceivingly warm glow across Fiddlehead Lake just a few yards away. Smoke rose from the chimney, letting her know *he* was in there, *waiting*.

Sophie had the distinct urge to vomit. Intense anxiety had that effect on her.

"This is so cool," Joshua exclaimed beside her, eyes wide,

taking it all in. "That's Fiddlehead Lake, then?" He leaned his head toward the large body of water, judging the angle of the afternoon sun. He'd been forced to study maps of the area, to learn every escape route, just in case.

Sophie nodded. "We're at the southern part of the lake."

He pointed toward a grove of white birch trees in the distance. "That's where the lake feeds into Wajo Stream, which leads to the Penobscot River."

"Yes," she said with approval. "Rhuddin Village is just the entrance of your father's territory. There's a clinic five miles north if you continue along the road we entered on, then your father's house, and another building for guards. They all circle along the outskirts of the wilderness reserve. And everything connects to the mountain—"

"—and the best way out is through the waterways," he finished. "Don't worry, Mom. I remember everything you've told me."

Sophie ran her hand down his arm, needing to touch him, fighting every urge to throw him back in that car and drive away before she lost him to this other world forever. But another fear, a greater fear, kept her grounded. "I love you."

"Love you too, Mom."

She had professed those words so many times over the years that his response was automatic. She didn't care. She had needed to hear it.

The front door opened and Dylan walked out. She straightened, letting her hand drop away from Joshua's arm.

Dylan remained silent, an announcement unnecessary. His mere presence demanded attention. He wore jeans and a black flannel shirt that hugged his massive frame. His once shoulder-length golden waves had been cut business short, only to make him look harder, more severe.

Dark eyes landed on her, black as sin, absent of light and utterly compelling, as if all the mysteries of the universe waited in their depths for someone strong enough to handle the darkness.

Or so she had thought, *once*, when she was young and

stupid and still believed in romance and happy endings. She wasn't so young anymore, and far less stupid, and she knew way too much about the darkness to hope for a happy ending.

And yet, those eyes continued to hold her captive with unspoken emotion. It was Dylan who broke the contact first—*not* her. His expression, however, changed upon seeing his son for the first time; it softened into something almost . . . *vulnerable*?

Joshua remained frozen to her side, not touching but not parting either. Sophie took a step forward to lead her son, knowing this awkward silence was her fault and her challenge to fix.

"Joshua," she said, "this is your father." She climbed the steps until she stood on the cedar planks of the porch. "Dylan, your son."

Dylan closed the distance, offering a hand. "There has not been a day I haven't thought of you."

Joshua extended his hand, only to be pulled into a fierce hug. At six foot three, he was only a few inches shorter than his father, and not quite as massive, but the resemblance was undeniable.

Dylan held on to his son with his eyes closed and his nostrils flared as if learning a precious new scent. Joshua didn't move, and his discomfort became obvious as the embrace prolonged into another awkward silence.

Dylan stepped back and gave a sad, knowing smile. "You're tall for your age." He gave Joshua a playful squeeze on his shoulder as if he couldn't stop touching him, not yet. "And strong."

Joshua grinned under the compliments. "I work out every day. And Mom makes me drink protein shakes."

Sophie felt a gentle hand on her arm as her own mother came up beside her. Some of her tension eased with the unspoken support. *You are loved,* that gesture said, *no matter what.*

Sophie squeezed her mother's hand, so very thankful to have her there at that moment. It made her wonder whether things might have been different back then if only one person had been on her side.

The seclusion might have been tolerable.

Francine cleared her throat, her sharp brown eyes assessing Dylan with haughty disdain. She was just as protective of her child as Sophie was of Joshua. "The amount of food my grandson puts away could feed a small army."

Sophie cleared her throat. "Mom, this is Dylan. Dylan, my mother."

"You may call me Francine." Her chin rose in challenge, although her voice remained polite.

"Francine." He gave her a brief nod. If he was displeased with her presence it didn't show. "Please call me Dylan."

"Can I look around?" Joshua interrupted, too overwhelmed to stay put for long.

"Help me unload first," Sophie reminded him. "Then maybe your father will give you a tour."

Dylan pinned her with those black eyes, his expression unreadable. "I would like nothing more, Joshua, but your aunt Elen is anxious to meet you. She's waiting for us at the clinic. I don't know how long her patience will last."

"Okay." Joshua's expression turned thoughtful. "Can we eat first?"

A slight smile tugged at Dylan's lips. "I believe a small feast is being prepared for you at this very moment."

"Cool. Can Mom come too?"

"Of course. Enid, *my cook*," Dylan explained, "is making your mother's favorite. Your grandmother is welcome as well."

"I'll pass," Francine interjected. "But I appreciate the offer. I'll stay behind and unpack."

"Are you sure, Mum?" Sophie asked. "We can just put the food in the fridge and I'll unpack our clothes later."

"It's been a long day and I'm tired." Francine pinned her daughter with a meaningful gaze. "But you need to do this."

"Did you hear that, Mom?" Joshua's dark eyes twinkled with mischief. "Enid, *the cook*, is making your favorite."

"I heard." Her stomach gave a small heave of protest.

Six

DYLAN DROVE IN SILENCE, A FEELING OF COMPLETE fulfillment spreading out from his chest and into his limbs. Sophie had cared well for their son. Joshua was strong and healthy. *And here*—where he belonged.

Unable to stop himself, Dylan took another sidelong glance. It was odd and more than a little overwhelming to see one's own features on another being. Joshua sat with his legs spread wide, taking up the whole passenger seat, his hands drumming softly against the dashboard.

Dylan had not felt such peace in a very long time.

A turn in the road came into view. On impulse, he veered his truck to the left, choosing the long way to the clinic. He heard Sophie shift in the backseat as she became aware of the detour.

Dylan watched her in the rearview mirror. Her profile was clean of paint, her complexion drawn by winter, or strain. Or both. Her jaw clenched as she stared out of the window, trying hard to ignore his presence. Her light brown hair cascaded down her back in thick waves. He'd always known her to keep it short.

She wore jeans and a navy sweatshirt and looked very much like the college intern he'd met sixteen years ago. She had not aged. He wondered if she realized that.

"What has your mother told you of me?"

Joshua straightened, his hands dropping to his lap, looking over his shoulder to the backseat. It angered Dylan that he looked to her first for approval.

"Just tell your father the truth," Sophie said.

"Um, well, I know you have a huge house that looks like a stone fort and a lot of people live there. You watch out for everyone in your town like they're your responsibility. I have an uncle named Luc. And an aunt named Elen who's a doctor. They were nice to Mom when she lived here."

The last was said as if everyone else was unkind to Sophie. How many other lies had she told?

"Do you know how your mother and I met?"

Joshua nodded. "You rented her the lake house. She worked as a wildlife biologist on a research team from the University of Maine and was trying to reintroduce caribou back into the Katahdin region. You guys ended up spending the summer together until Mom found out she was pregnant with me. She quit her job and moved in with you."

The accounting was too guarded for Dylan's satisfaction. "Did she tell you about her time in Rhuddin Hall? And please don't moderate."

"I'm not." Joshua's defense of his mother was immediate. "You were always worried about her and kept people around her. She was very sad because you wouldn't let her call Grandma. She found out my grandfather died from an obituary in a newspaper. You wouldn't let her go to the funeral. You guys had a really big fight over it." He paused, his eyes shifting to the backseat.

"Go on," Sophie urged.

"Mom didn't understand why you were so weird about her leaving. Then one night you showed her why." He didn't give specifics but his voice indicated he knew them. "Just before you"—he cleared his throat—"*changed*, you told her she could leave after I was born, but without me. So she left before I was born."

Although biased, the accounting was fairly accurate. Dylan had expected worse. However, there was an odd tone to his son's voice. "What are you not telling me?"

"Nothing," Joshua hedged. "I don't know. I just don't think you knew Mom that well or you'd never have made that offer. That's all."

That's all.

Dylan gripped the steering wheel, trying hard to keep the anger from his voice. It seemed Sophie had omitted an important piece of information that their son deserved to know. "My words and actions may seem unfair to you, but I had my reasons. Your mother and I were wedded that summer she spent at the lake house. When she moved into my house we were husband and wife."

Sophie hissed from the backseat, no longer ignoring his presence. "I don't believe that wedding was entirely legal."

He met her glare in the rearview mirror, deciding with some satisfaction that he preferred her anger to indifference. "Do your oaths mean nothing, *wife*? Because I assure you *I* don't make vows unless I mean to keep them."

"We were never in a church," she ground out, a forced calm in front of their son. "As far as I'm concerned, that ceremony was just a romantic gesture in the woods. There was no minister present, or a priest, or a justice of the peace, for that matter. And I know we never signed any papers—"

"We were in *my* church. And I don't need a clergyman or a clerk to validate my vows. And documents are useless items easily destroyed and irrelevant."

And you are my mate, his wolf growled silently, flexing its teeth along Dylan's spine. *An unbreakable bond. Your human vows are insignificant in comparison.*

Her jaw hung open, rendering her momentarily speechless. Joshua remained quiet in the passenger seat, although a slight grin tugged at his lips.

"Don't even think about it." Sophie found her voice and its warning tone was aimed directly at their son.

"Awww . . . Come on, Mom." He looked over his shoulder, his eyes aglow with potential trouble. "Grandma should know."

"Grandma won't recognize anything not blessed by a minister."

Dylan stowed that information away for later use and addressed another issue about his son's account that bothered him. "I had valid reasons for wanting your mother to separate from her old life, even her family. It was for her protection, and theirs, and for the people I'm responsible for. Now that you're here, you'll learn the whole of it."

And you'll understand my side.

Sophie cleared her throat. "I only recently gave Joshua the full details about"—her voice faltered—"the last time I saw you. I told him two weeks ago, when I could no longer delude myself that he wasn't experiencing similar traits."

Dylan grew annoyed with the evasive wordplay. "You know I can change into a wolf?"

Joshua nodded. "Yeah, Mom wanted me to know just in case I inherited the same . . . um, talent."

"And were you surprised to hear of such a thing?"

"Not really." He rolled his eyes toward the backseat. "But, if you haven't noticed, Mom's more than a little freaked-out about it."

Not really.

Curious now, Dylan pulled over to the side of the road and opened the passenger-side window. "What do you hear in the forest, Joshua?"

He nodded with understanding and accepted the challenge. "There's a bird making a nest a few yards away." He pointed to a grove of young cedars. "Two deer are foraging for food over there." He closed his eyes, concentrating on the sounds. "A man and a woman are whispering a short distance up this road." He opened his eyes and gave a confident smile. "They just stopped."

Dylan forced himself to stay calm. The man and woman he referred to were guards, Ceri and Gabriel, and they were more than a short distance away. "How long have your senses been . . . *heightened*?"

"I don't know," Joshua said. "Always, I guess. I've always known I've been different from other kids, *stronger*. But in the last three weeks I've felt . . . *more*." He shot a sidelong glance toward his mother. "I feel things I haven't before."

"Like what?" Dylan's heart slammed against his chest. "What do you feel?"

"Life." Joshua's voice dropped to a low growl not entirely human. "Power."

Dylan hissed, sensing the whispers of energy dance along his skin, called not by him but by his son.

Sweet Mother. Was it possible?

Did he dare allow himself to hope for such a thing?

"What *is* that?" Sophie asked, her voice anxious.

"A gift," Dylan whispered. "An unbelievable gift. Do you know what that power can do, Joshua?"

He blinked slowly. "I think so."

I think so. Not tested then, not fully.

"You'll learn." Dylan reached over, unable to contain his joy, grabbing his son by the shoulder to give a reassuring squeeze. "I'll teach you."

"When?" he asked, eager.

"Soon."

"Is Joshua going to be okay?" Sophie demanded, leaning forward, inches from his face.

He turned to her, a brush of movement before she jumped back. He ground his teeth against her fleeting scent. "As long as he stays with me, everything will be fine."

"And how long will that take?" Suspicion and fear laced her voice.

Dylan evaded her question with one of his own. "Did anything change in Joshua's life three weeks ago?"

She frowned then. "No. Nothing changed." Her eyes

turned toward their son, shrewd and assessing. "Unless I'm not aware of it."

"No, nothing," Joshua confirmed. "At least, I don't think so. I like where we live now. It's been nice not moving around so much."

"Ah," Dylan said.

"What?" Sophie's voice turned frantic.

"Joshua's wolf might have remained dormant because his environment was constantly changing . . . *unsteady.*"

Her brown eyes snapped with gold fire. "He's always been protected . . . and loved, no matter where we were."

"But he probably sensed your anxiety," Dylan explained. "He wasn't given enough time to settle, to feel secure in his surroundings . . . until recently. Am I right?"

She remained silent.

He pressed his point, "How long have you lived in your current location?" It took a great deal of self-control not to ask where that location was specifically.

"Four years," she admitted, although with obvious reluctance. "So this . . . *change* in Joshua has nothing to do with hormones? I thought maybe . . . I don't know . . . *puberty* might have brought this on."

"Oh, *God*, Mom." Joshua rolled his eyes, disgusted. "You're like a few years too late for that question."

Dylan had a hard time keeping his grin contained. "No, age is irrelevant."

"Okay." Sophie exhaled softly. "But is he going to be okay now that"—she swallowed—"now that his wolf's no longer dormant?"

"I promise you," Dylan said calmly, trying to ease her concern, "if he stays with me, no harm will come to him. There are things for him to learn that you can't teach him. You must understand that."

"I'm here, aren't I?" She pressed back into the seat, crossing her arms. "If Joshua wants to stay, we will. If not—"

"I wanna stay, Mom." Obviously sensing the undercurrents of his parents, he hedged, "Mom can stay too, right?"

Dylan swallowed a pleased snarl.

He had her.

"Only if she wants to."

"If *I'm* here," Joshua said with confidence, "Mom'll want to stay."

The unguarded statement revealed a great deal about their relationship.

His son had only known love from his mother.

Dylan felt his beast sigh with satisfaction. "Your mother is aware of my conditions. They haven't changed. There must be no contact with anyone outside our territory."

A look passed between mother and son, a questioning glance from Joshua answered by a sharp frown from Sophie.

Their distrust left a vile taste on Dylan's tongue. "There are five hundred and twelve people living in Rhuddin Village under my protection. I refuse to have their welfare compromised. Their lives are no less valuable than ours."

"That shouldn't be a problem," Joshua blurted out. "We have no one of importance to contact. Right, Mom? Grandma's already here. And I'm here. There's no one else. Well, besides Mr. Ayres. But he's not family."

Dylan frowned with the mention of another man's name, a man who he'd never heard of—a man who *wasn't* family.

"He's my boss," Sophie explained, her voice dry. "Nothing more. He does deserve a call, however. And will be getting one."

Seven

A CIRCLE OF TALL PINE TREES SHROUDED THE SMALL
clinic from outside eyes. The building was all on one level,
half built into the ground, a fairly modern design of cement
walls and metal roofing painted brown and green to blend
with its surroundings.

Sophie followed Joshua and Dylan along a dark path that
led to the only visible entrance. Her son hovered close to his
father, eager to please, and not acting the least bit un-
healthy.

She glared at Dylan's back, fuming at her own stupidity,
beginning to realize Joshua had never been in any real danger, and that Dylan had taken advantage of her ignorance.
He'd been too damn happy in the truck at the first indication
of—whatever the hell *it* was. *Power*, they'd called it.

Dylan opened the door to the clinic, a smile—an actual
smile—on his face as he laughed at something Joshua had
said.

Her breath clogged in her throat as she watched the bud-
ding relationship grow stronger with each passing minute.
Her son looked happy, more than happy—accepted.

Wanted.

Her shoulders slumped. Dylan deserved to know his son, and Joshua needed his father. She no longer had the right to deny them that relationship.

If she ever had.

"Mom, come on." Joshua held the solid metal door, waiting for her.

And suddenly a small weight of sadness lifted and she quickened her step. Dylan would never be able to take away the time she'd had with their son. No matter what the future held, Joshua would always know how much she'd loved him.

"Hold on," she said. "I'm coming."

Elen stood in a large open space reserved for incoming emergencies. She looked just as fair and lovely as Sophie remembered, with her hands crossed in front of her chest, watching Joshua approach with tear-filled eyes.

"Hello, Joshua. My goodness, you're tall. And handsome. I'm your aunt Elen. It seems I've waited forever to meet you."

Joshua held up his hand in a quick wave, uncomfortable with the personal greeting. "Hi."

Elen stayed back, obviously sensing his unease. She turned to Sophie and her expression turned colder than Fiddlehead Lake in February. "Thank you for bringing him home. If you don't mind, I'd like to ask you a few questions. Then I'll examine him in private."

Icy. Professional. And yet Joshua's alarmed expression gentled her voice. "Just a quick check of your vitals," she told him. "It won't take long. Your mom can come too, if you'd be more comfortable."

He straightened under the insinuation of still needing his mother. "Nah, I'm good."

"Joshua's never been to a hospital before," Sophie found it necessary to explain. "He's never been sick, until recently."

"I'm not sick, Mom."

Sophie waved away the interruption. "You know what I mean."

Elen frowned, tilting her head to one side, assessing. "Where did you give birth?"

"At home. With midwives." Sophie tried to ignore Dylan's silent glare. "I was afraid he'd be different. I didn't want him to be taken if he was."

Elen nodded, not denying the possibility. "Was the birthing normal?"

"I believe so. But it was long."

"*How* long?" Dylan asked.

"Twenty-five hours. He was ten pounds six ounces," Sophie said proudly. "And perfect."

Elen's posture softened at the last comment, although her voice remained reserved. "What did you feed him as an infant?"

"I nursed. My mother tried to give him a bottle once just to supplement feedings but he wouldn't take it. He was hungry *all* the time. He fed more than he slept. You should've seen me. *I was huge.*"

Sophie dropped her hands, realizing with some embarrassment she'd been demonstrating how big her chest had gotten.

Joshua groaned. "Way more info than I needed to hear."

Dylan had gone rigid, the small muscle on the side of his cheek flexed and relaxed, then flexed again.

Elen tactfully changed the subject. "And after? What's his diet been like?"

Sophie let out a soft laugh. "Pretty much everything I give him, and then some. He never seems to gain weight. I even supplement his meals with protein shakes."

Elen gave Joshua a brief smile. "He looks good," she admitted. "So whatever you've done has worked well for him. Has he had any immunizations?"

"No." Sophie shook her head. "Should he have? I was just afraid to expose him."

Elen shrugged. "They're unnecessary but wouldn't have harmed him. I asked only because a few cause lethargic symptoms until both immune systems adjust. It might have explained certain behaviors. You must have homeschooled him then," she said absently, "if he wasn't immunized?"

"Not always. I worked in the public school system when he was younger. I forged his heath records. If you look for them," she warned to discourage an investigation, "they are inaccurate."

"You've become quite resourceful, haven't you?" Dylan commented dryly.

Sophie sent him a too sweet smile. "I've always been resourceful. Now I'm just paranoid."

"Any unexplained broken bones?" Elen continued her questioning without pause. "High fevers? Problems sleeping?"

Again, Sophie shook her head. "He's always been healthy up until three weeks ago," she hesitated, still finding it odd to speak openly, "when the changes began."

Elen's eyes darted to Dylan. "Thank you, that's all I need for now. Joshua can answer the rest of my questions." She waved him over. "Are you ready, my handsome nephew?"

"I guess so." Joshua didn't look exactly thrilled to be led down the strange corridor by an unfamiliar aunt.

As he turned away, Sophie forced a reassuring smile. Letting him walk down that hallway without her was beyond difficult. It was, in a sense, the first step toward letting him go. She reminded herself to be reasonable. Elen's frosty reception was in defense of her brother and she would never harm her nephew. Joshua was almost sixteen.

Unfortunately, the heart wasn't guided by reason.

Adding to her unease was Dylan's looming presence—and the simple fact that they were now alone.

She was fairly certain her punishment was about to begin.

$\mathcal{E}$ight

DYLAN FOUND HIMSELF AT THE RECEIVING END OF AN
angry woman's displeasure, one who should be groveling
for forgiveness and not leveling him with a very astute glare.

"Joshua's not the least bit in danger of dying, is he?"

He saw no reason to carry the untruth any further. "No,
not unless vital organs are removed from his body."

She pursed her lips at his blunt response. "But he's different?" She exhaled softly, amending her words. "Well,
different even for your kind?"

Again, very perceptive. "Not exactly."

"Can you just give me a straight answer for once?"

"You speak to me with venom in your voice and yet I'm
not the one whose actions require atonement. So choose
your words wisely from now on, because your audacity has
reached its limit."

She sighed then, an anguished sound that called to his
soul, if he even had a soul. With her, it seemed that he must,
because he always felt tortured in her presence.

"You're angry, and you have every right to hate me for
what I've done." She lifted her hand in a helpless gesture

before letting it fall back to her side. "But if our situations were reversed, you would've done the same thing."

"Never, Sophie. I never would've kept you from our son."

Her features pinched. Whether from guilt or anger he wasn't sure, nor did he care.

"You're so certain," she said. "So quick to judge. But then you never considered my position in your life. You just expected me to conform."

"I expected you to trust me," he ground out.

Her eyes widened. *"Trust you?* How do you trust someone who's suffocating you? I couldn't breathe without you or someone hovering over me, watching me—*following me.* I was constantly guarded by people who despised me, not permitted to contact my family—"

"I was protecting you!"

"You were protecting your secret," she snapped. "And when my father died you wouldn't even let me go to the funeral."

"The man had already passed on. Your presence over his dead body would not change that fact."

She went completely still. "And how does that justify your response to my grief? You locked me in a room like . . ." Her voice shook with raw anger. "Like a dog. *You made me a prisoner—*"

"You were threatening to leave me!"

"—and then you dragged me through the woods and changed into a . . . *a wolf. And*, if that wasn't enough, just before your little demonstration, you gave me an option to leave, but without my child."

When he didn't respond she glared at him as if he were the king of idiots. "And you wonder why I left you?"

With great effort he managed to keep his voice restrained. "I would never have made that offer if I'd known how much you wanted our child."

She scoffed, "Every mother wants their child."

No, he thought, *not every mother.* "There are more lives at stake here than just yours or mine, or even our son's."

"I didn't betray your secret." She misunderstood his point. "Joshua's the only person I told."

"I believe you." Unfortunately, that wasn't the betrayal that had caused him over a decade of sleepless nights.

She sighed, pinching the bridge of her delicate nose. "Fighting will not solve our differences. Can I make a suggestion?"

"I'm listening." He crossed his arms, leery of her sudden tone of cooperation.

"I will answer any question you have for me, truthfully— if you do the same."

It wasn't, Dylan decided, an unreasonable request. "What do you want to know?"

"What's different about Joshua that you're not telling me?"

He regarded her for a long moment before answering. It was time, he agreed, to end her ignorance. "A shifter hasn't been born in over three hundred years. So, *if* our son is powerful enough to change into the wolf, it will be an incredible blessing for me and my people."

She frowned, absorbing that information, and not, it seemed, particularly pleased with the idea of her son becoming a wolf.

Tough shit.

"*You're* a shifter."

"Yes." He knew where this was going.

"How old are you?"

He hesitated only a moment, but then answered with blunt honesty. Whether she believed him or not was irrelevant. The time for lies had ended the moment Sophie had reentered his territory.

She was never leaving again.

"I was born 329 years after the modern calendar lists the birth of Christ. In a place called Penllyn. You would know my country as Wales."

She remained quiet for several moments. "I would call you a liar, *or a lunatic*, if I had not watched you change from a man into a wolf with my very own eyes." She gave a soft laugh, a calming means of self-preservation when the mind was forced to accept knowledge it didn't want or understand. "The only thing I'm sure of is how much I don't know about this world."

"That night in the woods was my attempt to open your eyes, to teach you, although I must admit now that I may have been overenthusiastic in my approach."

His attempt at humor was rewarded with a slight smile.

"Wales, early fourth century," she mused. "Celtic then? Pagan?"

He nodded, his eyes drawn to her full mouth as she worried her bottom lip, taunting him with desire that he didn't want.

Soft brown eyes lifted to his, unguarded and without malice. "That explains a lot."

This conversation had taken a dangerous turn. In the face of anger he could resist her, but not this—not her looking up at him with newfound understanding. It was her gentle nature that had drawn him to her in the beginning.

He could do nothing but respond. "Like what?"

"Your beliefs. The way you live. Your fortress of a home." She lifted one delicate shoulder and let it fall, causing light to dance around her long curls. "Your dominant temperament."

"The last is from my wolf." The treacherous beast that wanted to reach out and snag one of those curls to explore its texture.

"Joshua has your eyes," she whispered. "Those are not the eyes of a Celt. Or a wolf."

"Roman," he supplied, taking a step back before he gave in to baser instincts. "My father was a legionary commander during the Roman occupation of Britain, his mother an Egyptian slave."

She blinked twice and began to rub her temples. "Are your parents still alive?"

"Not my father. He wasn't of our kind."

"Neither am I," she said softly, wrongly assuming that Dylan and Joshua would exceed her in life. And yet it was not with resentment but awe that she asked, "How long could Joshua live?"

"Thousands of years."

Still, denial lingered. "But he's aged normally."

"Our children age at the normal human rate until adolescence. But then the aging process slows." He waited for her to assimilate that information before moving on to something he knew would truly unsettle her. "The same way your aging has slowed since carrying my son."

Her expression again turned wary. "You said your father's no longer alive because he wasn't of your kind."

"It's different for mothers," he explained. "You carried my child, shared your blood with his for over nine months. Because of that biological bond, an incubation of our blood with yours, you'll live much longer than you've assumed."

He did not, however, inform her of the rarity of a female conception with a male of his kind.

Sophie had initiated their affair that fateful summer. He had accepted the pleasant distraction only because he'd thought nothing would come of it.

Obviously, he'd been wrong.

Just one of many misjudgments concerning this woman.

"Let me get this straight." Her voice was thick with disbelief. "Are you saying I could live for over a thousand years?"

"That's very possible."

"As long as no vital organs are removed."

"Yes." He would kill anyone who dared try.

She slowly slid into a waiting chair, resting her face in her hands. He left her alone, a difficult stance when all his instincts itched to pull her into his arms.

Finally, she lifted her head. "You're not messing with me, are you?"

"Why would I lie about something that will only be proven in time?" He sighed at her lowered glare. "It's been

sixteen years and you look the same. Haven't you noticed?"

"Women in my family age very well," she said defen-
sively.

"Not that well." And just to prove his point, or so he justified to himself, he stepped forward and ran a finger down
the smooth perfection of her cheek. "The sooner you accept
that you're a part of my world, the easier it will be for you
to accept your fate."

She leaned away from his touch, visibly shaken. He let
his hand drop to his side as an inner battle raged.

He'd underestimated the effect of one simple touch.

He'd been denied physical comfort for too long.

"And what's that supposed to mean?" Sophie asked,
oblivious of her precarious position. "I don't believe in fate,"
she huffed. "I believe in choice and free will."

He gave a bitter laugh. "You'll learn there are some
things beyond our control, and that we are just pawns to a
higher power."

That annoyed her. "Fine. But how am I supposed to accept *my fate*, as you call it, if I don't even know what you
are." She held her hands up, waiting for an explanation.
"What are you? Werewolves? Shape shifters? How are you
possible? How are the shifts possible? Are you even from
this earth?"

"Shape shifter is an apt term." He did his best not to smile
at her naïve questions. "And yes, we are from this earth. But
werewolves, as far as I know, are just a legend."

"Then you're not allergic to silver?" When he hesitated,
she blurted, "I ask only for Joshua's sake."

"We are not allergic to silver." He let his eyes drop to her
waist, having noticed earlier she favored her right side. "That
gun under your sweatshirt won't protect you, whether it's
loaded with silver bullets or lead." She remained silent. He
suspected she had other weapons planted on her person or
she would have shown more concern. "Nor are we compelled by the full moon. However, some of our elders still

shift on the night of the dark moon to honor the Goddess Ceridwen. I would not be surprised if the werewolf legend began with an unknown witness to a ritual, thousands of years ago."

"And how do you shift?"

He gave thoughtful consideration to his answer, knowing a woman born of modern times would only understand the scientific explanation. "The earth is a powerful instrument; creation is constant. The same element that makes a seed grow into a tree, and animals age, and winter turn into spring, can be used in different applications, if you know what to look for and how to draw from its energy." He eluded the full explanation for another time. Better to let her adjust in increments. Sophie didn't react well to surprises she didn't like. "Now, I think it's your turn to answer my questions, and I expect the same honesty I've given you."

She crossed her arms in front of her chest. "I'm always honest. You've always just chosen not to listen."

"How could you have done it?" He didn't know who was more surprised by his first question, him or Sophie. "How could you have taken my son?" *How could you have left me?* "Did you even think of me, just once?"

"Of course." She lifted her hand as if to touch his arm but then let it drop. "How could I not? I almost called you the night Joshua was born. He was so beautiful and I wanted to share that with you. I even dialed your number."

He scowled. "Why would you tell me this other than to torment me?"

"I've given you no reason to believe me, I know . . . but I never wanted to hurt you." Conflicting emotions bled from her pores in a murky spiral of scents: sorrow, bitterness, frustration, and beneath them all, the pungent trail of fear. "Did it ever occur to you that I may have had valid reasons for staying away?"

His nostrils flared; he inhaled slowly, savoring the evidence of her remorse on the back of his tongue like a perfectly aged Scottish whisky. "I can think of none worth what you've put me through." He turned his back on her, feeling his wolf react in earnest. "Do you have any idea what it was like for me? Wondering if you were alive? Wondering about my child?"

He heard a whisper of movement before he felt a tentative hand on his shoulder. When he didn't shove her off, she moved closer.

"And for that," she whispered, "I *am* truly sorry. I was scared, Dylan. I was scared of losing my son."

He had no argument against an assumption caused by his own words. "Did you teach Joshua to fear me?"

"No." She released his arm and walked away. "I taught him not to trust the people around you."

His chest tightened with her admission. "Why would you do such a thing?"

She faced him with a hardened expression, reminding him of a warrior after a first kill, of innocence lost. "Because the people you're so eager to defend are not worthy of our trust."

"What have they ever done to you to warrant such dislike?"

She tilted her head to one side. "You have no idea, do you?" She shrugged. "But then why would you? I made certain you wouldn't."

"Speak openly . . . because your evasive words grow tiresome."

"Then I'll save you the details." A dead calm stole over her. "But there is something you should know . . . Siân found me in the woods the night I ran from you. I convinced her to let me go by telling her my child wasn't yours. However, she threatened to kill us if we ever returned, and I have reason to believe she'll try."

Her words robbed him of air. He had no memory of Siân from that night, but if she had found Sophie and not told him . . .

"Siân has been contained," he said quietly. "I will

investigate your claims. If they prove true then she'll be punished accordingly."

"If they prove true?" she sneered, shaking her head as if the betrayal of their past was his fault alone. "You are blind when it comes to your people. I was stupid to believe that anything I might say would change your mind."

"I'm protective," he corrected. "And I told you I would investigate your claims."

She gave him an odd smile. "Do you want to know the main reason I didn't call you?"

He remained silent, waiting to hear her reasoning, no matter how irrational, because whether they were true or not, he was quite certain that Sophie *believed* her accusations.

"It was for *Joshua's* safety," she continued. "I've waited until he was strong enough to defend himself against the people *you* are so eager to protect."

Her lack of trust in his ability to keep their child safe left a foul scent in the air. His voice lowered to a soft growl. "No harm will come to you," he vowed. "*Or* to my son, while you're in my territory. I will make certain of it."

"Thank you," she said, sounding genuinely relieved.

Her gratitude annoyed him; their safety should have been expected, *not* appreciated. "I still have a few questions I'd like you to answer."

"I'm sure you do."

"Has anyone helped you since that night in the woods?" He found it incomprehensible that she'd been able to hide from him all this time. She had no idea of the lengths he had gone to find her.

"Not in the manner you're suggesting. The only help I received was from family and old friends, nothing that was connected to you. And not once did I betray your secret."

"Where have you been?" Thanks to Porter, he knew she'd made her first call from Providence. It had taken the guard a good amount of time to locate her signal, but by morning he'd been able to report some useful findings—and yet not nearly enough for Dylan's satisfaction.

"I didn't leave the country," she admitted, still protecting something, *or someone*. "I taught grade school until the fingerprinting laws started to take effect. Then most recently I've been working as a chef and housekeeper for a nice employer."

"Mr. Ayres," he supplied dryly.

"Yes." Her tone dropped in warning. "And I would be very angry if you tracked this person down and questioned him. He knows nothing of my past. He's innocent."

"I promise not to track him down if you promise not to run."

"I'm not going anywhere, Dylan, as long as Joshua wants to stay." She lifted her hands and let them fall back to her side. "I only ask that you work with me, to at least be civil with me in front of him."

He frowned, not knowing how to respond to such a rational request. "Agreed."

"I know my son." She sighed with resigned acceptance. "I'm not sure how long he wants to stay, but I have a feeling it might be for a while."

"*Our* son," he corrected quietly, "is old enough to make his own decisions."

"I know that," she said softly. "He'll need to enroll in school. And I'll have to commute to find a job." She began to pace, a delicate frown creasing her forehead. "But Bangor's only an hour away. If it's not in your territory then it must be somewhat close. You can make a compromise, I'm sure, if you really want to." A sparkle of hope lifted her features; her voice turned wistful. "I'd love to teach again."

"Teach? Commute? *A job?*" Being with Sophie was equivalent to standing on a small ship during a nasty storm, the ground beneath his feet constantly unstable and threatening to toss him on his ass.

"Will you rent me the lake house?" she asked cheerfully.

"*Rent you the lake house,*" he spat, livid once again now

that her words had sunk in. "You're not a servant. I don't expect *payment* from you to live here. I'll provide whatever you need. You're my—"

"Don't even say it." Her eyes narrowed. "Don't you dare! I don't acknowledge those vows as a marriage. If you still do then I'm sorry, and I release you from them. Even ancient Pagans recognized divorce," she said with just a tad too much knowledge for her own well-being.

Dylan bared his teeth as his beast clawed at his spine, demanding a voice. "We have a son together. There'll be no divorce."

You are my mate!

She opened her mouth to object, then snapped it shut. "We can discuss this at a later time."

He shrugged. She could talk whenever she wanted and for however long she wanted. Years, decades, *centuries*, it was irrelevant; his decision on this matter was nonnegotiable. However, he needed to think further on her request to teach. If it would pacify her, perhaps he could find a way to make it happen without compromising her safety.

"We have eight children here in the village," he said. "Gwenfair is their classroom teacher. I'm sure she'd appreciate your help anytime. She can also tutor Joshua if necessary."

"You can't be serious?" Sophie stared at him in stunned shock. "You haven't been listening to me, Dylan. The people in your village *hate* me. And that was before I ran away with your son. I can't even imagine how they'll react now that they actually have a reason to." She laughed, and it wasn't a pleasant sound. "They certainly won't let me anywhere near their children, that's for sure."

"They are wary by nature," he explained, keeping his voice calm to her prejudice. "You just didn't give them enough time."

"Whatever you say." Submissive words laced with malevolence, as if arguing suddenly became a waste of her time.

"You can't live as you were!" He sensed her determination,

her unbreakable will; she fully intended to do whatever she pleased, even if it went against his wishes.

"Really?" Her chin lifted, only to validate his concern. "Why can't I?"

"There are precautions that must be taken." He clenched his hands by his sides in frustration. "The knowledge of our kind can never be revealed. You must come to terms with that."

"And how high a price will I have to pay under your terms?"

He tried to defuse her ire with truth. "There are others of my kind who will eliminate any threats to our race."

"I'm not a threat. Unless," she amended, her eyes narrowing with a dangerous light so unlike her former self that it took him by surprise, "they come after my son."

A real possibility that he kept to himself. "I'm grateful that you and Joshua are here now, healthy and unharmed."

"Are you trying to scare me?"

"My motivations have always been to keep you safe."

From the other side of the building, Dylan heard the soft click of a closing door. Footsteps approached, one heavy and one light. Joshua and Elen appeared around the corner a moment later, halting the conversation.

Elen commanded his attention with her expression, her face aglow in awe. She whispered in the old tongue, "He's whole. The Goddess has blessed us, brother. *Your son is whole.*"

Dylan closed his eyes briefly at the confirmation of what he'd already suspected. Still, he refused to celebrate, not until he saw his son change with his own eyes. Porter was whole, according to Elen's special gift, and he was unable to call the wolf.

Soon, Goddess willing, they would know for sure.

Sophie pulled Joshua aside, the concern in her voice palpable. "Are you okay?"

He rolled his eyes. "Chill, Mom. I'm fine. Aunt Elen just listened to my heart rate and did a few other tests." He grinned then. "I think I passed."

Aunt Elen, is it? Dylan smiled.

So did his sister. "You passed."

His wife, however, wasn't smiling when she leveled Elen with a searching glare. "Should I be relieved or concerned?"

Elen looked to Dylan. "Can I speak openly?"

"Yes, we will no longer protect my wife from the truth. I believe she's ready to hear it."

His sister nodded with approval, not inclined to soften her words. "Joshua is powerful enough to shift into the wolf. Are *you* strong enough to handle that? If so, then be relieved. If not, then be concerned."

Sophie flinched, unaware that Elen had been her greatest defender. "You have no idea what I'd do for my son."

"No, I don't." Elen crossed her arms in front of her chest. "But then whose fault is that?"

Sophie turned her back on them and ran a gentle hand down Joshua's arm, searching his face. "I'm strong enough to handle anything but losing you."

"I know, Mom." He nudged her with his shoulder. "Are you ready for a new adventure?"

By the look on Sophie's face, the simple question had personal significance. It made Dylan painfully aware of his exclusion from their life.

Sophie laughed, and it was a musical sound of pure love and acceptance. It was, Dylan recognized, a sound he'd never heard from her.

It made him ache.

"You're accepting the news better than expected," he said dryly.

Her smile faded when turned upon him. "I had already accepted the possibility when I called you."

Of course she had, he thought bitterly, *or else she would never have made that call.*

Nine

RHUDDIN HALL WAS A FORTRESS OF FIELDSTONE AND iron, with four long rectangular buildings enclosing the main house and central courtyard. The roof held a catwalk around the perimeter connecting the outer buildings, with watchtowers in all four corners.

No one was allowed admittance or departure without Dylan's permission.

And the guards were good.

Sophie knew this firsthand.

With Joshua by her side, she followed Dylan and Elen up the cobblestone drive. Each step took conscious effort. She felt laden with knowledge, overwhelmed by information.

Their earlier words disturbed her mind and challenged her convictions.

You'll live much longer than you've assumed.

The sooner you accept that you're a part of my world, the easier it will be for you to accept your fate.

Joshua is powerful enough to shift into the wolf. Are you strong enough to handle that?

She couldn't think of the last, not yet. Not without losing what little composure she had left. Despite her misgivings, she'd been given a small view into Dylan's world. Her mind wanted to reject that knowledge but it explained too much about his behavior.

There are others of my kind who will eliminate any threats to our race.

She began to understand his motives. She also understood that her son was a part of his father, and therefore a part of his world. If she wanted to remain in Joshua's life, she needed to conform to Dylan's terms.

The very thought went up her ass sideways.

The sound of hushed voices and curious whispers pulled Sophie away from her morose meanderings. She lifted her eyes toward the evening sky. Gas lanterns encased in wrought iron cages hung above the second-floor windows, casting an eerie light along the stone façade. Along the catwalk there stood over a hundred shadowed faces, all looking down on her with unguarded resentment.

Raw human emotion on perfect human faces. One would never know the secret they protected, until it was too late.

She felt a warm hand on her back, comforting, strong—*and not her son's.* Joshua would have nudged her or crowded her. He *would not* have stroked her back with a steady hand.

"Ignore them," Dylan whispered next to her ear, gently ushering her forward. "They're just curious."

"Okay," Joshua said under his breath, "I have to agree with Mom here. That's a little creepy."

Dylan frowned but didn't comment. The front building housed most of the guards; in the center was a silver gate wide enough for a large vehicle to drive through. Dylan nodded to a female guard Sophie knew as Taran.

Siân's sister.

Golden eyes fell on Joshua with a somber expression, then quickly narrowed in on Sophie. "She's carrying weapons."

Sophie lifted her chin, not surprised by the woman's accurate assumption. "I'll not enter this place unarmed. And

I'll not allow my son to go in without me . . . as long as there are people here who mean him harm."

Taran sneered as the insult registered. "You'll do whatever our leader tells you to do."

"Leave it alone, Taran," Dylan ordered with displeasure heavy in his voice, directed more toward Sophie than the woman guard, who was simply performing her assigned duty. "I would have removed Sophie's weapons before we arrived, if it had been my inclination to do so."

"You might have tried," Sophie said quietly, an automatic response to his threat, one she regretted a moment later. Thankfully, Dylan chose not to call her challenge but he gave her an odd look, as if just realizing the woman he had once known as his wife no longer existed.

A scowl marred Taran's features as she retracted the gate inside the stone walls without further comment.

Joshua lifted his head toward the sky as they walked through the stone archway, his eyes drawn to the gathering crowd above. "Do they all live here?"

"Most have homes in the village," Elen said.

"Then why are they here?"

"To meet you." Dylan led them through the gardens in the courtyard; the perennial beds were cut to the ground, waiting for new growth to emerge. He went around to the side of the main building and opened the kitchen door.

As they entered, Enid leaned against the center island with her arms crossed in front of her chest, like a general guarding her domain against an intruding force. She was a stout woman with reddish-brown hair and flushed cheeks. Her lips thinned downward with disapproval.

As other members of the house filled the room, Enid glared at Sophie without comment, then turned her sharp gaze on Joshua. There was an odd expression on her face. Sophie might have called it remorse if she thought the woman capable of such an emotion.

"Joshua," Dylan said, breaking the hushed silence, "this is Enid, a dear friend." He waved his hand around the room, listing off names of huddled faces. "Everyone," he announced with pride, "my son."

"Hello." Joshua looked about the room with wide eyes.

Enid gave him a lowered nod. "You'll learn all our names in time. I hope you enjoy the dinner we've prepared for you. Are you hungry?"

"Starving." His favorite answer to that particular question.

Enid shooed everyone away. "Then go have a seat in the dining hall and we'll be right in with the first course." Her voice was cheerful.

The sidelong glare she shot in Sophie's direction was not.

Sophie kept her shoulders squared as she weaved through the crowded kitchen. She recognized most of the faces staring back at her. Their nodded greetings did little to relieve her apprehension; they had always been nice to her in front of Dylan.

It was the other times that concerned her, when Dylan wasn't watching.

The dining hall had not changed. It was a gothic affair of formality, with torch sconces, dark oak floors, stone walls, mounted swords and large tapestries.

Luc was seated at one end of the long table with five other empty place settings around him. Sophie gave an inward sigh of relief that Dylan had thought to make this a small gathering.

Luc stood as Dylan waved Joshua forward. With long black hair and features too harsh to be handsome, he formed an intimidating presence. His eyes were light silver circled in navy, liquid mercury on ice, an eerie contrast against his dark skin.

With her new perspective, Sophie recognized the Egyptian heritage in Luc more than in his siblings. Although, in her opinion, Dylan's features were just as unusual, with thick blond hair, golden skin, and black eyes that followed her every move.

"Sister," Luc greeted Elen as she entered the room, pulling out the chair next to his.

Elen accepted her brother's assistance with tight-lipped annoyance. She was the only sibling who hadn't inherited any dark traits, except for her current expression.

All three, without question, were the purest combination of ancient races.

Perhaps sensing Joshua's unease, Dylan stepped forward. "My son," he said to his brother. "Joshua, this is your uncle Luc."

Luc held out his hand. "Welcome home, nephew."

"Thank you." Joshua shook his hand.

"Sophie," Luc acknowledged with a sharp nod. "Glad you finally came to your senses and brought our boy home."

She was not offended by his blunt tone. She had expected worse. "Hello, Luc."

Luc assessed Joshua with the eye of a warrior. "I train the children of the village for"—he shot a glare in Sophie's direction, changing his tone and modifying his words—"*in* defensive fighting techniques. I have a session tomorrow afternoon. You're welcome to come and watch."

"I'd rather help," Joshua said.

Luc snorted at the cocky reply, a slight grin tugging at his lips. "Can you defend yourself, nephew?"

"Yes," Joshua said with confidence.

Luc's eyebrows raised in challenge. "With weapons?"

"With anything you put in front of me." He shrugged. "Or with nothing."

That gained Luc's attention. The edge of humor left his voice. "We'll see. Tomorrow morning then, around eight, you can show me what you know."

"Sure. Where?"

"The courtyard."

"No," Dylan interrupted, "not the courtyard. You can spar at the lake house. I'll be there as well."

Luc nodded. "I'm good with that."

"Me too," Joshua answered, showing no sign of concern. On the contrary, he looked excited at the prospect of sparring with his uncle.

Lord help me, Sophie thought as she took a seat next to Joshua, across from Elen and Luc, while Dylan sat at the head. Not long after, Enid marched into the room, serving their first course, gray sausage links and wilted greens, possibly European sorrel smothered in a sour white sauce.

It smelled like fermented meat and had the consistency of lake slime. The poor animal that had sacrificed its life for the sausage was a mystery. Pig, perhaps. Or its tendrils.

"This was your mother's favorite dish." Dylan watched Joshua push a link around his plate with a three-pronged golden fork. "It always surprised me that she enjoyed this. I never favored it much myself."

Sophie stared down at her own plate and tried not to gag.

Joshua shot her a sidelong glance, knowing full well the predicament she was in. As a lesson on the consequences of withholding information, she had shared with him a few of Enid's creative past torments—like serving unpalatable food.

Joshua's shoulders began to shake. He was laughing, the little shit. She tried not to join in, but laughter, embarrassingly enough, was more infectious when denied, and even worse in uncomfortable situations.

"Did I miss something?" Elen asked.

Joshua stifled a sound, half snort, half giggle. And it triggered the end of Sophie's restraint. She burst out laughing, pulling the napkin up to hide her face.

Luc and Dylan frowned at each other. Elen looked annoyed.

And that just made it worse.

"I'm sorry," Sophie coughed out, feeling her face turn hot with embarrassment.

Enid had gone completely still, glaring at Sophie over Dylan's head. In the past, Sophie had always taken her little attacks in silence.

Dylan spoke to Joshua, aggravation clear in his tone. "May I ask what you've found so amusing?"

His father's disapproval silenced his antics. He turned

toward her, his gaze searching for permission to break her confidence.

She gave him a nod. "It's okay."

"Mom hates this dish," Joshua admitted. "It used to make her puke every time she ate it."

Dylan's dark eyes landed on Sophie, quieting her giggles. "Then why did you keep asking Enid to make it for you?"

Sophie ignored Enid's glare. "I didn't."

"Liar," Enid sneered. "Dylan, she's a liar."

Sophie said calmly, "Enid knew the effect this dish had on me. In fact, I think she enjoyed it."

"And yet you never told me." Dylan's tone had gone dangerously low. "Why?"

Enid started shaking her head; her voice turned frantic. "You can't believe anything this woman says."

Dylan held up his hand. His stance, even while seated, emanated power. He spoke in a language Sophie didn't recognize, nor had she ever heard it from him; it was the same dialect as Elen's first words after examining Joshua. It had to be their original tongue, an early version of Welsh.

It was a strong dialect, almost guttural, and more than a tad foreboding when spoken in anger.

Enid turned away, her head lowered in submission.

Dylan's dark eyes turned to Sophie, his anger controlled but still present. "Please answer the question."

It was the "please" that softened her answer. "I never told you because I was young and stupid and wanted your friends and family to like me. I thought that by keeping silent they would learn to trust me. I now realize what a foolish notion that was and no longer care if they like me or not." Sophie smiled, and she knew it wasn't a nice smile. "But hear me now, Enid." She waited for the woman to look up. "And be sure to pass this information along to all your cohorts in crime—I am *not* the same woman you once knew, and if anyone treats my son as I was treated when I lived here, they *will* regret it."

Enid took a step back, frowning at Sophie's changed behavior.

Joshua spoke up at that point, voicing his own agenda. "I don't have to eat this, do I?"

Sophie patted him on his arm. "I want you to try it. If it's not to your liking, then no, you don't have to eat it."

He leaned over and whispered, "Will you make me a pizza later?"

"Mac and cheese," Sophie offered back.

"Homemade?"

"Sure."

"Deal." He took a bite; his swallow was visibly forced. With flared nostrils and a sad shake of the head, he announced, "I don't like it."

"Enid," Dylan said, his voice heavy with displeasure, "clear our plates and bring the next course."

Ten

NIGHT HAD SETTLED INTO FULL DARKNESS DURING THEIR time at his home. From the warmth of his truck, Dylan watched his wife linger on the porch after he dropped off her and Joshua at the lake house. The porch light pinched her drawn features in harsh shadows, yet there was a resolute quality to her stance; despite her obvious exhaustion, she was waiting for him to leave before entering the house.

As her early vow had promised, this was *not* the same woman he had once known, a woman who had danced in the rain just to make him laugh. *That* woman had abhorred weapons and would never have kept them on her person.

This woman was stronger, mature . . . *defensive*—wiser in her instincts to fear her surroundings, *to fear him*.

Her loss of innocence saddened the man, but her quiet strength pleased his beast. And the way she had cared for their son, protected him with boldness akin to a mother wolf . . .

That more than pleased him. His blood ran hot and hard through his veins, straight to neglected areas long overdue for attention.

Before his need overruled his good judgment, Dylan shoved his truck in reverse and pulled out of the dirt driveway, angry that his family was in one place while he drove to another.

He had wanted an invitation to join them.

He was a damned fool.

Punching the gas, he headed straight for Rhuddin Hall with unpleasant matters to deal with. Taran nodded as he drove through the gate; her golden eyes refused to meet his, a warning that didn't bode well. Unfortunately, he had a lesser incident to deal with before confronting Sophie's accusations against Siân.

Dylan parked next to the main house; he found Enid in the kitchen, surrounded by her daughters, Lydia and Sulwen. The room reeked of fear and hostility; fear from the daughters, hostility from Enid.

"Enid," he ordered, not inclined to defuse their apprehension, "follow me to my office."

She took her time wiping the remaining dish before falling in behind him, a final defiance from an old stubborn pagan. Lydia and Sulwen tried to follow but Dylan halted them with a glare. They frowned, anxious but obedient to his silent command.

Sophie wouldn't have obeyed so easily, he mused inwardly. She would have either confronted the situation, if deduced worthy of her time and convictions, or, if not, simply moved on. A lack of argument didn't necessarily mean compliance.

It was an intriguing insight into his wife's character, one he'd overlooked in the past, to his great regret.

His office was located on the main floor, secured by Porter for sensitive meetings and disciplinary actions. His desk had been a gift from Koko, carved from maple, with three wolves in howling position, supporting a crescent top in the shape of a Celtic moon.

Koko had been an incredible artist, an unknown master of her craft who chose anonymity for love. There were reminders of her throughout the house; it was no wonder his brother still mourned.

Her spirit lingered.

Dylan settled behind the desk and waved his hand, motioning for Enid to take a seat across from him. Enid had been with him from the beginning. He owed his brother's life to her.

So it was with offended bewilderment that he asked, "Why, Enid?" Her mouth opened to refute but he held up his hand. "No, don't embarrass yourself with further lies. I sat up too many nights worrying about my wife emptying her stomach after every meal you served."

"That woman is weak," she sneered. "*A temptress.* I did not believe her child was yours."

"And now that you've seen him?" he said quietly. "How did it feel to have my son laughing at your attempts to humiliate his mother?"

Enid remained silent, her head lowered.

"You shamed me with your abuse to my mate."

She shook her head, beginning to realize, as her daughters had earlier, her precarious position. "I did it for you. That woman is not worthy of you."

"She is my mate," he growled. "The Goddess has found her worthy."

Enid looked away with a sneer, at war with her beliefs. She feared the Gods and their judgments.

And with good reason.

She whispered under her breath, "She is not strong enough to lead by your side. *She is not strong enough to protect us.*"

Ah, as he had suspected, therein rested the true motive. Sophie's kindness, in effect, had been a form of submission.

Wolves only respected strength.

"My wife returned for a purpose." He had not intended to share this information until confirmed with his own eyes, but the night's events made it necessary. "Our son has called the elements . . . I witnessed it myself today. Tomorrow night he'll try to complete the transformation."

Enid snapped to face him. "That cannot be." Her voice was thick with disbelief—*or denial*. "Do not get your hopes up on this, Dylan," she warned. "Neither Lydia nor Sulwen was blessed with enough power to call the wolf. The disappointment is . . . *difficult* to handle. I would not wish that upon you."

"We'll see," was all Dylan said, unwilling to belittle Enid further on this issue. But on another matter . . . "My wife made several negative references to her stay in my home. I didn't believe her until tonight."

He had trusted his people over Sophie, because he'd known them for centuries and her only months. The fact that at least two members of his household had mistreated his wife was an abhorrent discovery.

He shook his head, disgusted more with himself for not seeing the truth sooner. In retrospect, viewing past events from his wife's perspective didn't bear well in his favor. All she had asked for was contact with her family, and in return she had been confined and mistreated—and then, in his greatest act of ignorance, brought into the woods on a cold, desperate night.

"I will amend my wrongdoing," Enid conceded with a brisk nod.

"Yes," he said, "you will. But your blatant disrespect for my authority is inexcusable. I cannot let it go unpunished. You and your daughters will move from Rhuddin Hall in the morning. Constance has an empty cottage available in the village."

It was a direct demotion of her intimate status in his home. It would humiliate her.

She did not take the punishment lightly. "Because of this woman, you would deny me your home? When it was *I* who found you, huddled under a tree, with a wolf cub in your arms? When it was *I* who taught you how to care for Luc?

When it was *I* who gave you a home when you were forsaken by your family?"

"It is because of our history that I am not removing you completely from my protection. If you don't agree with my judgment . . . *leave.*"

She visibly stiffened. "I have nowhere else to go. My daughters . . ." she whispered. *"The Guardians will kill them."*

"A valid reason to accept my offer."

"I . . ." She pressed her lips into a thin line of fear mingled with pride. The fear won, of course. "I accept."

"Good. I will inform Constance to make her cottage ready for you." He waved his hand. "You are dismissed."

"Breakfast will be delayed tomorrow." Her tone had a sarcastic edge.

"It has yet to be decided if you'll continue in the kitchens. I'm leaving that judgment for Sophie. You will be informed of her answer by tomorrow evening."

She hissed softly, "You might as well tell Porter to find a replacement for me."

"We'll see. And, Enid," he said as she stood to leave, "I do *not* want to be blindsided like I was tonight. Pass the word around. Anyone who has done my wife wrong should come to me first, because if I hear it from her there'll be no forgiveness. No one other than you has earned that consolation."

Her expression was solemn. "I will pass your word on."

SOPHIE PEEKED IN ON HER MOTHER. FRANCINE HAD wanted the bedroom overlooking the lake; as the smallest room on the second floor it offered more privacy from the rest of the house. The gentle sound of even breathing came from the tiny lump under a country quilt.

She closed the door with a soft click. Joshua's bags were stacked by the door of the second bedroom, still unpacked, as were hers in the master bedroom on the first floor. That project could wait until morning.

Stifling a yawn, she followed the sound of cupboards opening and closing from the kitchen. By the time she arrived, Joshua had most of the ingredients for mac and cheese lined up on the counter next to the gas stove.

"You can't still be hungry." She shook her head. Enid had rectified her dinner after the first course. "You must've had two loaves of bread with the roast."

"You promised," he reminded her.

"I know, sweetheart. But it's been a long day and I'm exhausted. I'll make it up to you in the morning."

His shoulders slumped, disappointed. "With what?"

"Homemade cinnamon rolls."

He turned his head, his interest piqued. "Blueberry pancakes *and* homemade cinnamon rolls?"

She tried not to smile but it was a pointless attempt. "You drive me crazy."

"I make your life interesting," he teased, using humor to lighten her mood, as he'd always done. "What would you do without me?"

She reached out and squeezed his hand, marveling with some sadness that she could no longer enclose his within hers. He was a young man now, not her little boy, and it was time to prepare him for adulthood, and for his other life.

"As long as I know you're happy, Joshua, wherever you are, I'll be okay. This is *your* time. Don't concern yourself with me. I can take care of myself."

"Jeez, Mom, I was just messing with you." He shuffled out of her grasp. "I didn't mean for you to turn all serious on me."

She pressed her point. "I need you to watch your surroundings. And don't trust anyone . . . except me and your father."

"I understand." He squared his shoulders and leveled her with a dark look, resembling Dylan so much it jarred her. "I understand more than you think. I know the woman who opened the gate, the one with the weird yellow eyes, wasn't happy to see me."

"Good," she said with approval. "She is the sister of the

woman I told you about. Neither can be trusted." She turned him around and gently pushed him toward the stairs. "Now go to bed and get some sleep . . . unless you want to talk more about your father and what we learned today."

He shook his head immediately. "Nah, I'm good."

"You sure?"

"Positive."

She didn't force the issue. He would come to her in his own time, when he was ready. "Good night then."

"Night, Mom," he mumbled between heavy footfalls up the stairs.

Sophie returned the mac and cheese items to the fridge and cupboard and took her first good look around. Not much had changed, and unlike Rhuddin Hall, this place carried too many *good* memories. She had flirted with danger and lost her innocence in this house.

And gained her greatest joy.

She ran her hands over her face, feeling the weight of her choices as she walked the main floor. She loved being a mother, so much so that she'd shut off everything else, everything that threatened her place in Joshua's life.

A custom pine bed filled the master bedroom, a foot longer and wider than a king, leaving just enough space for an overstuffed chair and a long bureau. She walked to the bed and ran her hand over the quilted comforter.

She remembered Dylan in this bed, his weight on hers, the heat of his skin, his breath across her neck, his thickness pushing into her . . .

A shudder of pure desire pooled in her stomach, eliciting a physical response she hadn't felt in years. He had teased her body into pleasures she hadn't known possible. They had been happy once.

They had loved . . . *once.*

Don't go there, she whispered to herself. *You lost that right sixteen years ago.*

Leaving Dylan had been the most difficult choice of her life. In the end, fear over Joshua's safety had been the only thing that strengthened her resolve. Returning served to remind her of what she had lost, and how weak she was in Dylan's presence.

For reassurance, because she sensed her hard-earned resolve begin to crumble, she removed her gun and turned it in her hands. It was a .45-caliber Glock, a slimline model that held six rounds. She kept two spare magazine cartridges in holsters on both calves, and yes, the magazines held silver bullets, alternating with hollow-points. She hadn't been sure about the myths concerning silver bullets and magical creatures that shouldn't exist but do, however hollow-points had the capacity to shred a target upon impact, and so alternating bullets inside the magazines seemed the most logical choice.

She remembered the first time she'd held a gun, and the instructor who had taught her how to use it. She had lived in Texas at the time, and Joshua had just turned a year old. It seemed a lifetime ago, but in actuality was only fourteen years, when she had forsaken her very nature to become the person she needed to be to protect her baby . . .

THE INSTRUCTOR'S NAME WAS JULIE, A RETIRED COP WITH *hooded eyes that constantly observed her surroundings. With her hard body, and challenge-me-if-you-dare attitude, men tended to watch but few approached. Sophie envied her confidence, her strength, and knew in order to protect Joshua she needed to become more like her instructor.*

Julie taught self-defense lessons and a firearms safety course for battered women, and had kicked Sophie's ass every Wednesday night for six months. Joshua usually slept in his car seat close by, never far from his mother's sight, while she learned to kick back. Julie taught her how to use momentum and balance as a weapon, and how to use a perpetrator's strength against them.

Their lessons advanced to Sunday afternoons at a local outdoor firing range. Joshua stayed home with his grandmother during those sessions. Empty brass casings littered the ground, an eerie combination of gilded metal, packed earth and spent power. She fumbled through learning how to load bullets, jumping when one slipped from her fingers and landed on the ground, half expecting the tiny projectile to explode. She gave a nervous laugh to hide her mounting anger.

She hated Dylan in that moment, for forcing her to become this person who learned how to kill. This was not the person she was meant to be.

Julie remained calm, ever watchful, patiently waiting while Sophie mastered each new skill. "This is a .45-caliber Glock," she explained. "They make a slimline model that I recommend for women because it's light and easy to handle."

"Is it powerful?" Sophie gave the black pistol a doubting glance. More important, "Can it kill a wild animal?"

"Most people prefer shotguns for critters, but try reacting quickly with a shotgun." Julie snorted softly. "The .45 will do the job, especially if you use hollow-point bullets. It's gun etiquette to pull the slide open. Like this . . ." She demonstrated the proper handoff, revealing the empty chamber. "It shows the gun isn't loaded."

Sophie accepted the weapon.

It felt like death in her hands.

Throughout the tutorial, Julie adjusted Sophie's grip, leveled her arms and changed her stance. "I have earmuffs in my truck if you want to use them."

"No. But thanks." Sophie couldn't afford the luxury of muffling her senses. A paper target was stapled to a wooden stand less than twenty yards away. Her hands shook when she fired. The sound jarred her more than the kick of the gun, loud and vile, followed by a much softer sound of rustling leaves in the nearby woods. The softer sound, she realized, had been her bullet missing its very large target.

Unacceptable. She finished the round and loaded another. The acrid scent of gunpowder and lead filled the air and clung to her skin, and only one bullet out of twelve had hit the paper target.

"You're shooting low because you're tensing last minute," Julie explained. "Relax, site your target and just pull the trigger gently. Don't tense up."

The lessons continued over the next few weeks, until one Sunday Julie asked the inevitable. "Why are you doing this? Who are you afraid of? An ex-boyfriend? Husband? I may be able to help."

"You have helped." Sophie gave her instructor a sad smile. "More than you know." It would be the last time they saw each other. Once the questions began, Sophie moved on.

The following day, she bought her first gun from a little man with a ZZ Top beard who called himself the Country Cowboy. His home was located on a ten-mile-long dirt road decorated with No Trespassing signs. More important, he believed in the second amendment and in not prying into other people's business when it concerned their constitutional rights. Afterward, she found a remote gun shop that sold the equipment to make handmade bullets; press machines, brass casings and molds all sat neatly on the shelf like groceries in a convenience store. The kiln to melt silver came later.

Within a month she could load bullets in the dark, because she practiced every night. Within six months, as long as the target was in range of her vision, moving or stationary, it didn't matter, she never missed her shot. Never.

OVER THE FOLLOWING YEARS, SOPHIE HAD MOVED ON TO other instructors, other lessons, and other weapons. She hoped never to have cause to use them but would—without question—if necessary.

For now, she tucked the gun under the mattress. Normally she removed the magazine, but tonight she kept it in. Two knives followed, one from the holder strapped to her left calf, the other from behind her waistband; she placed one under a pillow and one under the bed. All were within arm's length if needed.

The woman Dylan had loved was gone; the wildlife activist with nothing more than a tranquilizer gun and innocent ideals had died in these very woods. Now she was older, in mind if not in body, and not so innocent.

She felt jumpy as hell when unarmed, too anxious to sleep. To keep her mind busy, she removed her pants and placed them neatly inside the bureau. The purple scar that ran the length of her leg caught her eye. Bracing her foot on the nearest chair, she smoothed her hand over the puckered flesh, wondering if Dylan would find her scars repulsive.

Chastising herself for caring, Sophie let her foot drop to the floor. Vanity had no purpose in her life. She hefted her suitcase to the chair to search for her sweatpants and nightshirt. The brown paper bag Matthew had given her fell forward onto the floor with a loud thump. Frowning, she tugged on her sweatpants and then retrieved the bag, set it on top of the long bureau, and opened it.

Eleven

NOT BOTHERING TO KNOCK, DYLAN WENT IN THROUGH the side door of his brother's apartments, located on the top floor of the west outer building. Paintings of animal life and wilderness lined the walls, all Koko's. The furniture was an eclectic assortment, some pieces masculine, some hand carved from wood.

Dylan found Luc pouring a glass of water in his private kitchen.

"Your boy is healthy," Luc said, downing the water and setting the glass in the stainless steel dishwasher. "But immature."

"I know." Dylan leaned against the doorway and sighed. "His mother coddles him."

"There are worse alternatives."

Luc's eyes darkened with the reminder. "Elen told me her findings."

"According to Sophie, the changes began three weeks ago. I have no reason not to believe her."

"Why now, I wonder?"

"From what I've gathered, Sophie and Joshua moved around a lot, except for the last few years."

Luc nodded with understanding. "His move today won't help."

An initial shift wasn't possible if one of their kind felt threatened, a contradiction to the Guardians' original belief. Even simple environmental discord kept the other half dormant. Age was irrelevant. Luc had remained in wolf form until after they'd settled into the Katahdin region, almost six hundred years after his birth. Regrettably, their earlier years in Cymru had been turbulent ones, Luc's presence barely tolerated, and only in the camps of other outcasts.

"Yeah, well," Dylan said, "we both know once the wolf awakens, it doesn't back down easily." The first shift was the most difficult. After that, the wolf's instincts often dominated. Transformations, once completed successfully, were no longer hindered by one's environment. If threatened, the beast would most certainly emerge.

His brother gave a crude snort. Having been born in wolf form, his dominant nature was that of the beast. It was his human side that fought for control, and more often than not, lost that battle. "When will you try for a shift?"

"Tomorrow. I'm taking him to the gathering place after nightfall. I want you and Elen there . . . but no others. Not until I know for sure what Joshua's abilities are, *if* any. Either way, he doesn't need the whole village watching."

Luc dipped his head in acknowledgment. "I'd be honored."

"I spoke with Enid," Dylan added before being asked. "She will be moving to Constance's cottage in the morning, along with her daughters."

"A good solution," Luc replied, keeping his voice neutral. "From what I've seen tonight, I believe your mate has learned to defend herself. If she continues, she will earn the respect of our people without your interference."

"In time, perhaps. Until then, I have a greater problem." Dylan walked farther into the kitchen and braced his arms on the counter, letting his head fall forward. "Sophie informed me tonight that Siân found her in the woods . . . *after* my wife ran from us." Dylan looked up and met his brother's narrowed glare. "Siân found her and let her go, but not before issuing Sophie a death threat if she returned."

Luc whistled softly under his breath. "And you believe Sophie?"

"I'm choosing to believe her." His only regret was that he hadn't sooner. "Do you remember Siân from that night?"

Luc frowned, shaking his head. "No, but we weren't looking for Siân. Also," he added with some hesitation, as if recalling a distant memory, or revealing a personal confidence, "Koko felt Siân had the potential for violence."

Rarely did Luc mention his late wife in conversation. For him to do so now gave Dylan pause. "We *all* have the potential for violence."

"As I'm well aware. But Koko knew the difference. She married the Beast of Merin, did she not?"

Dylan scowled. "I despise that name." The moniker was coined by the Guardians upon Luc's birth. "Why do you continue to flaunt it?"

"Because I can." His sardonic smile turned serious, changing the subject back to the matter at hand. "What are you going to do about Siân?"

Dylan sighed, finding no pleasure in his next decision. "I have no other choice but to banish her."

Luc remained silent for several seconds, his stance subdued. "I'll come with you."

"I want time with her alone first." Dylan headed for the door. "Give me an hour. I'm stopping by Alise's office before I head over."

Alise was Rhuddin Village's official town secretary. Her unofficial job was to create new identities every eighty years or so, over a normal human life span. Those who worked outside Rhuddin Village on assignment were more of a challenge for her. In most cases, they returned within fifteen years—before it became noticeable that they were not aging.

At that time, Alise planned a life-changing—or -ending—event to suddenly occur in their "human" lives. "Gather Taran and her brother," Dylan continued. "I'll allow them to say farewell to their sister . . . or go with her, if they so choose."

"Cormack," Luc said, his voice thick with displeasure, "is probably with Elen."

DARKNESS HAD FALLEN ON RHUDDIN VILLAGE, NOT ONLY in the few hours of night, but also in the hearts of his people. There were no voices or laughter as Dylan walked the shadowed streets toward Siân's cottage, just a few faint whispers filled with concern. Most of the villagers had kept to their homes.

Siân lived on the outskirts of town, secluded by choice, her driveway obscured by tall pine trees. Gravel crunched under his boots as he made his way toward her front door. She had left the outside light on, revealing faded yellow paint and rotting posts as he drew near, neglected, much like the woman who lived within its walls.

As Dylan climbed the front steps he couldn't help but wonder if the human mind was strong enough to withstand immortality, if the conscience was meant to handle a thousand years of unfulfilled wanting.

The door opened before he could knock, and Siân stood before him in modern jeans, a white winter vest over a navy sweater and hiking boots. The red hair of a Celt hung down her back in a long plait.

She gave him a sad smile, and stood back for him to enter. "I've been expecting you."

He eyed the sparse room, and the four trunks lined up by the door. "You know why I've come, then?"

She cocked her head to one side, frowning at his calm tone, and looking somewhat confused. Thankfully, it was not an aberrant confusion; the glint in her eyes this night was lucid.

"I'm sure that woman has filled your ears enough," she said.

"I'd like to hear your side."

"Does it truly matter now, Dylan?" He expected anger, even defiance, but instead found sorrow. "I saw your son," she whispered, her words barely audible, even to his ears. "He has your eyes."

Her despondent attitude only confirmed Sophie's accusation. "Tell me what happened the night my wife left me, Siân. Tell me what happened when you found her."

As if he hadn't spoken, she looked out the open door toward the woods, lost in the torrent of her own thoughts. "I know Sarah and Michael are out there. They're watching me." She remained quiet for a moment. "I used to laugh when that woman fought you for keeping her guarded, and here I am now, sharing her fate." Her shoulders slumped, and her voice grew heavy with regret. "Except I don't have you in my bed . . . or a child of my own."

"You didn't answer my question," he said.

Her eyes glazed over then, and she was uncomprehending, or unwilling to answer. She had moved on to that other place, Dylan realized—her place of madness and avoidance. Was it a misguided sense of responsibility that her misery still provoked him? Perhaps it was, but he would rather feel compassion than hatred for a woman who'd once been his lover, and more important, his friend.

"Come here," Dylan said and opened his arms. She turned back toward the room. She frowned at him, but then the haze of confusion cleared and a soft sob escaped her lips. Three strides and she fell into his embrace, tucking her head under his chin. She smelled like dried lavender and mint. He kissed the top of her hair, more like a father would a frightened child than an ex-lover. "I know why you did it, Siân. But it doesn't change what I must do."

"I understand," she sniffed. "I can't live here now any-way . . . I can't bear it."

"I had Alise create a new identity for you, with six hundred thousand dollars in two separate accounts, under the name Pamela Johnston."

A soft growl grew close and Dylan dropped his arms, waiting for Siân to withdraw herself. She did so with some reluctance. He reached into his jacket and handed her a portfolio with her account information, her new birth certificate, her social security card and her driver's license. She accepted the packet, hugging it to her chest, nodding without words.

Heavy padded steps fell across the porch as a red wolf prowled through the door. Cormack took a protective stance between Dylan and his sister.

Siân rested her hand on Cormack's head. "It is all right, my brother. I'll be okay." But her voice cracked with emotion despite her brave words.

Dylan nodded to Taran as she entered and stood with her siblings. Taran took her sister's hand within hers and waited.

Dylan found no satisfaction in issuing this judgment. "Siân is banished from my territory . . . and my protection, for her own personal actions. I've provided her with the means to make a fresh start."

A low growl hummed through the room. Dylan pinned Cormack with a glare, letting his own wolf have a voice. Both sisters leaned against their brother in a silent bid for respect. In a fight, Dylan would dominate. Cormack broke eye contact first, but his stance remained arrogant.

"I don't expect you to agree with my decision," Dylan continued, "but I expect you to respect it. If you cannot . . . then you must leave with your sister."

Taran nodded. "We'll go with Siân."

"No." Siân shook her head, not willing to force her fate onto her siblings. "Cormack will never have a normal existence among mortals." The wolf made a noise in the back of his throat, almost human, and clearly offended. "You are trapped in this form." Siân stroked her brother's neck. "The Guardians will kill you. And the humans . . . at best they will confine you. Here you're free. *Here* . . . you're safe."

Cormack pushed up against her, releasing a mournful howl.

"No, I'll have no argument with you on this." There was vehemence in her voice and fire in her eyes. "You *will* stay here with Taran."

Was it divine justice, *or comeuppance*, Dylan wondered, that he'd been given a final glimpse of the woman he'd once admired. She had petitioned him for sanctuary almost four hundred years ago, with a red wolf by her side and a young sister in her arms. Sane and selfless. The protector of her family. And eventually his lover, until her need for a child had driven her to other men, searching for the one who could give her what she'd longed for most: *to be a mother.*

She never conceived with him, or with any of the others. Over time her behavior turned erratic . . . *desperate.* She had started to worship fertility gods, in the old way of the ancient druids, with mating rituals and animal sacrifices, until he put a stop to the senseless animal deaths. By then, whom she'd chosen to take into her bed was not his concern.

For a while, Siân's restlessness had seemed to settle into a form of acceptance, or so he'd thought.

Not long after that time, hardly even forty years, Sophie and her team of nature scientists had petitioned for temporary residence in Rhuddin Village. Dylan had agreed only to keep an eye on their efforts, *and to sabotage them if necessary.*

However, he hadn't been prepared for Sophie herself, with her gentle nature and fiery conviction, or her innocence in a sweet woman's body. She had taunted him, teased him, unaware of the wolf she aroused, with a need long denied.

She had conceived almost immediately.

His greatest joy had been Siân's worst humiliation. He had little doubt that she had threatened Sophie and his child. And that offense—regardless of their personal history—was unforgivable. "You have an hour to decide."

With a vile taste on his tongue, he walked out of the cottage. Elen and Luc waited on the front steps, supporting him with their silent presence. He turned to his brother. "Will you escort Siân out, and whoever decides to leave with her?"

"And if Taran stays?" Luc asked.

"Then she'll need to prove her loyalty before returning to her position. I want you to watch her," Dylan added for clarity. "*Personally*. She accepted her sister's banishment too easily."

He nodded without argument. Elen entered the cottage. Her concern, Dylan noticed, went to Cormack, as she knelt beside the wolf and buried her face in the thick fur at his nape.

"I'm going for a run," Dylan said, taking off toward the woods. His people had wronged Sophie. He was convinced of that now. And still she had come home to him, of her own free will—for their son.

His wolf clawed at his spine for release. Its fury, its need, its desire for the woman who'd had the courage to return for their child was no longer controllable.

The wolf wanted out.

Having her near and within reach was akin to pain.

Perhaps it was a good thing Sophie hadn't invited him to stay, Dylan thought as he entered the forest, ripping off clothes as he walked. For if she had, he wasn't sure if he could have controlled his hunger.

It had been too long.

Twelve

Matthew's gift was a large rounded golden box. The metal was worn, like a statue Sophie had once seen in a church, caressed by thousands of hands over time. And there was a rendering of a man with antlers inscribed along the lid, holding a horned snake, flanked on either side by two hounds. Or were they wolves?

A foreboding chill crept up her spine.

The box was Celtic in origin.

She had studied the religion of ancient cultures in college. In the Celtic religion, there was a horned god named Cernunnos, worshiped by ancient Celts as the lord of animals, the hunter and the balancer. His image appeared on several artifacts from Celtic gravesites.

Sophie slid the lid off the box and gently set it on the polished surface of the bureau.

A thick metallic rope lay coiled within, gold and silver combined in the shape of a horned snake. Tentatively, with her heart pounding in her chest, she grasped the tail of the snake and let it uncurl to the ground, about eight feet in length and an inch in diameter.

She studied the details of the ornament with morbid curiosity. The eyes of the snake resembled opaque jewels, cloudy white and set an inch apart, the fangs attached to holes along its tail. A belt of some sort? An odd yearning had her circling the metal around her waist; it looped three times until the clasp enclosed around the tail, hanging low on her hips.

She ran her hand across the delicate scales, then back against the grain—and felt the sharp bite of metal into skin. She drew back with a hiss, turning her hand to assess the damage. Blood pooled across her palm. The scales of the snake, she discovered too late, formed hundreds of thin razor edges.

With surreal clarity, she understood Matthew had given her a weapon—a whip with knives, with the tail as its grip, and the serpent's head a fanged barb.

Holding her palm up, she walked to the kitchen and held it under the faucet, watching the water turn from pink to clear. The wound wasn't deep, more like a nasty scrape, but with pressure and momentum true damage would have occurred.

Not a pleasant image. Her hands shook as she tried to unfasten the belt. The clasp wouldn't release. She tried again, only to receive more nicks in the process. As she searched for her phone, she pulled the hem of her sweatshirt down to cover the sharp metal scales. The purse hung on the coat hook by the door, her phone still in the side pocket. Checking the battery, she quietly stepped outside, hoping for better reception, and dialed Matthew's number.

He didn't answer. And his message recording had been changed to a generic automated system. She left a message. And just to be sure, she redialed his number. And left another message.

This isn't happening, she thought, certain then that Matthew had lied to her from the beginning; he knew why she had returned to her son's father. Why else would he have given her a weapon of Celtic origin—a weapon of *Dylan's* origin?

She paced across the cedar planks of the porch. The night was crisp, just above freezing, but the fresh air soothed her racing thoughts. A rustling sound drew her attention to the woods. She froze, not moving her eyes from the edge of trees where the forest ended and the driveway began.

A wolf stepped into the clearing, making his presence known. Moonlight danced across the gold tones of his fur, caressing him like a mother would a child, proud of her creation, loving his existence.

"Dylan?" she whispered, grasping the porch railing. Relief washed over her when she should have been more afraid, as if her heart recognized what her brain refused to acknowledge.

Intent dark eyes leveled on her as he prowled closer and into the light. Strands of gold and green bled into the darkness of his gaze. *Wolf eyes.* She hadn't noticed that change before.

He bowed slightly in answer to her question.

He was large in wolf form, too large for a normal wolf, well over two hundred pounds—equal to his human weight. Why that scientific observation came to her now, she had no idea. Perhaps her mind was grasping at senseless facts to ward off insanity.

Or perhaps she no longer cared. Why else would she have made her next offer? "If you have clothes nearby, you're welcome to change and sleep on the couch." She almost laughed at the double meaning of those words. God, it had been a long day. "Or I'll sleep on the couch. But I'd rather you come inside than watch us from the woods."

Then she turned and entered the house, not wanting to witness the transformation. She closed the door behind her but left it unlocked. Dylan would accept her offer. She had no doubt he would accept her offer, if only to be near his son.

She made another attempt to remove the snake, or belt, or whatever the hell it was, but without success. Not willing to take a knife to it just yet, she decided to call Matthew again later on, one last chance to explain his intentions. If he still didn't answer, then the belt was coming off, even if she had to use pliers to pry its mouth open, antique artifact be damned.

She pulled her sweatshirt down to cover the snake and turned her energy toward an activity that didn't make her head pound with unanswered questions. She had promised her son cinnamon rolls. The cabin was cool, and morning wasn't too far away, so the rise time should work out well.

It was an awkward process due to a rearranged kitchen and the limited use of one hand. Still, cooking had always been soothing for her, a productive distraction when anxiety tangled her thoughts. No more than a half hour later, just after she cleaned her mess and covered the dough with a floured towel to rise, she heard the soft click of the door as it opened and closed.

Dylan entered the kitchen, wearing jeans and a torn T-shirt that only served to accentuate the hard curves of his chest and arms. His feet were bare. He stared across the short distance that separated them, greeting her with a sharp nod.

Green and gold streaks remained in the black depths of his gaze.

She took a step back. He stood before her as a man but she sensed his wolf. *She felt it*, almost as if the animal had been forced to withdraw unwillingly and lingered just below the surface of humanity, ready to attack at the slightest provocation.

"Your eyes, Dylan . . ." She had invited him to stay for the simple reason that it had felt wrong to deny him access to his son, especially here, in a place that belonged to Dylan. But she hadn't expected this. "They're different," she said softly. "Why did I never notice them before?"

"Because I never showed you before." His voice was raw, gravelly, as if it hurt him to speak.

She didn't move, knowing that calm composure was the better response. "Then why show me now?"

"Because at this particular moment"—his voice dropped to a low growl, barely audible—"I'm having a difficult time controlling my wolf."

She swallowed. "What do you need me to do?"

Those eerie eyes narrowed in on her with a look of pure

carnal hunger. Her breath lodged in her throat. Of all the emotions she had expected from Dylan upon returning, desire had never crossed her mind. Anger, yes. Hatred, probably. But not desire.

"Dylan . . ." She grasped the back of a kitchen chair for support as her heart cried out and her body responded in kind. And that frightened her more than anything, for she fully understood her weakness toward this man, and what that might mean for her future freedom.

Slowly pushing away from the chair, she edged backward, her eyes darting to the door and then the hallway.

He moved in swiftly, shoving the chair out of his way, using his bulk to dominate her path until her back touched the wall.

"Don't run, Sophie . . ." He placed his hands on either side of her head, trapping her between his outstretched arms. "Don't move. Just keep still . . . *please*."

He smelled like pine and fresh air, and something other, something undeniably sensual.

"All right." Fear of her own reaction to his nearness kept her motionless.

"Don't be afraid." His head dropped and his lips hovered just below her ear. "I won't hurt you. I could never hurt you."

She shuddered, leaning her head forward until it came in contact with his chest. To be this close to him, to touch him, to know he still welcomed her touch . . .

A ragged breath fell from her lungs.

This was a dangerous temptation—because she wasn't afraid of him. Oh, no . . . She was afraid of her own weakness, of what she might let him do—of what she *wanted* him to do. It was sad, really, how rapidly her walls of defense had tumbled.

"What do you want from me?" She cringed at the desperate sound of her own voice.

He inhaled; she knew because the intake of air drew chills across her nape. "I think you know what I want."

"Joshua and my mother are upstairs," she reminded him in a panicked whisper.

"Both are sleeping." His hands tangled in her hair, tugging gently. "I can hear them breathing, soundly and unaware."

She clutched at his torn shirt, her knees threatening to buckle. "We can't . . ."

"One kiss, wife." It was a soft-spoken demand, but a demand all the same. "You asked me what I wanted . . . and what I need from you. For now . . . *for tonight*, just give me one kiss to calm my beast and then I'll leave you alone."

One kiss. She closed her eyes and rubbed her cheek along the soft material of his shirt. *Just one kiss.*

Dylan lifted her head, cupping her face with both his hands, forcing her to meet his gaze, his dark eyes still stricken by the wolf. He did not ask for further permission. Slowly, as if sharp movements might frighten her into bolting, he lowered his mouth onto hers.

It was a gentle kiss that didn't invade, a warm kiss of promises and restraint.

She closed her eyes and sighed against his lips. God help her . . . but she loved his mouth, the way it fit against hers. She didn't know what base emotion compelled her . . . Selfishness, perhaps? Instinct? Sexuality too long denied? Maybe even a touch of wickedness? Because it *was* wicked to play with this fire.

But rationality was lost, destroyed by a greater compulsion as Sophie curled her arms around his neck, turned her head and deepened the kiss. Dylan stiffened, surprised. She felt his struggle for control as his hard frame shook around her, just as she knew the instant he lost the battle.

It was as if something in the air lifted, some unseen restraint, and whatever control Dylan maintained shattered on a broken breath. His hands became rough as they moved over her body. His thighs pressed between her legs, forcing her to straddle his hips, trapping her between him and the wall. Those demanding hands found her backside and lifted her onto him.

He paused for the barest of seconds, waiting, she supposed, for a protest. When none was given, he gave a ragged groan and pressed his tongue along her lips, insistent.

She opened for him. She was powerless to do anything else, trailing her hands into the soft curls of his shortened hair, melting into the hardness of his body supporting hers, matching the thrusts of his tongue with those of her own.

The evidence of his arousal was trapped between their bodies, hard against her belly. If they were not clothed, he would have been inside her. She ground against him in frustration that he wasn't.

His mouth broke from hers. "Sophie . . ." He stilled her motions by pressing his entire weight into her, his hands a vise on her backside. "I will warn you not to tease me." She squirmed against him. And he swore under his breath, a guttural sound of frustration. "Unless . . ." The last was a whispered growl. "Unless you're willing to finish this properly."

Blood pulsed through her veins, the soft pounding in her ears combined with their labored breaths. Her entire body was shaking. She couldn't talk. She couldn't breathe.

"Sophie . . . ?" Hope hung heavy in the air, like the first rays of sun after a hard rain, warm and promising. He shuddered, rightly taking her silence as indecision, and pulled back slightly . . . only to return, pressing into her again, and again, a rocking motion that went straight to her core.

"Oh, God," she groaned, feeling the first pulses of pleasure start to build.

"Are you willing?" He continued to ride her clothed body, his tone both arrogant and pleading, a mixture of confidence and . . . *vulnerability*? "It's been so long."

Somewhere in the recesses of her mind she knew this was wrong—knew regret would follow. "If we do this," she warned, "it does *not* mean I'll stay."

Her conscience refused to promise him anything beyond the physical, simply because she wasn't willing to conform to what he really wanted—the complete submission of her will.

A low growl rumbled from his chest, vibrating against her hands. He tore at her sweatshirt, his movements almost brutal. He was angry, she realized, but not enough to refuse what was offered.

She lifted her arms to help him pull the unwanted item over her head. She wore a white tank top underneath, and felt exposed as his hands ran over the thin material, brushing across her breast to linger, thumbing the sensitive peak until she cried out.

His mouth dropped to her throat; heat and rough kisses teased her sensitive skin. His hand moved lower. She closed her eyes, letting her head fall back until it rested against the wall, waiting, breathless . . .

He froze. "What . . . ?" In an instant, his body went from liquid heat to a cage of iron. He lifted his head to look down to her waist and then back up, pinning her beneath his harsh gaze. "What is that . . . ?"

Realization invaded slowly. She pushed against his chest, the cool air a shock against her heated skin as he stepped away. Still dazed, still shaking from pleasure unfulfilled, she leaned back against the wall for support. A frown marred his features as he stared down at the gold serpent wrapped around her waist.

The cold silence that followed helped extinguish the last haze of passion.

"Dylan . . ." she began, finding her voice.

He held up his hand. "Answer me this one question . . ." His eyes met hers, entirely black and fully human, and suddenly she wished for the return of the wolf. "How is it that my human wife has returned to me after all these years wearing a weapon of my world?"

"I . . . I'm not sure," she stammered, as her hands fell to the serpent. Her suspicion that Matthew had lied to her was fully confirmed in the hard set of Dylan's jaw, and yet there was a part of her that instinctively wanted to protect her friend.

Matthew had always, always been kind to her.

However, on a matter that concerned a world she knew little about, it was not a difficult decision to give her trust to the only person who had more invested in her son's welfare other than herself.

"It was a gift," she said, relying on her most valued asset—*honesty*. "From my employer. He gave it to me this morning. He told me not to open it until I arrived here." She held up her hand, showing him the cut on her palm. "I had no idea this was a weapon until I tried to get it off."

Dylan reached out and grabbed her hand, examining the fresh cuts. "Is that who you were calling earlier?"

"You were watching me on the porch?" Sophie fumed at his narrowed expression. Of course he'd been watching her. There were probably others out there now, still watching. "Yes," she confirmed, "I was calling Matthew." Dylan glowered at her. "And you need to direct your anger elsewhere because I've done nothing intentionally dishonest. I had no idea Matthew was a part of"—she waved her hand around in a frantic gesture—"of this! Of your world! I'm here for our son. I would do nothing to harm him, or those who would protect him."

"I'm not angry with you, woman! I'm . . ." Dylan sighed, running his hands over his face. His chest rose and fell on several pronounced breaths that slowly evened out. "Truth be told, I find I'm hard-pressed to hold my anger . . . when I can still taste you on my tongue." A slight grin tugged at his lips at her annoyed gasp. "What was your Matthew's explanation when you called?"

"I didn't speak with him," she clipped. "His recording's been changed. I left two messages."

He searched her face, trying, she supposed, to discern honesty over deceit. He must have come to a satisfactory conclusion because his stance relaxed. "It needs blood."

Surely she hadn't heard him correctly . . . "Excuse me?"

Dylan reached out to snag the head of the serpent, but the instant his hand touched metal with aggressive intent it was repelled—and Sophie sucked in her breath as currents of energy screamed through her nerves, pulses of heat from her stomach to her fingertips.

"What the hell was that?" she asked through clenched teeth.

"I don't know." Dylan stared down at his hand, flexing his fingers. "I've never touched the serpent before."

"It didn't like it," she said, elevating the object to an anthropomorphic status.

"It allows you to touch it." If it hadn't been laced with concern, his accusation would have annoyed her.

"I know. I'm wearing the thing," she pointed out. "I just don't know how to get it off."

His lips thinned at her sarcasm. "There should be a latch just between the serpent's eyes . . . a feeding source. It needs blood to release."

"You're serious?" At his glare, she tentatively felt around the serpent's head, tensed for another shock. When nothing happened, she stroked her thumb between its clear-jeweled eyes, and felt a sharp catch. "I found something. Now what do I do?"

"Feed it your blood."

Feed it my blood. "Yeah . . . *okay,*" she coached herself, and then again, "okay," as if repeating the word would somehow make it so.

Like pulling off a bandage, swift and sure, she impaled her thumb on the protruding latch, and then inhaled a shaking breath as currents once again coursed through her veins, only this time they were warm, *comforting,* a nurturing sensation, as if nursing a child. "Okay . . . that's really weird."

A growl came from Dylan as he reached out.

"Don't touch me," she warned, sensing if he did so the warmth would turn to pain.

He pulled back, letting his hand drop to his side, fisted in frustration.

Feeling both awed and repelled, she watched as twin diamonds slowly turned burgundy. The clasp released with a soft click as the serpent opened its mouth and fell from her waist in a tangled heap about her feet.

She stepped over the crumpled metal. "How did you know?"

"I know its owner," he said in a quiet voice. "What does your Matthew look like?"

Sophie walked over to the counter and found a roll of paper towels, tore off a section, and wrapped it around her throbbing thumb. "Will you go after him?"

"If Matthew is who I think he is, your concern is unwarranted. He would look like he's in his young twenties. Blond hair. A woman once likened the color of his eyes to that of a robin's egg."

"You know him then?" Her eyes narrowed. "Is he a friend of yours?"

Dylan snorted. "Your Matthew has no friends that I'm aware of."

She had another thought. "Is he your enemy?"

He didn't answer immediately, giving the question ample consideration. "No. But he isn't a man who gives gifts without expecting something in return."

His evasive answers tried her patience. "What are you not telling me?"

"There are things at play here that you have yet to understand."

"Nothing has changed here, has it?" She bent down to retrieve the serpent from the floor. The weapon had been given to her and she fully intended to keep it. Dylan watched her gently coil the serpent in her hands, glaring as she went through the motions unaffected. "I'm still being watched . . . and you're still keeping secrets."

"Sophie . . ." Dylan stilled her with a hand on her arm as she turned toward the bedroom. "Are you truly ready to know everything? Do you think you can handle the truth?"

She rolled her arm out of his grasp. "Keep me in darkness and the only thing I want to do is run."

His jaw clenched. "What do you want to know?"

"You can start by telling me who Matthew is to you."

His lips pressed in a thin line. She turned her back on his silence and walked to the bedroom, cautious as she placed the serpent back in the golden box. Dylan allowed her to go, watching her from the hallway.

He was pacing when she returned, his movements sharp

as he stopped to stand in front of her. "I know him as Taliesin." His tone was blunt, spoken like a challenge, as if he dared her to doubt him. "He is the son of Ceridwen. And he is the reason I exist."

"Ceridwen?" She tried to keep the skepticism from her voice but failed. "As in the Pagan goddess of Celtic mythology?"

His lips tilted upward, mocking. "You'd be surprised what walks among us that most humans believe to be myth."

Ah, no, she wouldn't.

"I believe in God," Sophie said, compelled by doubt, or perhaps guilt, to profess her faith.

He gave a weary sigh. "As do many of my kind. There are those among us who were alive when the world went dark on the death of your Christian God's son. There are those among us who feel we are indeed the forsaken children of the underworld."

"I don't believe that." Sophie shook her head. "Joshua is your son. And he is not a child of the underworld. He is everything wonderful and good."

He smiled at her, as if her conviction had soothed some unseen hurt. "Then use whatever name makes you more comfortable . . . God, Buddha, Mother Earth, Great Spirit, Gici Niwaskw, Brahman . . . *Allah.* Good and evil, heaven and hell, earth and the otherworld . . . I have come to understand that we are the pawns of a much higher existence. And all that's different between us and humans is that our kind has been given a greater awareness of the other side."

Sophie took a deep breath, able to accept that explanation without forsaking her own beliefs. "And you think Matthew is this Taliesin?"

Dylan nodded toward the box that sat on her bureau, its carvings visible through the doorway like a gilded affirmation. "He is the only person I've seen wearing that weapon. And it would explain a great deal . . ." His voice trailed off. "I have always wondered why I could never find you."

"I'm having a difficult time picturing Matthew as this

person you speak of." She had lived next to the man for almost four years, cleaned his house—cooked his dinners. "How is it that you could possibly exist because of him?"

"The first of my kind were given the power to shift into wolves to protect Taliesin, to live by his side, to raise Ceridwen's son where she could not. She taught them how to see beyond our realm of existence, taught them how to pull power from other living things. They called themselves *Gwarchodwyr* . . ." Sophie frowned at the word and he translated it into English. "Guardian. At first, the term was meant for Taliesin alone, but now they consider themselves the guardians of our kind."

"These are the others you spoke of earlier?" She hadn't forgotten his warning. "The ones that will eliminate any threats to your race?"

"Yes."

"I see," she said, not overly thrilled that this fantastical world was beginning to make sense, *and* that Dylan's motives were quickly becoming more honorable than confining. "The Guardians that raised Matthew . . . are they still alive?" She went on to explain, "Because he had no visitors that I'm aware of while I worked in his home. He was always alone."

Dylan nodded as if that information didn't surprise him. "Some are still alive, but not all, and Taliesin holds little affection for the *Gwarchodwyr Unfed* . . ."

"*Gwarchodwyr Unfed*?" She fumbled with the pronunciation. "What does the *Unfed* stand for?"

Again, he translated, "Guardians, First in Order. They're the men and women who personally cared for Taliesin as a child. Sometimes we refer to them as the Original Guardians. Or the Originals." His voice was calm, even patient, like a teacher explaining a lesson to a teenager. "There are only twelve Original Guardians left. Those remaining twelve have formed a council meant to govern our kind. They call themselves the Council of Ceridwen."

She rubbed her hands over her eyes. "So, the term Guardian doesn't necessarily refer to an Original Guardian?"

"That's correct. A Guardian can also be a descendant of an Original who can shift, one who has aligned their beliefs with the Council."

"You can shift," she pointed out. "Are you a Guardian?"

"No," he clipped. "The Council and I don't share the same beliefs."

"You say that with disgust in your voice."

"The Guardians have earned my disgust."

"How so?"

He sighed, running a hand through his hair. "That's a story too long for this short night. Just trust me when I tell you it's a blessing only twelve Original Guardians remain."

"Where do they live?"

"Everywhere," he said bluntly. "But mostly throughout Europe. They convene in Wales . . . they still hold rituals in our homeland."

"How many Original Guardians were there in the beginning when Matthew was a child?"

He frowned at her continued barrage of questions but answered without complaint. "Forty-eight."

"And when . . . *exactly* was the beginning?"

"The Guardians have been around for over two thousand years, give or take a hundred. We didn't have a written verse at the time, so the actual date is debatable."

"But they can die?"

"Yes . . . they can die." He gave her a pointed stare. "There's not a being that walks this earth that can survive without its head, not even the first of my kind. Why do you think that serpent whip was forged? Why do you think I mount swords on my walls, and not guns?"

She assumed his bluntness was meant to frighten her, maybe even challenge her, but it only fueled protective instincts. "Are these Guardians a threat to Joshua?"

His stance changed, a subtle movement into aggression, reminding her he wasn't entirely human. "It will be better for our son if he can shift. The Guardians don't value human life, or others of our kind that can't shift. They would see them terminated to strengthen our race back to where we were in the beginning."

She wrapped her arms around her stomach. "You speak of genocide . . . of a demented view of a perfect race."

"I don't share their beliefs, Sophie . . . I'm just telling you what they are."

She took a deep breath and let it out, a moment of contemplation before digging deeper into this secret world. "You told me earlier that a shifter hasn't been born in over three hundred years. Is that true?"

"Yes, as far as I know. We are losing our connection to the earth, and therefore our power to shift. Many who live in Rhuddin Village came here for protection from the Guardians, for sanctuary. Those who can't shift are vulnerable; their bodies don't heal as well. It's the reason I'm so protective of them. It's the reason my sister became a doctor."

She began to understand why he turned a blind eye to their faults. "Why has your kind begun to lose connection to the earth? And why would Joshua have it now after all this time?"

"I wish I had an answer to those questions. Unfortunately, I don't." He reached out to cup her chin. She flinched, startled by the gentle touch. He frowned at her reaction but didn't remove his hand. "And I think that's enough for tonight. When was the last time you slept?"

She blinked, adjusting to the changed subject, distracted by the way his thumb caressed the side of her cheek. "I don't know." *Sleep?* What was that? "It's been a while."

"You need to rest," he said, letting his hand drop. "You can have the bed. I'll sleep on the couch tonight."

"Ah . . . okay." She felt awkward discussing sleeping arrangements after what had almost happened. "Do you mind leaving in the morning before my mother wakes up?"

His eyes narrowed with annoyance, the first indication he wasn't pleased about her mother's presence. "Fine. I have responsibilities in the morning. But I'll be back before eight." He frowned then, as if reminded of another unpleasant matter. "There's one more item I need to discuss with you. Enid is moving to a cottage in the village. Her living quarters will no longer be in my household. Would it offend you if she continues her duties as my cook?"

She cocked her head to one side, confused. "Why are you asking me this?"

His jaw tightened. "Because you are the reason she's being punished, and because you are my wife."

He had punished Enid.

"You need to stop calling me that," she said softly.

"I will call you nothing other than what you are."

She pressed two fingers into her temple, too tired to continue this argument tonight. "I don't care if Enid continues as your cook." His eyes narrowed, obviously displeased by her lack of thought on the subject. She sighed. If he had taken the time to address the woman over a past digression, the least she could do was give his request ample consideration. "Who is her backup cook?"

"We don't have a backup cook."

"Who cooks on Enid's day off?"

"Enid doesn't take a day off."

"Maybe that's the problem," she said. "I suggest you let her keep her position but allow someone else to cover for her on . . . let's say . . . Mondays. The competition might do Enid some good."

He took a moment to ponder her suggestion, ending with a sharp nod. "It's a fair judgment. I will announce the Monday position in the morning." Then a slow smile touched his lips. "This ought to be interesting."

Another thought crossed her mind. If Dylan had punished Enid . . . "Have you spoken with Siân?"

"Siân has been banished from my territory." His harsh statement didn't welcome further inquiries.

She nodded, feeling . . . *Good lord*, how did she feel about Dylan's punishments toward those who had wronged her? Relieved? Surprised? *Protected?*

Her throat tightened with another emotion she refused to consider. "Good night, Dylan."

He gave a brief nod of acknowledgment. "Good night. Try to get some sleep. Tomorrow will be . . . an eventful day."

She felt an insane urge to laugh. "More eventful than today? How is that possible?" She held up her hand. "No, don't answer that. I'm not sure I can handle any more enlightenment tonight."

"Luc plans to be here in the morning," he continued, searching her face with worried dark eyes. "Afterward, I would like to take Joshua around my land. Show him more of the village. I want some time alone with our son."

Specifically without her present. It was not said, but she understood his intention. A tight knot formed in her stomach and she shook off the protective reaction. Dylan had every right to request time alone with their son.

"He would like that," she whispered, wondering if he understood how difficult it was for her to make that concession.

The weight of his gaze lingered until she closed the bedroom door. She stripped out of her sweatpants, leaving on her tank top and underwear. Out of habit, she checked the location of her weapons before slipping into bed. The stairs creaked as Dylan walked upstairs, pausing by the room above hers. He was checking on Joshua. A few minutes later his footsteps returned back downstairs, stopping briefly to pause by her door before moving toward the living room.

She let out a breath, unaware she'd been holding it. It took some time for her mind to relax with Dylan just around the corner. Exhaustion eventually pushed her to sleep. Oddly enough, it was not Dylan that crept into her dreams, but a serpent instead, one with red eyes and the horns of a ram.

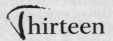

Thirteen

HIS HOUSE WAS TOO DAMN QUIET.

He missed them.

He missed Sophie with her soft brown eyes, Joshua with his curious mind, and Francine with her fiery wit, a woman who had taught her daughter strength and conviction, and how to love a child with a selfless heart.

Taliesin sneered at his perfectly made bed. Sophie would have fluffed his pillows and turned the right corner of his covers down. A cold glass of water would have been sitting on his nightstand. His dinner would have been cooked fresh, not frozen in plastic containers he had to heat himself.

What was the point of that? It wasn't the same unless she made it for him, unless she was in his kitchen, filling his house with warmth and laughter. And family.

Now he was alone.

Again.

He slumped down on his bed. What day was it? *Tuesday?* He ran his hands over his face. *Fuck . . . they had only been gone one day?* It wasn't even Thursday yet? Thursday was pizza and movie night, a tradition in the Thibodeau women's household, and Sophie made the best damn pizza.

Taliesin had bought the new Jackie Chan movie, an impulse even though he'd known they wouldn't be here to watch it with him. Joshua loved Jackie Chan.

He pulled his cell phone out of his pocket, flipped it open, dialed his message box and listened to her voice one last time. He heard her fear, the questions, and the mistrust; it ate at him like roundworms in his gut.

She was with Dylan now, as it should be—as it was meant to be.

I must not interfere any more than I have. I must not interfere. It was a chant in his mind, repeated again and again. He squeezed his cell phone so tightly it snapped in half. *If I do, if I warn them, if I help them any more than I have—the consequences will be severe.*

Taliesin threw the broken pieces of his phone against the wall. Knowing the future sucked.

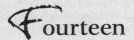

Fourteen

THE SERPENT WEAVED A HEAVY PATH UP HER BODY. ITS
weight surprised her, as heavy as a man, rubbing between
her legs and under her shirt, and then a smooth slide across
her belly. The texture of its skin reminded her of a knotted
rope made of silk, its temperature indistinct, as if it matched
hers.

Sophie arched into the sensation, shivering with a mixture of pleasure and revulsion.

The snake hissed, pleased with both emotions. "I see why
Sin chose you."

"I haven't sinned in a very long time," she said, wondering why she was debating her virtues with a dream.

"Such a shame, that." Its voice was a compelling whisper
in her thoughts, strong and very old, as if it spoke in a meld
of ancient accents.

"What do you want?" The cloying scent of apple blossoms and pollen hovered around the edges of her muddled
awareness.

"Only to offer a gift. Will you accept my gift, Sophie
Marie Thibodeau, wife of Dylan ap Merin?"

Even a serpent in her dream branded her as Dylan's wife. That couldn't be a good sign. "That depends on the gift."

"Knowledge." Its head rested on her chest, heavy with horns that circled its head. "My gift has always been knowledge."

"And just what is the price for this knowledge? The destruction of paradise, perhaps?"

"Do you like walking in the dark when wolves watch from the woods?"

Oh, the serpent was good; it knew how to elicit fear, knew what offer might tempt her most. But then, it *was* her subconscious weaving this dream. *Wasn't it?*

"What knowledge do you offer?" The words fell from her mind, unbidden by her lack of consciousness. Were dreams realities in a different realm?

The serpent slid down between her breasts, snuggled, comfortable—*pleased.* "You will know danger from security. You will see lies in truth. And you will learn how to defend those you love most. Do you want to protect your son, Sophie Marie Thibodeau, wife of Dylan ap Merin?"

"Yes, of course," she thought.

"Good." The serpent reared back with a hiss and sank its fangs into her skin.

SOPHIE SHOT AWAKE, BLINKED AT THE SUNLIGHT FILTERING through the window, and relaxed back into her pillow as reality overcame the nightmare. Unfortunately, a dull ache in her chest disallowed complete serenity. She yanked up her tank top. Two red dots swelled on the underside of her left breast.

Spider bites, she reassured herself, *not the dream.*

She said a brief prayer just to be safe.

Other events of the night began to filter through her panic over a dream. She swung her legs over the bed and peeked around the door. The couch was empty and the house was quiet. As promised, Dylan had left before sunrise.

Shaking off the last remnants of sleep, Sophie rummaged through her suitcase for her sweatpants, sports bra and jogging shoes, followed by her concealed holster shirt. She resembled one of Enid's gray sausage links after donning all her layers. She tucked her Glock in the side pocket of the customized shirt, and grabbed two extra magazines, along with two knives. She forced herself to run five miles every day, a routine she hated but never neglected. If another escape became necessary, she would be prepared.

After pulling on her sweatshirt, she checked on Joshua, not surprised to find him still sleeping. As she sat on the edge of his bed he groaned and tried to pull the covers over his head.

"I'm going for a run," she whispered. "Do you want to come with me?"

"Not today." He turned onto his back and cracked open one eye, and then lifted an arm over his face to block the light streaming in through the window. "What time is it? Did you make the cinnamon rolls?"

"It's around six in the morning and the rolls are still rising. I'll cook them when I get back." She felt a twinge of concern about leaving him alone, even for a short time. "Will you be okay alone for an hour or so?"

"Mom, come on . . . if anything happens I can defend myself. Not that anything will."

"Your father has people watching our cabin," she warned him.

"I know," he said. "I heard them talking in the woods last night. I caught parts of their conversation. They're . . . protecting us."

Protecting or spying? Both, probably. But she knew in her heart Dylan would never allow his son to be harmed. Just as she knew he would do everything in his power to keep him from leaving. And for the first time she felt secure in that knowledge, appreciating Dylan's protection, especially when it came to Joshua. "You have your weapons nearby?"

He sighed. "Of course."

"Okay." Satisfied, she patted his leg and stood. "I'll just be running a circle around the cabin. If you need me, all you have to do is holler."

"Mom . . . *Go.*" He rolled in a cocoon of blankets, covering his head and already falling back asleep.

"Don't forget your uncle will be here at eight," she reminded him as she headed to the door. "That's only two hours away."

He grunted.

Sophie checked on her mother before going back downstairs, closing the door softly after finding her still asleep. She pulled her hair into a rough ponytail and brushed her teeth. Under her sweatshirt rested her gun, tucked tightly against her side. She secured the knives and extra magazines to each calf, her own special jogging weights.

According to Dylan, a gun wouldn't kill one of his wolves, but she was betting it would slow one down. *Or piss it off.* Hopefully she would never find out. Regardless, she wasn't leaving the house unarmed. She even debated wearing the serpent but opted against it; yesterday's events combined with the dream had left her feeling edgy. Accepting gifts from talking serpents had that effect on her, even a serpent of dreams.

The outside air was crisp. She stretched on the porch, keeping her ears open for signs of the guards' whereabouts. Somewhere close, she was sure. Patches of snow lingered beyond the trees but the road was dry and clear, perfect for a morning run.

A sad feeling settled in her chest as she took off down the gravel-covered road, starting at a steady jog. She missed her dog . . . *Well, Matthew's dog.* Tucker had always run with her in the mornings. She had felt safer with the Great Dane by her side.

Matthew, *or Taliesin*, or whatever his real name was, hadn't returned her call, nor had she tried to call him back. What was the point? She had left a message and he knew her number. And frankly, she was tired of being lied to.

Birds sang in the forest, the sound a delicate accompaniment to the steady rhythm of her strides, nature's orchestra soothing her tattered nerves. She increased her speed; her side started to ache and her calves protested but she fought through the pain, focusing on her breathing and her surroundings.

DYLAN WATCHED ELEN TAKE A SIP FROM HER MUG AND then set it down on her kitchen table. The scent of coffee drifted through the room, mingling with dried herbs tied with string that hung from the kitchen rafters.

Elen sat across from him, still in her sleeping garments, covered by a soft pink robe. The sun filtered in through her front window, making her hair shine golden white around her shoulders.

A massive wolf stood by her chair, his eyes filled with human resentment. Even confined to all fours, Cormack towered above Elen.

She stroked her hand down the wolf's neck and whispered something into his ear, low enough to mask the content of her words from Dylan but not the tone, a tone of warmth, of tenderness.

Cormack retreated, although with obvious reluctance.

Dylan waited until the steps of the beast had left the house and retreated to the woods. "You've become close with Cormack?"

Her eyebrows rose, mocking. "You can lose that fatherly tone. Cormack and I are friends. He keeps me company when others are . . . *uncomfortable* around me."

"Who's uncomfortable around you?" Dylan sat up in his chair. "Not our people from the village?"

"Don't be angry with them," she said. "They still call on me when they're hurt." She waved her hand around her cottage. "Can you blame them for being wary of me? They know I'm different." Her voice turned melancholy. "Do you remember the witch who lived in the hills when we were children?"

"Maelorwen." Dylan supplied the name.

"Yes." A brief smile touched her lips, suggesting her memories of the witch were not unpleasant ones. "Maelorwen taught me a great deal about plants and their uses. I always wondered why she befriended me. I was such a nuisance, constantly underfoot asking questions, but now I understand how she must have felt; she was lonely."

"Are you lonely, Elen?"

She gave a delicate shrug with one shoulder. "Like Maelorwen, I've become a healer . . . and yet the people I help are too wary to come to me unless in need."

Troubled by the comparison, Dylan glanced around his sister's kitchen. It had been a while since he had visited Elen in her private quarters. Although a short distance from the clinic, her cottage remained secluded, and like her front yard and private garden out back, plants grew around the windows and over the walls, a greenhouse effect in early April that gave Dylan due cause to worry. "Your gift is growing stronger."

She looked down at her hands. "I know."

Elen might not have the ability to call the wolf, but she wasn't powerless. Quite the opposite, in fact. Like Dylan and Luc, she could call on nature and any living thing in her immediate surroundings. But unlike her brothers, or any others of their kind, she could give that gift away. In her own way, she had the ability to give life. And when the power ran strong it showed in her surroundings, because she always gave it back to the earth.

Dylan crossed his arms and leaned back in his chair, pondering the consequences of his next suggestion, but having enough faith in his sister's innate goodness to make it. "Perhaps it's time you explore your gift beyond plants."

"I cannot." She kept her eyes downcast but the conviction in her voice refused argument, and yet there was deep longing that filtered through the fear. "I'm afraid once I open that door . . . I'll never be able to close it."

"You may be able to use your gift to help others . . . You may be able to use it to help others like Cormack."

"Not without taking an equal life. And I'm not willing to do that." She shook her head with vehemence. "I will *never* do that."

Dylan gave her a low nod, respecting her choice. "I'm always here for you."

"I know," she whispered.

"Your apartments are still available . . . if you want to move back in with your brothers."

"Oh no," she said with a tad more force than necessary. "I may be lonely at times . . . but I still value my independence, such as it is." She stood quickly, her chair almost toppling over in her haste, and walked toward the sink and away from her brother's good intentions. "I'm assuming you didn't come here to discuss my problems," she continued, effectively changing the subject. "Luc informed me he's called everyone back home from the cities. I'll make a point to stop in and see Beatrice when she arrives. She'll probably stay with her mother. And Joseph . . ."

Dylan nodded absently. Luc had indeed called everyone back home, and some had begun to arrive, but his mind was on another matter entirely. "Sophie has possession of the Serpent of Cernunnos."

Her mug fell from her hands and hit the tiled countertop, shattering on impact. She ignored the broken porcelain and turned to stare at her brother. "Are you sure?" At Dylan's raised brow, she asked, *"How?"*

"It was a gift from the man who's been helping her hide from me since California. She calls him Matthew but he fits the description of Taliesin."

"But Sin hasn't involved himself in our affairs for many years. Not since we've come to this country." Her perplexed expression quickly became one of concern. "Unless it involves the Guardians."

"I didn't realize you knew him that well." He frowned at her casual use of Taliesin's nickname. Only a select few called him Sin.

"I know Sin well enough." She gave him a sad smile as she

gathered the broken pieces of her mug and placed them in a trash bin under the sink. "He helped me when I was young."

"When?"

"During the time when you left with Luc. Sin protected me from the Guardians . . . and our mother."

As always, when he thought of her alone, left to the Guardians' manipulations, guilt stirred in his gut. "Why have you never told me this?"

"Because I know it upsets you to speak of that time." She walked back to the table and placed a hand on his arm. "But, as I've told you before, I believe there's a reason for everything." She let her hand drop. "I know the purpose of Sin's weapon."

He shrugged at the obvious. "To kill our kind."

"Not just our kind. *Not us*. Not descendants. Not even *Drwgddyddwg*." Blue eyes met his and held. "I believe Sin's weapon was forged to kill Guardians." Her voice became hushed, as if speaking of things better left untold. "I've seen him use it."

"On a Guardian?"

"On an Original Guardian," she added. "On a *Gwarchod-wyr Unfed*."

Apprehension tightened his spine. "Whose death do you speak of?"

"Madron's," she said without remorse.

Dylan closed his eyes briefly, running his hands over his face. He had heard of the execution, Madron's head found separated from his body in a bedchamber occupied by children. It happened before Dylan had traveled across an ocean to new lands, *before* he had gone back for Elen.

Whispered rumors had traveled far amongst their kind, even to the camps of the outcasts, Taliesin being the only viable choice as executioner; his hatred toward the Guardians well known, even then, especially toward the men who had raised him—the *Gwarchodwyr Unfed*.

However, to Dylan's knowledge, no witness had come forth to validate the suspicions. Until now. "You were there? You saw it happen?"

"Yes," she confirmed in a quiet voice, rubbing her hands up and down her arms as if warding off a chill. "After you left, after our father died . . . our mother lived with Madron for a while."

"I didn't know." Bile rose in his throat as rage clouded his vision. "You should have told me. Why have you kept this secret?"

"It was my secret to keep."

"Even from me?"

"Yes, brother . . . even from you."

A question he shouldn't ask fell from his mouth. "Did Madron ever touch you?"

"No." Her denial eased his tension somewhat, but not enough, not when her eyes remained distant and her voice haunted. "Even at fourteen years of age I was too old for his peculiar tastes. I shared a chamber with one of his favorites."

A shattered breath fell from her lips and Dylan remained quiet, in part because he was afraid of his own voice, afraid his anger would, in some way, debase her confession.

"Her name was Leri," Elen continued. "She was ten, not yet showing signs of womanhood. Madron would send his sister to our chamber at night to bathe Leri. And dress her in fine silks. She never told me what happened when they took her each night, but I knew . . . She made me promise not to tell anyone. She made me promise not to speak of it. And I never have . . . until now."

When he spoke, it was only to say, "I am sorry."

"It had naught to do with you." She waved away his apology as if it were an annoying insect about to feed on one of her precious plants. "I'm not sharing this story to put more weight on your conscience. You do that well enough yourself. I'm sharing this because I want you to understand the importance of Sin's weapon."

Dylan understood full well the importance of Taliesin's weapon. "Go on."

"One night, when Madron sent his sister, Leri refused to go. He returned to our chamber in person . . . but this time

Sin was with us, telling Leri and me a tale of evil men and courageous knights, and why some men needed to die. Sin was waiting for Madron. I realize that now." She took a deep breath and let it out. "He told us to turn our backs, to cover our eyes. Leri obeyed . . . but I didn't. I wanted to see. The beheading was instant. You would not believe how fast unless you saw it with your own eyes."

A human's spine was strong, a Guardians' even stronger. A beheading didn't happen in an instant, not without momentum, weight, muscle, gravity, or a device that embodied all those qualities. "He used the Serpent to do this?"

Understanding the direction of his thoughts, she added, "I don't believe the Serpent of Cernunnos is entirely of this world."

"I would have to agree." Dylan had felt its power, *its anger*, when he had tried to take it from Sophie.

Elen started to pace. "If the Guardians knew that Sophie has possession of it . . ."

A reminder he didn't need. "Then Taliesin will have condemned my wife."

She stopped in front of his chair and gave him a pointed look. "Sin may be trying to protect Sophie. He obviously cared enough to get involved."

Condemn or protect?

"Are they not one and the same?" Dylan felt as if a vise had tightened around his heart. Anyone who knew Taliesin's history understood the frightening significance of that statement, because every person that man cared about always ended up dead.

Elen didn't deride him with false words of solace. "Then it has finally come." Her voice deadened with acceptance. "The time has finally come for us to face the Guardians."

"Yes." It was a soft answer, one he'd given before, one he didn't enjoy giving again. She'd held on to hope, he knew, to the possibility of another explanation for the banner, but Sophie's possession of the Serpent was a new warning too significant to deny the impending arrival of the Guardians.

He reminded her, "We are proceeding with a course of action in two days hence. I expect arrivals to begin Friday after sunset. If you're not going to use your apartments, I'll have them prepared for Isabeau."

"Of course." Elen waved her hand absently. "Sophie should be told of the gathering."

A sound came from his pocket and for once he wasn't annoyed by the interruption. He retrieved his cell phone and flipped it open. "What?"

Gabriel's voice filtered through the line; he was one of the guards assigned to the woods surrounding the lake house. "Your wife is running."

His vision blurred as he gripped the phone. Utter, immobilizing fear clawed at his spine. *"How far did she get?"*

He listened to the directions as Elen hovered close with a worried frown.

"What's wrong?" she whispered.

"Sophie's running away."

The phone fell from his grip as he slammed out of Elen's house, her voice a distant warning by the time he hit the forest at a full sprint.

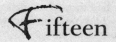

Fifteen

Sᴏᴘʜɪᴇ ꜰᴏᴄᴜsᴇᴅ ᴏɴ ᴛʜᴇ ᴇᴠᴇɴ ᴘᴏᴜɴᴅɪɴɢ ᴏꜰ ʜᴇʀ sᴛʀɪᴅᴇs until she sensed a second echo, a second rhythm interrupting hers. It was her only warning before her feet left the ground.

It happened so fast, *inhumanly* fast, she had no time to react other than to hold out her hands to accept most of the fall. One moment she was running and the next she was on the ground, face first, gravel cutting into her palms with a large mass on top of her.

The form of a man—*not a wolf*—held her down with forearms and large hands.

"Don't move," an all-too-familiar voice growled next to her ear; the weight of his body forced air from her lungs.

"Good God . . . *Dylan?*" She practically melted with relief that she hadn't retaliated, and yet the hard earth beneath her cheek was a cold reminder that she should have. If it had been anyone other than Dylan, that split-second hesitation could have cost her life. She twisted out from under him, using a root from a nearby tree for leverage to crawl forward. *"What is wrong with you?"*

"Did I tell you too much yesterday?" He grabbed her leg

and pulled; her sweatpants caught on a rock or fallen branch, she wasn't sure which, just something sharp that exposed her calf as he continued to yank and her clothing refused to follow, bunching up around her knee. "Is that why you're running away?"

"What?" she seethed through clenched teeth. "Running away? Are you crazy? I'm not running away. I'm jogging."

"Jogging?" He sounded confused.

"Yes, jogging. You know . . . like . . . *exercise*." She lunged forward, grabbing at the ground for more leverage, kicking backward and hoping to land a solid blow on his chest if her calculations were correct. "I would never leave my son."

He grunted as her foot landed on something solid. Unfortunately it didn't dislodge his hand, which continued to remain a vise around her ankle.

But then his motions stilled and his voice took on a strange tone, low and barely audible. "What is that on your leg?"

"It's called a knife," she snapped, twisting onto her back to face him, forcing him to let go of her ankle or be tangled in her legs. He loosened his grip enough for her to turn. Her new position freed her right leg. She braced her foot against his groin, eyebrows raised in challenge and ready to kick.

His eyes were not on her knife.

But on her exposed skin instead.

With proficient motions, he yanked off her calf holster and threw it onto the path, uncaring that it fell within reach. He left the other leg alone, obviously not threatened by either weapon. Instead, he tried to push her pants farther up her exposed leg. After a few seconds of fighting with the elastic material, he decided to yank them down, *and off*, instead.

Aware now of what he'd seen, of what he wanted to see more of, Sophie kicked out, only to have her free leg caught and disarmed, his movements a blur to her human eye. Her sneakers followed. She fell back with a groan, knowing a struggle would only prolong the inevitable. Genetically, he was stronger than her. She was human. And he was . . . *more*.

Besides, she was beginning to accept the fact that she

really didn't have the heart to fight this man; her heart had an entirely different desire.

He peeled the pants completely off and threw them to the side. She had removed her sweatshirt during her run and tied it around her waist. It had untangled sometime during their scuffle, offering no protection from his heated glare.

Irritated, more with herself than him, she rose to a semi-sitting position and leaned back on her elbows, looking down the length of her bared body. All that remained were her sleeveless concealed holster shirt over a sports bra, purple underwear and white ankle socks. Her gun bulged outward from her side. Pine needles and dirt clung to her sweat-coated skin, but not enough to hide the purple scars that puckered her left leg from hip to mid-calf, more prominent because of the chilled air and her matching hip-hugger briefs.

"Who did this to you?" His voice was raw, almost broken as he knelt before her.

Her answer lodged in her throat as Luc chose that moment to barge into the clearing. Wild silver eyes scanned the area until he looked down and found his quarry. Six others followed: three men, two women and a brown wolf. One of the women was Taran. Without being asked, the guards formed a circle around Dylan and Sophie.

There was a gasp and several murmurs as they assessed the situation—and Sophie's exposed leg.

"Who did this to you?" Dylan asked again, uncaring that they now had an audience.

"It happened the night I left you . . . but it looks worse than it was," she told him, only because she wanted out of there as quickly as possible. "I think if I had gone to a hospital it would have healed better."

His voice lowered to a deadly whisper. "Are you telling me that Siân did this to you?"

"Yes," she answered with more calm than she felt, feeling the weight of eight sets of eyes. "I told you that Siân threatened to kill us if we ever returned. And that I had reason to believe she'd try. I don't make false accusations."

A strangled sound came from Taran, a moan of feminine denial laced with fear.

"You didn't tell me she had harmed you," Dylan ground out, tracing his hand over the puckered scars.

Gritting her teeth, she placed her hand over his to stop the movement. "The scars are sensitive to touch," she explained.

"Your nerves were damaged." A tremor entered his voice, an odd sound coming from a man who never showed emotion. "You were not treated well here . . . were you, my wife?" It was a question he obviously didn't expect an answer to and so she remained silent. "I brought you into the woods that night to help you understand why I kept you away from your family. And in return you were attacked by one of my people. It's no wonder you never returned."

At a loss for an appropriate response, she clung to the obvious. "I'm here now."

"Yes," he challenged. "But for how long?"

"I will always choose the path I believe best for our son. That path has led me back to you. Joshua needs you. And I will stay as long as my son wants me to."

Looking somewhat consoled, Dylan shifted onto his side and stood, helping Sophie up. With calm proficiency, he found her sweatpants and handed them to her. Ignoring the pine needles and dirt stuck to her skin and bottom, and probably other areas she didn't want to think about, she yanked them back on. She walked over to her discarded sneakers, paused to unroll her wet socks, and shoved her bare feet into the shoes. Next, she retrieved her knives, letting the holsters dangle from her hands rather than bending over to strap them back on.

Feeling more secure dressed, she looked up only to find Luc watching her with one black eyebrow raised to her weapons and a slight grin on his face. He dipped his head in acknowledgment.

Dylan took a step toward the circle of guards. "Taran, did you know of this?"

"I didn't." Taran fell to her knees, her head bowed. "I swear, *Penteulu*, I didn't know."

"You sensed nothing," Dylan spat.

Her breath fell from her lips. "I . . . I knew something had happened. My sister changed after that night, her mind became whole again for a while." Absolute fear laced through the woman's voice, a plea more than an explanation. "Siân thought . . . She thought you were free again. She refused to believe that woman's child was yours. She refused to believe you were mated."

Sophie frowned at the woman's choice of words. *Mate* was a very specific term, especially when referring to the habits of wolves.

Luc stepped forward and the others moved out of his path. His hair was loose and black around his shoulders, his chest bare. Several tattoos of black symbols and scrolls covered his back and upper arms, more noticeable as he hovered over the bent woman.

"There would have been blood," Luc sneered as he grabbed a fistful of red hair and pulled her head back with enough force to lift her knees off the ground. "A good wolf would have sensed it on her sister."

Sophie took a step forward but then stopped. She was becoming more aware, and sadly, more comfortable with their dominant behavior now that she knew its source.

"I didn't," Taran pleaded, her eyes rolling back and then away. "Siân reeked of skunk for days."

"I was sprayed by skunks that night," Sophie admitted. Upon hearing her voice, Luc's grip on Taran's hair eased enough so that her knees touched the ground. "I hid in a hollowed trunk occupied by skunks. It may have hidden my scent. It took days for the smell to leave my skin."

Frowning, Luc looked to his brother. "How should I proceed?"

Sophie took another step forward and placed a hand on Dylan's cheek, guiding him to look down at her. Gold and green streaks had bled through the blackness of his gaze.

She swallowed, keeping her voice calm. "Taran wasn't there that night. Punish her if you think she's a threat to our son, but don't punish her for what her sister did to me. She wasn't responsible for her sister's actions."

He rubbed his cheek against her palm, unshaven and rough against her skin, before turning his head toward his brother. "Luc, take Taran home and question her at your discretion . . . for I cannot without prejudice. If you feel she's innocent, I will default to your judgment. But"—he looked to Taran as he made his last order—"I want her removed from guard responsibilities."

Luc gave a sharp nod. "Understood."

Dylan looked to the others. "John and Malsum, return to your posts. The rest, follow Luc."

There were murmured farewells and a few nods in Sophie's direction. As their footsteps retreated, she tried to ignore the pounding of her heart, although Dylan surely must have heard it. "Will Luc harm her?"

Dylan shook his head, holding her hand to place a kiss inside her palm before answering. "Not unless she gives him due cause. He will remove her from her duties and keep her contained and watched until we know she can be trusted."

"Good," she said, tugging her hand from his grasp and turning away, not because she didn't like it, but because she did.

Not dissuaded, Dylan walked up behind her and wrapped his arms around her waist. "No," he said as she tensed, "don't resist me. Just let me hold you."

His heat seeped into her muscles, so warm, so enticing, as if she could melt into his arms and all their troubles would go away. How long had it been since she'd allowed someone to hold her? To comfort her?

Forever, it seemed. Not since the birth of her son. Not since Dylan had brought her into these very woods sixteen years ago.

With her back to his chest, she slowly relaxed into the sensation of being protected. Unfortunately, something Taran had said continued to ride her thoughts and refused to be ignored. "How much are you compelled by the instincts of the wolf?"

His arms tightened around her. "More than I would like."

"Taran said her sister didn't believe you were mated. Mate is a very specific term, especially for wolves."

One hand loosened from her waist and found the elastic in her ponytail, tugging until her hair fell around her shoulders. "I like your hair down."

"You're changing the subject."

"Then stop hedging and just ask me what you want to know."

"Fine." She took a deep breath and let it out. "This is going to sound silly, because I know wolves don't always mate for life." She was rambling, she knew, but couldn't seem to stop. "If one mate dies, the survivor will find another."

He nuzzled her hair; his breath whispering against the exposed flesh of her neck. "You don't feel dead to me."

Her stomach twisted. "Oh, God."

"That's right." His lips dropped to her neck, a whisper of movement against her sensitive skin. "Our son isn't the only thing I lost when you left me."

"But you're also a man," Sophie emphasized, trying to ignore the sigh of his breath across her nape. "Humans are not bound by those convictions. Surely . . ."

"I'm compelled by both human and wolf instincts. For our kind, the melding of the two strengthens the mating bond, as if human emotion reinforces the wolf's choice. Most of us mate for life." His cutting tone left little doubt that he considered himself among the ones who did.

"So there are others of your kind who don't? How do you know for sure that you're not one of them?" Inwardly she cringed, aware that she had opened a precarious door to a difficult subject.

"Like all humans," he stated bluntly, "I could bed anything I wanted. I could carry out the act. But because my wolf has chosen its mate, because you conceived my child, mating with anyone other than you would feel unnatural, a violation."

She closed her eyes. "Like a rape?"

"I wouldn't know." He dropped his hands from her hair and returned them to her waist. "I've never had a taste for that act, but there a few of my kind who have no distinction between the two."

"The Guardians, I assume."

"You're learning." He plucked at the waistband of her concealed weapon shirt, changing the subject once again. "Where did you get this garment?" Annoyance darkened his voice.

"From a biker convention. They had booths of this kind of stuff. It works great for jogging."

With her eyes still closed, she felt his hand inch downward, pause, and then snake under the elastic band of her sweatpants and briefs.

Her eyes flew open. "What are you doing?" She dropped her holsters and grabbed at his forearm.

"I'm going to give you pleasure," he announced as if it were a nonnegotiable fact.

"Here?" *Oh, God. "Now?"*

"It's taking every ounce of my will not to throw you on the muddied ground and come inside you." He pressed a finger between the moist folds of her skin. "I need this." He moved up and over the sensitive peak of her sex. "Let me hear my name on your lips when you—"

"*Stop!* Just stop talking." Because his words taunted her, *aroused* her. She grabbed at his wrist but it was too late; he had found his target, plucking at the sensitive bud with skillful fingers.

His arm pressed into her thigh, holding her in place. She lost her footing, falling back into the full support of his embrace. Her insides tightened, and tightened some more, and soon her grip on his wrist was encouragement as he stroked her toward a violent release.

And, yes, she cried out his name.

The sounds of the forest invaded slowly. She was mildly aware that Dylan had gone utterly rigid and that he no longer supported her weight.

"I'm going for a run," he growled, and left her struggling for balance, in more ways than one, in a suddenly empty clearing.

WITH HER SCENT IN HIS LUNGS, AND THE ECHOES OF HER cries in his ears, Dylan couldn't breathe.

Pausing in the shadows of the forest, the memory of her flesh and soft body haunted him. He wanted to go back and shove her to the ground, rip her pants down around her knees, wrap his hands in all that thick hair and pin her beneath him until he felt her sweet flesh pulse around his deprived cock . . .

His wolf prowled, caged in his body, in full agreement with that plan, anxious and ready to be satisfied. It translated desire into hunger and it wanted to feed.

It wanted to mark its mate.

Leaning against a tree for support, Dylan clawed at the hardened bark beneath his fingers, welcoming the pain. He was in no mood to be nice. It had been too damn long. If he returned to her now in his current state, he might hurt her.

With that knowledge, he moved forward with one heavy step, and then another, a focus of will that helped put distance between him and his ultimate temptation.

There was one thing he knew for certain, one point of clarity that gave him strength: Sophie's return was a tentative gift, one that could just as easily be taken away if not handled properly. Their reunion couldn't be an act of domination. Not with their history. Not with how she'd been treated in his home.

No, his wife needed to come to him, because he wanted more than just her physical submission. He wanted her loyalty—and her trust. He wanted her to accept their marriage, and he would bloody well wait for her to do so, even if it killed him.

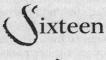ixteen

"WHAT THE HELL?" SOPHIE RAN HER HANDS OVER HER face, trying to regain her composure. When she realized he wasn't coming back, she returned to the lake house, creeping through the front door like a guilty teenager.

Her mother was up—*of course*—and dressed for the day in navy slacks and a simple white blouse. She turned and assessed Sophie with shrewd brown eyes. "You couldn't put off running for a few days?"

"No." Sophie felt her face turn red, even though the question had nothing to do with her embarrassment.

Her mother's eyes narrowed further. "Did something happen? Did you run into Dylan?"

"No. Well, er, yes," she fumbled.

"Why is your face red?" She sniffed the air as if something didn't smell quite right. "And what's on your clothes?"

"I tripped and I'm sweaty. And I need a shower." Sophie rushed to the bathroom before her mother could probe further. "I won't be long."

Locking the door behind her, she stripped quickly and turned on the shower, groaning when the hot water ran down her back. As Dylan's words replayed in her mind, she rested her forehead against the tiled shower wall.

Our son isn't the only thing I lost when you left me.

A soft sob escaped her lips. Only here, only when she was alone and the water washed away her tears, could she express her true feelings. How many times had she pictured Dylan with other women? With Siân? God help her, but she felt immense satisfaction knowing he had never returned to that woman's bed.

After rinsing off, she wrapped a towel around her middle and gathered her dirty clothes from the floor. Once in her bedroom, she chose the first thing out of her suitcase, gray trousers and a square-neck black sweater; both items hugged her frame but also allowed movement and were presentable and functional.

After combing out her hair and putting on tinted moisturizer, the extent of her morning routine, she made her way to the kitchen, ready to face her family.

Joshua sat at the kitchen table as Francine leaned against the counter. The smell of cinnamon and baking bread filled the room, along with a sudden awkward silence.

"Thanks for finishing the rolls, Mum."

After no response, Sophie asked, "Okay, what's up?"

Francine lifted her coffee mug to her lips, took a sip, and set it down on the kitchen counter. "Joshua and I have been having an interesting conversation."

"Oh, yeah?" Sophie glared at her child, whose six-foot-three frame was trying unsuccessfully to sink under the table. "About what?"

"Um," Joshua mumbled, "is the bathroom free?" Not waiting for an answer. "I'm gonna take a shower now."

Not a woman to waste time, Francine got right to the point. "Joshua told me you're married to his father. Is this true?"

Sophie glared at her son's retreating back. "Dylan and I made promises to each other. Nothing more. No papers were signed, no minister, no witnesses. I thought, at the time, it was a romantic gesture."

Francine pinned her daughter with an assessing look. "But Dylan thinks differently."

"He does," she admitted.

Her mother remained silent, thoughtful—*never* a good sign. "I'm going to ask you a few questions, and I want you to be truthful with me."

"Can't this wait?"

"No, it can't. Did your husband ever hurt you?"

"Mum . . . you don't understand, it wasn't like that. It's . . . *complicated*."

Her mother wasn't deterred. "It's a very simple question . . . yes or no . . . Did your husband ever hurt you?"

Regardless of their sordid history, Sophie was unwilling to allow her mother to think the worst of Dylan. "No."

Her eyes narrowed. "Then why were you injured when you came to me?"

"Dylan had no knowledge that I was hurt when I left him."

Francine's shoulders eased somewhat. "When your husband threatened to take his child from you, was that because he knew you were leaving?"

Sophie's stomach tightened, not liking the way her mother kept referring to Dylan as her husband. "Yes."

"Did your husband want you to stay with him?"

And tightened some more. "Yes."

"And what type of promises did you give your husband in this ceremony that had no witnesses? Did you promise to support him, and to love him, through good times and bad . . . ?"

"Stop." Sophie held up her hand. She knew where this was going but didn't know how to defend her actions without betraying Dylan's secret. So she voiced the only truth she could. "I lost my freedom as Dylan's wife."

"Sweetheart," Francine said in a tone that would have been condescending if it hadn't been laced with concern. "What do you think marriage is? Sunshine and roses?" She snorted, a feminine snort, but a snort all the same. "Your freedom ended the day you spoke your vows and accepted that man as your husband." She held up a pointed finger. "*And* consummated the union. There are reasons to end a marriage, of course. So, I will ask you again . . . Do you have a justified reason? Do you think your husband is capable of harming either you or Joshua?"

"No," Sophie said again, shaking with frustration, "Dylan would never hurt us. And I don't want to talk about this any more." Feeling overexposed and miserable, she slumped into the nearest chair and put her face in her hands. There was a soft shuffle across the kitchen floor as her mother approached, and then a gentle touch on the top of her head.

"In all these years," Francine said softly, "you've never so much as looked at another man. And yet, in Dylan's presence, you're all blushes and fumbled words. Do you still love him?"

Sophie hated the sudden thickness of her throat. "I told you it's complicated."

"*Life* is complicated. The heart isn't. Do you still love him?"

"I . . . Oh, hell . . ." she stammered, turning to mush under her mother's comforting hands and facing what she'd denied for sixteen years. "I love him so much that when I look at him it hurts."

"That's what I thought." Francine let out a loud sigh. "I know you. And I know I didn't raise a coward. I think it's time you explained to me what the hell is going on. If it's not your husband, then what—*or who*—have you been running from all these years?"

$\mathcal{S}$eventeen

I LOVE HIM SO MUCH THAT WHEN I LOOK AT HIM IT HURTS.

Dylan stood outside the lake house, letting his forehead rest on the painted wood of the front door, listening without guilt to his wife's conversation with her mother. Sophie's admission resonated through his chest, soothing his beast more than a run ever could.

Francine's reproach to her daughter had been an unexpected insight into her character. He was pleased, but also troubled by his own past mistrust. How different would their lives have been, had he allowed Francine into his home when Sophie had needed her most?

After two knocks, he opened the door. The women jumped apart. Sophie looked shaken, and . . . *displeased.* Perhaps she sensed her charade was about to end.

"It's time to tell your mother the truth," he said.

Her jaw gaped as understanding dawned. "No. Don't do this." Sophie started to shake her head, her tone beseeching. "I've told my mother nothing. *She knows nothing.* She can still leave here if she wants to."

Dylan walked over to his wife and lifted her chin. A wet

streak stained her face and he dried it with his thumb. "It's too late for that."

Francine poked at his shoulder. Not one poke, but several, until he turned and acknowledged the petite woman.

Undaunted by his glare, she placed both hands on her waist, her questioning gaze on Sophie and then on the bathroom door as it opened. "Would someone please tell me what's going on here?"

Joshua's hair stuck out in unkempt spikes, as if he had just shaken his head to expel the dampness. He assessed the situation, probably having heard most of it before stepping into the room. "Grandma, I want to ask you a serious question."

Francine threw up her hands. "What now?" Her narrowed glare held the fierceness of a worthy opponent but then gentled as she looked to her grandson. "Fine," she sighed. "Out with it. Ask me your question."

Joshua gave her a respectful nod. "Would you rather live with us and never be able to leave, or leave us and have your freedom? *But*," he emphasized, "the price of your freedom is to never see us again. What would you choose?"

Dylan interrupted, saddened that he had to contradict his son. "Your grandmother no longer has a choice. She knows where I live . . . *where you are*."

Rolling his eyes, Joshua turned his back to both women and mouthed silently, *Watch and learn.*

Surprised, but also intrigued, Dylan waved his hand for him to continue.

Francine tilted her head to one side. "We're not talking a hypothetical situation here, are we? This is a real choice you want me to make?"

"Yes," Joshua confirmed.

"Why?"

"We can't tell you unless you agree to stay."

"Fine," she said, directing her answer toward Dylan. "I choose my daughter and my grandson." There was no hesitation, not even a question or a doubt, or even a moment for thought. "So, that's settled. Do you mind telling me what's going on?"

"I can change into a wolf," Dylan said bluntly.

Francine laughed. "No, really, what's going on?"

"I can change into a wolf," he repeated. "Do you need a demonstration? One of my men is nearby, or I could do it myself."

The laughter fell short. She looked toward her daughter for reassurance and found none. "He's serious?"

"I'm afraid so," Sophie said.

"I would like a demonstration." The quiet request had come from Joshua.

"From me?" Dylan asked. "Or from one of my men?"

Joshua shrugged as if he didn't care, but Sophie whispered, "Not you."

Unwilling to deny her any reasonable demand, Dylan opened the door and held out his arm for Francine and his family to go ahead of him. A mixture of emotions surrounded the slow procession, doubt, sadness, and last, from his son, anticipation. He followed them to the front porch and let out a sharp whistle. Within seconds, Malsum appeared beside Sophie's vehicle, still in wolf form.

"Dear God," Francine whispered, her doubt now edged by fear. "That's a wolf."

Committed to this display, Dylan nodded to Malsum and ordered, "Shift."

The wolf gave a low nod and shivered as he drew in the surrounding energy. Dylan heard a startled gasp from his son, not of surprise, but of pleasure as the tendrils of power bled in their direction.

Keeping his face to the ground, an act of respect for Dylan's family, Malsum began his transformation. Within seconds, a human body took shape in a graceful dance of sinew and receding fur. He was often harassed by other guards for being a pretty shifter.

A deep inhalation expanded newly formed lungs as Malsum unfolded into a standing position as a man; his waist-length hair shrouded much of his muscled form. His dark coloring turned gold in the morning light. With his arms relaxed by his sides, he waited for further instruction, although laughter danced within his brown eyes and a slight grin tugged at his mouth.

Malsum's father had been a native of this land, and much like his ancestors, he had a calm nature, an ability to evaluate a situation at a higher level. However, he also had the blood of a Celt running through his veins—the source of his wolf. If provoked, if given just cause, the man had no reservations about eliminating anyone who threatened his home and family, quickly and without emotion.

"Thank you, Malsum." Dylan nodded for him to leave and turned to assess his family's reaction. Joshua had his hands fisted by his sides, riding out the aftereffects of lingering energy. Sensing his tentative hold on control, Dylan placed a hand on his shoulder. "Soon."

Tension eased as Joshua gave a sharp nod of understanding.

After shooting an icy glare in Dylan's direction, Sophie went to stand in front of her mother. "Mum, are you all right?"

The woman answered with a quiet request. "Would you get me my purse, please?"

"Sure," Sophie said with some hesitation, "if that's what you want."

"That's what I want."

Sophie disappeared into the house and returned with a small leather satchel. "I told you things were complicated. I warned you not to come with us."

Francine ignored her daughter as she rummaged through the bag, giving a ragged sigh when she pulled out a metal cigarette case. She removed one cigarette, put it to her lips with a shaking hand, and then frowned. "Lighter? Where are you? Oh, there you are, my sweet thing." She lit the cigarette and took a long draw, exhaling with a smoke-filled sigh.

Sophie started to pace. "Mum . . ."

"No, no . . ." Francine shook her head. "Not yet. I haven't had a cigarette in eighteen years. Don't ruin this for me."

"Are you unwell?" Dylan asked, quickly becoming concerned with her odd behavior. Perhaps he had misjudged her mental strength?

"My mother used to smoke," Sophie explained. "She quit when my father was diagnosed with cancer."

"I saved my last pack for a stressful situation," Francine added on a breath of smoke. "I'd say this qualifies."

"Indeed." Dylan gave her a low nod, thankful that she seemed quite lucid.

However, once the initial shock wore off, Francine leveled him with a look of reproach. "Does this . . ." She waved her hand in the air, searching for an apt description. "Does this *thing* that you do also affect my grandson?"

"We believe so," Dylan said.

"I see." She turned to her daughter. "You should have told me."

"*How*, Mum? How was I supposed to tell you something like this? I asked you once if you believed in any of the old legends, if maybe you thought there might be some truth behind the stories . . . and you accused me of doing drugs."

"Did I?" Francine shrugged. "I don't remember that, but if I did accuse you of doing drugs, it was only because you hung around all those hippie people with knots in their hair . . . who smelled like dirty socks."

"Dreadlocks, Mum . . . The knots in the hair are called dreadlocks. And those people were educated professors, and scientists, and wildlife activists. And why are we talking about this?" Sophie threw up her hands. "That was a long time ago, before Joshua was even born."

Francine huffed. "You'd think an educated person would know how to use a bar of soap."

"They did use soap."

"Then why did they have knots in their hair?"

Dylan pretended to cough only to hide his laughter; he

was quite sure he had met a few of the people Francine referred to, just as he was sure this inane argument was an outlet for their anxiety.

"Sophie, I will take my leave now and give you and your mother some privacy to talk and to . . . *adjust*." He ignored his wife's indelicate snort and turned toward Joshua. "Luc has been detained this morning. Your sparring session will have to wait until later. I would very much like to give you a tour of my lands instead. How does that sound to you?"

"That sounds cool." Joshua looked to his mother for consent.

Distracted from her argument, Sophie ran her hands over her face. "How long do you think you'll be?"

"I'll have him back before noon," Dylan said.

"My grandson hasn't eaten yet," Francine added. "Let me pack some cinnamon rolls up before you go."

"Thanks, Grandma." Joshua leaned down and gave the older woman a kiss on the cheek.

Both Sophie and her mother did not look pleased, but they made a valid attempt to disguise their fear, a true testament to their love for his son. Not to mention the three pounds of frosted spiced bread that was shoved into Joshua's hands, and a whispered warning from a tiny woman who, without question, had been a warrior in a past life.

SPRING HAD YET TO REACH THE HIGHER PEAKS OF Katahdin. Dylan guided Joshua along one of his favorite paths, covered by packed snow, trodden by the steps of his wolves. "Your aunt Elen told me she informed you of our history."

"Yeah, she talked a lot about scientific stuff, our anatomy and longevity, and the transformation process." Joshua walked in rhythm with his father's stride. "How long does this trail go for? Are you really going to help me shift tonight?"

"I am," Dylan confirmed. "After nightfall." He wondered if his son's rapid change of focus was common among modern teenagers. He made a mental note to ask Sophie about it later. "This trail runs north for approximately forty miles. Do you have any questions about the transformation?"

"I don't know. Not really. Aunt Elen was pretty descriptive."

Knowing his sister well, Dylan felt confidant Joshua had been gently but thoroughly prepared. "Then is there anything else you would like to know? Perhaps about my family?"

"Sure." Keeping his gaze forward, Joshua kicked a chunk of snow out of his path. "What's your last name? Mom said it was Black but I searched your ancestry at the library. I couldn't find a connection to the name Black."

"Currently I use the surname Black. We keep our records as secure as possible, although that has become a challenge with the Internet open to the public. We have a woman in the village who manages false birth and death records, with your aunt's assistance."

Joshua nodded. "So then what was your last name when you were born? Aunt Elen told me it was around the Middle Ages. That was like . . . King Arthur's time, wasn't it? Was he real? Did you know him?"

"I knew *of* him," Dylan replied, keeping his voice neutral. "Arthur was just a man. His accomplishments were highly exaggerated by a drunken bard and bored monks who wrote down the ramblings of a fool."

He didn't mention that Taliesin, aka Matthew, had been that drunken bard. Taliesin had spent much of the Middle Ages intoxicated, an impressive feat since, like Dylan, his metabolism was more active than a mere human and wolf combined. He'd had to consume a massive amount of alcohol. Unfortunately, too many stories of his antics were documented by humans during that tumultuous time.

"When I was born," Dylan continued, purposely steering the conversation back to Joshua's original question, "we did not use surnames. Humans were differentiated by their father's name. Villagers called me Dylan ap Aemilius, as in Dylan of Aemilius. My father was human."

"Did your kind call you something different?"

"*Our* kind," Dylan emphasized, "uses the name of our more powerful parent, regardless of gender. In my case, my mother is more powerful. I am called Dylan ap Merin. Although I haven't heard that reference in a very long time."

"Powerful?" Joshua paused on the path, taking a pine bough in his hands and running it through his fingers. "As in able to shift into a wolf?"

"Yes."

"Is your mother still alive?"

"She is, as far as I know," Dylan said carefully. "Merin is not a kind person. Unlike your mother, she was very cruel to her children. We don't speak of her."

"Oh." Joshua looked to the horizon with a contemplative stance, tactfully changing the subject. "So, I would be known as Joshua ap Dylan."

His heart clenched with pride. "That's correct."

"Cool." Joshua's gaze focused on his feet.

Sensing a sudden shyness, a trait he had yet to witness from his son, he asked, "Is there anything else you would like to know?"

"Yeah. I was wondering . . . What do you want me to call you? I mean . . . Mr. Black seems kinda weird."

"Don't call me Mr. Black," Dylan said, more harshly than intended and took a moment to calm his reaction. "What do other young men your age call their fathers?"

"Dad."

"Then let's go with Dad."

"Okay . . . *Dad*."

Swallowing past the thickness in his throat, Dylan reached out and squeezed his son's shoulder. "I would like you to know something . . . I was unaware your mother was mistreated in my home. She will never be so again."

Joshua's posture stiffened. "Good to know, but since you've brought it up . . ." He looked up with dark eyes that didn't waver. "What are your intentions toward my mom?"

Letting his hand drop, Dylan didn't hesitate with the

truth. "I want you and your mother to move back into Rhuddin Hall where you both belong. I want us to be a family. How do you feel about that?"

Joshua shrugged; the nonchalant gesture didn't match his lowered tone. "I'm okay with it, I guess . . . as long as Mom's happy here."

"I will do everything in my power to make that happen."

"And my grandma?" Joshua probed. "Can she stay with us too?"

Dylan nodded, refusing to repeat this past mistake. "Your grandmother is welcome as well."

Tension eased from his son's stance. "You're going about it all the wrong way, you know."

"I'm well aware of that," Dylan said, unashamed to ask for advice. "Do you have any suggestions?"

"Give Mom the choice to leave," he said as if it were the simplest thing in the world to do. "She'll choose us, like my grandmother did . . . but she needs to know she has the choice."

"You don't understand this yet," Dylan tried to explain. "And a part of me hopes one day you will—and another part of me wants to spare you the anguish. As I'm sure you're somewhat aware, our kind is compelled by the instincts of our wolves. When you were conceived, your mother became my mate. It goes against everything I am to let her go."

"See . . . that's what I'm talking about." Joshua rolled his eyes. "Saying stuff like that will only freak Mom out."

"I've noticed." The dialect of a modern teenager made a grin tug at Dylan's lips, a brief moment of joy that quickly turned to concern.

Having been protected all his life, Joshua's personality was carefree and unsullied by cruelty. Was he ready for this world? Would he have been better left to his mother's care, ignorant and safe, away from the Guardians?

Maybe, for a while, but time had a way of hardening the innocent. And may the Goddess help them all, Dylan vowed silently, if keeping his family here, if this one selfish decision, resulted in their harm. Because he would spend the rest of eternity punishing those responsible, and anyone who got in his way.

"Okay," Joshua said, "if you really want this to work . . . you're gonna have to listen to me."

Taken aback by the offered assistance, Dylan couldn't help but respond, "What do you have in mind?"

Eighteen

IF SOPHIE COULD HAVE PREDICTED THE COURSE OF THE day, watching her son carry their suitcases back out of the lake house and down the porch to her car would *not* have been one of her choices. Neither would she have predicted her mother's easy acceptance of Dylan's little demonstration.

"If you don't stop frowning, you're going to get ugly lines on your forehead." Francine leaned against their car and dug through her purse, pulling out a compact. "It runs in our family, you know."

"Somehow I'm not worried," Sophie said, wishing Dylan was there to take her frustration out on instead of her gullible family—who had, in less than a day, fallen for his charm. "I can't believe you're siding with *him*."

"Grandma's siding with me, Mom." Joshua strode by with a cooler over his head. "*I* want to go live with Dad. It was my idea. And I want you to come with me, but I understand if you don't want to."

Dad? Sophie crossed her arms and studied her child. "You're up to something. I can feel it. Did your father put you up to this?"

"Leave the boy alone," Francine said. "From what I've seen, Dylan's been very gracious under the circumstances. It's not an unreasonable request to have us stay where he can get to know his son better. You should be thankful he included us in the invitation. If I were in his position, I wouldn't have."

"You're not helping." Sophie watched with growing disbelief as her mother casually applied another coat of lipstick. "You're primping like we're going on some grand vacation. Believe me, we're not."

"Why would I want to go on a vacation?" Francine closed her compact, her rose-colored lips turning in a smooth, well-cultured smile. "Sweetheart, have you *seen* the men in this place? I'm fifty-eight, *not* dead."

"Oh. *My*. God." Sophie ran her hands over her face. "This is ridiculous. They're wolves, Mum. That doesn't frighten you? Not even a little?"

"Of course it does." Her mother gave a nonchalant wave. "But living alone and without my family frightens me more. And I'm not *that* egotistical . . . I realize there's more to this world than I alone will ever know." Her direct gaze never wavered in her conviction. "But I would rather live life to the fullest, with my eyes open, around the people I love, than fear the unknown alone."

"It's not the unknown I fear." Sophie pointed toward the lake house. "At least here, if things get bad, we have a chance to escape. We won't inside Rhuddin Hall."

"You've made this bed, Sophie Marie." Her mother sent her a narrowed glare, full of reproach. "Dylan is the father of your son. And the man you chose to marry. It's time to stop running and deal with the consequences of your choices."

Joshua threw the last suitcase in the trunk and slammed it shut. "Dad said you could stay at the lake house if you wanted to, Mom. I can bring your bags back in if . . ."

"I don't think so." Without the support of her family, Sophie felt a bit lost, especially as she realized her adorable and conniving child may have counseled his "Dad" on how to manage *her.* "I'm not letting you go there alone and you know it."

His lips turned into a devilish smile as he threw her the keys. "Thanks, Mom."

Uncertainty was not a state of mind Dylan particularly cared for, or wished to repeat anytime soon. He had taken to the outdoors an hour ago, the walls of his home an annoyance as he waited, wondering if he had given Joshua an impossible task. The sound of a vehicle arriving lightened his mood considerably.

"Bloody hell, it took that woman long enough," Porter muttered as he opened the gate, pointing for Sophie to park by the side of the main house. "As if we don't have enough to do with preparations for the gathering."

"Sophie has no knowledge of the gathering," Dylan warned. "So be sure to keep your comments to yourself."

"I'm thinking you might want to tell her before Friday," Porter muttered under his breath, shrugging off Dylan's glare.

Sophie stepped out of the car, her displeased gaze landing on Porter and then Dylan. "I see your pit bull is still here doing your bidding."

With exaggerated motions, Porter cocked his head to one side. "Am I hearing a harpy screeching . . . or is that just the wind?"

Holding his tongue, Dylan ignored the exchange, shoving two suitcases at Porter to keep the man occupied. The mere fact that he had reacted to Sophie's comment gave an indication of . . . well, not fondness, but perhaps respect, as in the kind reserved for a worthy opponent, one who had eluded a very aggressive chase. Otherwise, he would have just ignored her.

"Your rooms have been prepared," Dylan told his son and mother-in-law as they crowded around Sophie. "Follow me and I'll send someone to get the rest of your bags."

Francine looked around with widened eyes. "This is a fortress." At the sound of the closing gate, her lips thinned with displeasure. "Whenever it's convenient for you, Dylan, I'd like to have a word in private."

"Find me after you get settled."

She gave a brisk nod. "I'll do that."

As they made their way through the courtyard, Sophie remained sullen, ignoring his presence until they passed several rows of mounded roots and broken earth. She paused, her head turning toward the side garden located just below the master bedroom. "What happened here?" Her hand lifted above her eyes to screen the afternoon sun. "Is that George? Why is he digging up his roses?"

"Because I ordered him to pull them up," Dylan said without remorse.

"But why?" she asked, obviously confused. "They were so beautiful."

"Because George informed me this morning that he chastised you once for cutting a rose." Dylan inclined his head toward the ground. "This is his punishment."

Unfortunately, George hadn't been the only one offering a confession. Several others had come to Dylan throughout the morning, prompted by Enid's move to the village, to confess their past transgressions against his wife. To George's misfortune, his admission had annoyed Dylan most, simply for its sheer pettiness—a denial of a flower from a plant that only thrived from being cut.

Sophie blinked, taken aback, and her frosty attitude thawed with disbelief. "You did this for me? Because I was denied a rose?"

"I did this because you were treated unkindly in my home. And their unkindness resulted in your unhappiness." Very aware of their audience, he closed the few steps that separated them, and whispered next to her ear, "And I was denied you because of it."

A charming blush crept across her cheeks as she swept a nervous glance toward their son. Hugging a leather satchel to her chest, she stepped away. "I enjoyed the rose garden when I lived here. Does it have to be destroyed?"

"Not if you don't wish it to be," he said.

"I don't."

He bit back a grin at her suddenly formal tone. "Then I will have it put back."

"Please do."

The gardener had paused in his digging, leaning against his shovel, unabashedly eavesdropping.

"You heard my wife, George," Dylan called over. "You may put your precious roses back in the ground."

"They may well still die," he called over, but with obvious relief. "Ground's not fully thawed. Not good," he grumbled, "not good at all." Some of his roses were original strains, cultivated and perfected throughout centuries.

The fact that he had shown more concern for his plants than the possible arrival of the Guardians was, in Dylan's mind, a greater concern. George, like many others, relied on his protection. Moreover, they *expected* it.

Don't choose our safety over your own happiness. I'll not allow that a second time.

His sister had known this would happen. She had told him once, when he had chosen to love a human, that their people would become a burden. Had they sensed his dissension? he wondered. If so, then he had a role in their hatred toward Sophie.

Dylan showed his family through the front door of the main house, stopping on the threshold before heading up the central staircase. He was committed to starting a new beginning with his wife and son, and no one, not even the people he protected, was going to get in his way.

"My home is open to everyone who lives in Rhuddin Village," he explained. "But the second floor is our private quarters, for immediate family only."

"Why is the kitchen empty?" Sophie ran her hand along the railing as they walked up the stairs. "Is it because Enid didn't like my suggestion?"

"Enid accepted your offer," he told her, "but asked for a week's vacation before coming back."

"And that's a problem?" Sophie paused on the landing, too astute for her own good.

Dylan sighed, having hoped to save this conversation for a better time. But would there ever be a better time? The gathering was only two days away, and preparations had already commenced, as Porter had needlessly reminded him.

Wary of her reaction, he offered only minimum details. "I'm having guests this weekend, a gathering of sorts with leaders from other territories. It was planned before your arrival." He waited for an assault of questions and didn't know whether to be concerned or relieved when none came. But then Sophie had only lived in his house for a few months. She would have no knowledge of his interactions with others outside his territory. In her world, a weekend with associates was a normal affair. "A feast is a traditional offering for these guests."

"You have no one willing to cover Enid's vacation?" Her lips thinned as he shook his head. "That was clever of her, wasn't it?"

He placed a hand on her lower back, gently guiding her up the stairs. Her proximity affected him. A snarl of satisfaction rumbled against his spine. The mere fact that she didn't shun his touch was all the encouragement his wolf needed.

His endurance, he had no doubt, was going to be tried beyond comprehension over the next few days. "I'd rather not force the issue, but I will if it comes to that. Meanwhile, the guards have become used to eating here. Expect some crankiness this week."

"I have a better idea," Francine suggested behind them, clearly having listened to their conversation and not the least bit embarrassed for doing so. "My daughter is a competent chef."

"I could manage a dinner party," Sophie offered. "As well as feeding the guards . . . if you need me to."

"You're not a servant," he reminded her.

"Oh, please," Sophie scoffed. "If I don't have something to do, I'll go crazy. Besides, if I cover Enid's vacation, it will make things easier for the poor person who has to work with her in the future."

"We have several guards and their immediate families that we normally provide for during the week," he warned her.

And potentially a hundred more if other leaders brought their own assembly of guards, but he kept that information to himself for the moment.

She hedged for a number. "I need to know how many, if I'm to prepare enough food."

Dylan knew her inquiry about the people who lived in his home, who guarded his family, had an ulterior motive. He found it difficult to be annoyed, however, after overhearing her confession to her mother.

I love him so much that when I look at him it hurts.

He could forgive a great deal, he realized, knowing he still had a place in her heart. "Sixty-two."

"What about the people who live in the village?"

"They care for themselves, as can those who live within Rhuddin Hall, if needed."

"If you can provide the supplies," she said without pause, "I can manage the preparations."

"Fine," he conceded, warming to the idea of having his wife occupied with a productive task rather than planning her escape. "The kitchen is at your disposal. And I'll introduce you to the butcher this afternoon."

Dylan walked ahead once they reached the upper landing. The scent of lemon oil lingered from a recent polishing of woodwork and pine floors. Joshua and his mother-in-law seemed pleased as he showed them to their apartments. He waited in the hallway as Sophie fussed and stalled in each room. Eventually, she did emerge, but with obvious resignation.

"I know you and Joshua conspired together for this

move," she said once they were alone. "Please don't make me regret my decision to cooperate."

"Can you not have faith in me, Sophie?" He made sure his voice held warmth and not ire, a promise of sorts, and a plea. "Just this once? You might find that I've done everything within reason to make you comfortable here. You might find that I am worthy of your trust."

TRUST? SHE ALMOST LAUGHED AT SUCH AN IMPOSSIBLE outcome to their broken history—which was partially her fault—but kept her cynicism to herself. Not an easy task as he opened the door to the adjoining bedroom next to his (assuming he still resided in the master suite) and held his arm out for her to enter.

Surprise overrode caution as Sophie walked around the double bed with an unfinished child's quilt folded neatly across the footboard, a project she'd been working on during those last few months before leaving this place.

The room remained exactly as she remembered it: pine floors scattered with Oriental rugs, cream wallpaper and a four-poster bed with blue velvet curtains tied back. She opened the top drawer of the tall mahogany bureau. Tiny cotton shirts and infant socks were folded neatly in two rows—just as she'd left them sixteen years ago. Because of the connecting doors that led to the master bedroom, she and Dylan had planned to make this smaller room into a nursery.

Out of the corner of her eye, she saw the broken pieces of a wooden cradle stacked under the window. The cradle had been a gift from Luc, the first given to their unborn child. It had also been intact when she left.

"Porter was supposed to remove that," Dylan said with discontent heavy in his voice. He didn't deny he had been the one to destroy it, nor did he offer an excuse.

Sophie knew full well why Porter had kept it there—to remind her of what she'd taken from Dylan, and to show her the stark evidence of the anguish her leaving had caused.

She didn't need the reminder.

Moving the shattered wood with her foot, she stood in front of the window, her gaze unfocused; the gardener below was a blur of brown color, and the thud of his shovel a distant sound, although she stood only one story above.

Dylan could hate her for leaving, if he wanted. They *all* could hate her and she wouldn't care, because her actions had kept her son alive until he was old enough to defend himself.

Her decision to stay away, Sophie reminded herself, as she always did when guilt poisoned her conscience, *had* been justified.

Run, human. Run far away and never return . . . because if you do, I'll kill you and that bastard child you carry in your womb.

Dylan's steps were almost silent as he approached, not that it mattered; she sensed his presence more than she felt the racing of her own heart. He leaned down, his chin brushing the side of her cheek, smooth from a recent shave. "What are you thinking about?"

Cool air radiated off the window and she let her forehead rest against the glass. "That I never thought I'd be standing here again . . . in this room . . . with you."

"You belong with me." A soft statement filled with quiet conviction.

She sighed, not so sure. "Before I agree to stay, I feel I must be frank with you."

"I'm listening."

"I have come to accept a few things about myself. My instinct to protect our son is not rational or reasonable, and sometimes . . . it's even cowardly and selfish. But it will never change. I will always put Joshua's welfare before all others, even my own, by any means necessary."

"You should save your breath, if you're trying to warn me away." His hands lifted to her shoulders, warm and gentle as he turned her. The glare from the window reflected off his black gaze; a glint of hunger moved from within before he pushed it back. "I have begun to realize why the Goddess has chosen to favor you, my human wife, who not only accepts both the dark and light aspects of herself, but also embraces them—in order to protect our child."

My human wife? "You're not going to stop calling me that, are you?"

"No." His hands tightened on her shoulders briefly before trailing down her arms.

"You act as if we can just forget the past."

"Not forget." He turned her wrist and pushed something cold and jagged into her palm. "But we can learn from it and move forward."

Avoiding his hardened glare, she unfurled her fingers and stared down at a modern brass key. "What does it open?"

"Both doors to this room. It's the only copy," he added. "So don't lose it."

"You changed the locks?"

"You stole the master," he reminded her.

Not trusting her voice, she closed her fingers around the key. One of the first skills she'd acquired after escaping was how to pick a lock. But Dylan wouldn't have known that.

"I need to do a few things," he said, turning toward the outer door. "You know where my office is. Meet me there when you're ready. I'll show you around the kitchen and larder." His hand rested on the doorknob, and he watched her with hooded eyes, as if he expected her to renege on her offer to cook, or run for dear life.

She didn't intend to do either. "Just give me fifteen minutes to wash up and change my clothes."

It was time to stop running, as her mother had irritatingly, and rightly, suggested. And perhaps . . . her belly gave a little flip at the mere thought . . . perhaps she may even fight for what her heart wanted.

In response, his features stilled, darkened, as if he sensed her thoughts. The effect was disquieting, reminding her—and maybe him as well—that not all their memories in this room were unhappy ones. Her gaze lingered on his mouth, feeling as if the pine wood floors had just given way under her feet.

"Sophie . . ." His knuckles turned white around the doorknob, and the wooden door gave a groan as if too much pressure had been applied. He released his hand and stepped into the hallway. "This room is yours," he said through the open doorway, putting space between them. "I want you to feel safe here. I'll not disturb you, or come to you at night. But you need to remember that I've been sixteen years without my mate. I'll do my best to keep my distance until you're ready to accept your future here . . . until you're ready to accept me." His voice took on a sensual timbre, full of dark promise. "However, the next time you stare at my mouth as you've just done . . . I will use it upon you."

Nineteen

D YLAN WAS QUITE CERTAIN HIS WIFE WAS GOING TO BE the death of him before this was over. Leaving Sophie in the kitchens had not been an easy task; her innocent excitement over inane objects, like an industrial bread mixer (of all the bloody things to get excited over), had almost driven him mad.

He wasn't sure how much longer he could endure her proximity without claiming what was rightfully his. His body ached; his skin felt like strung leather over taut nerves and his temper ran short. Luc and most of the guards had begun to avoid him. Not that he blamed them. He was in no mood for companionship other than that of the one who could ease this torture.

Francine's lecture on how *not* to smother her daughter had prompted him to get some fresh air, and much-needed distance. Well aware of his tenuous limits, he took a walk around the back of his home, moving away from the more visible trails and into a dense section of his woods, and, more important, away from his beautiful wife. He wanted nothing other than to carry her up to *his* bedroom where she belonged, and do exactly what his mother-in-law had warned him not to.

As he traveled farther into the forest, his instincts heightened to alert. He stepped onto a small, winding trail, where branches and knotted roots formed a tangled path, and listened. For what, he wasn't sure, but he felt something was amiss.

Malsum and Porter had this area firmly secured, he knew, and yet he continued to have a distinct feeling of being watched—of a powerful presence that didn't belong.

Were the Guardians getting closer? Had they already arrived? Or was this someone connected to the gathering?

So many possibilities, none of them reassuring.

The sound of footsteps, four-legged and aggressive, warned of his visitor's approach. Dylan tensed, ready to shift. The white hound that came crashing through the barren brush was unexpected, as was the man with golden hair who stepped out of the shadows and whistled a sharp command. The creature heeled, teeth bared, eyeing Dylan with malicious distrust.

"Taliesin," Dylan acknowledged with a sharp nod. It was customary to kneel; he remained standing. "You look like shit."

Resembling a vagabond, Taliesin wore plaid pants and a ragged shirt—sleeping garments perhaps?—stained and wrinkled, as if he'd worn them for days, or at least since Sophie's departure from his home.

"Be careful, warrior," Taliesin said, "I might actually think you care."

"You kept my family." Dylan held back a growl, not an easy task when anger was like acid on his tongue. "I should challenge you for what you've done."

"You would lose," he said simply.

"Are you so sure?" A searing pain shot down his spine as his wolf rose to the challenge and was denied release.

"Calm your wolf, warrior." White heat filled the air, a warning to behave, and a promise to retaliate. "Your jealousy is vile and unwarranted. If not for my protection, you would have lost your family."

The hound let out a soft whine, letting Dylan know he wasn't the only animal who felt fire invade his skin. "Why do you care? More to the point, what has my wife done to deserve your attention?"

Taliesin gave a nonchalant shrug, and a cool breeze brushed through the clearing as if the forest began to breathe. "Sophie's devotion to Joshua intrigues me." He walked up beside the creature and ran a soothing hand over its rust-tipped ears. "I kept her until she was ready for what will come."

"Your riddles annoy me."

Taliesin turned; an arrogant tawny eyebrow rose in question. "Annoy you or frighten you?"

"Both," Dylan said without pretense.

"Ah." His mouth twitched with a hint of amusement. "I find your honesty refreshing." Then he quieted. "You must wait another night before attempting a transformation with Joshua . . . His mother needs some time to adjust."

"Are you giving me advice on how to handle my wife?" Dylan sneered; it galled him that this man knew more about her than he did.

"Soon, your son will run as a wolf." His voice was impatient but firm. "The transformation will go easier for her, and for Josh, if Sophie learns to trust you first."

As a father, Dylan could not ignore such a warning, or the promise of an almost unbelievable gift. The lure of gaining his wife's trust would have been enough, but to ease the effect of the change on his son . . . "If one more night will help achieve that goal, then consider your request granted." Then he allowed himself a moment of weakness; his shoulders sagged with relief over his son's affirmed ability, until he thought of all the others, like Cormack, who had endured the dark side of their gift for centuries. "Why has my son been chosen? And why now?"

Taliesin let out a crass snort. "Fuck if I know. You think the gods converse with me regarding their plans?" His voice held a cold edge, and once again the forest responded with a shudder, sending droplets of rain to the ground. "I'm not allowed to play with their toys, as you're well aware. My sight is contained to this world."

Taliesin's crudeness came as no surprise; after the Middle Ages, he had chosen to live amongst the basest of humans, preferring the company of commoners over royalty, a trait Dylan grudgingly admired.

As Taliesin lingered without cause, given that his request had been easily granted, Dylan sighed, quite sure he wasn't going to like the answer to his next question. "What is your true purpose for being here?"

Deep blue eyes looked up and held his, haunted with a knowledge no being should carry. "Sophie's not wearing the Serpent."

"I know." The warning was like a punch to the gut, confirming what Dylan had already surmised. "You know what will happen if the Guardians learn she has possession—"

"Who do you think I'm protecting her from?" Taliesin snarled. "Your eyes are open, warrior, and still you're blind. You must convince Sophie to wear the Serpent or you will lose everything you love most."

His anger deflated under the dire warning; Dylan began to pace, agitated by fear and frustrated by what he could not control. "As you're well aware, I've had little influence over my wife's decisions in the past. What makes you think she'll listen to me now?"

"Just try. Wait until morning . . . She'll be more inclined to cooperate." His gaze became unfocused, as if plagued by memories, past or future, Dylan wasn't sure which. Not that it mattered with Taliesin because he had lived one and foresaw the other.

"Why? What have you seen?" Unlike some, Dylan had never asked Taliesin to share his divine sight. He had never loved something enough to risk the consequences. Until now.

A pained expression pinched his features. "Just convince her to wear the Serpent."

"Convince her yourself."

Tawny eyebrows rose in what seemed like genuine surprise. "Are you inviting me into your home, warrior?"

For Sophie and his son, his generosity, it seemed, had a higher limit. "I am."

"Your offer tempts me more than you know." Taliesin shifted from side to side, chewing his bottom lip. "She's making pizza tonight," he said in the tone of a petulant boy.

"Who?" Dylan frowned. "Sophie?" He cocked his head to one side, beginning to realize, with gratifying relief, that the nature of Sophie's relationship with Taliesin was maternal. "Maybe, I don't know."

"She is," he said with slumped shoulders, his eyes downcast, shaking his head as if to clear a forbidden thought. "I can't. I've already interfered more than I should." His words were laden with guilt, and he turned on his heels and took to the woods. "Tucker will help your cause."

"Who's Tucker?" Dylan called out in frustration, only to receive a soft growl in return. He eyed the creature standing on the trail as if it owned the forest. "You can't be serious?"

But there was no spoken reply, only an offended huff as the beast lifted its head, snout up, and walked along the path that would take it directly to Sophie.

ENID'S CHEEKS TURNED FLORID AS SHE STOOD IN THE kitchen glaring at Sophie, as if half her blood had just risen to her face. "You're making Roman fare in my kitchen," she spat. "Sweet Mother, I'll never get the stench out!"

"Since you've decided to stop by," Sophie said calmly, "will you tell me where the pasta is?" A blank stare prompted further explanation. "Spaghetti . . . Macaroni . . . You know, it comes in a box. You put it in boiling water."

"I don't keep dried pasta." A smug smile turned her lips. "*I* make everything fresh."

Sophie bit back a smart reply as she leaned against the counter. She didn't have time to make fresh pasta, but remembering seeing yeast starter in the fridge, she disappeared into the pantry and returned with honey and oil. She had discovered a large bin of white flour earlier, stored in a closet next to the lovely Hobart mixer. "We'll have pizza instead."

"Porter," Enid ordered hysterically, "*do* something about this . . . This woman is contaminating my kitchen."

"You forget yourself, Enid." Porter stood with his back to the farthest door. His biceps bulged as he crossed his arms, guarding the exit like a demented gargoyle on steroids. "Dylan was born of a Roman and this is his house. I believe pizza is a fine meal for his people. Though," he added, "I'm hoping it's the American version."

Sophie raised her eyebrows, surprised by his support. "Thank you, Porter. It will be, once I find the cheese." She pinned Enid with a challenging stare. "I assume you have cheese."

The woman crossed her arms, her lips pressed in a thin line.

Porter supplied, "In the cooler by the side entrance."

"Will you taste this?" Acting as if she were oblivious to the exchange, a convincing ruse to everyone but Sophie, Francine brought over a spoon filled with sauce. "Tell me if it needs more garlic?"

Biting back a smile when her mother rolled her eyes, Sophie blew on the spoon and took some sauce into her mouth. "Garlic is good, Mum. But add more wine. And maybe a pinch of red pepper."

"I don't keep red pepper in my kitchen," Enid huffed.

"Good thing we brought our own," Francine returned with a tight smile. She was behaving herself, so far, but Sophie recognized her tone, and perhaps so did Enid, because the woman made no response.

Sensing the start of an ugly dispute, Sophie encouraged Enid to move on. "You should take this time and enjoy your vacation. Go somewhere tropical. Your position's secure here, and I promise not to burn down your kitchen before you return."

A look of disgust crossed her florid features. "Somewhere tropical? You . . ." She made a choking sound. "You are such a frivolous . . . *stupid* . . . *girl*!" A shadow passed behind her eyes, turning blue to orange, a color that most definitely was *not* human. "We must stay put until the Guardians make—"

"—Enid," Porter interrupted, "control yourself. And hold your loose tongue!"

A warning Enid obeyed—but not Francine. "Don't *ever* speak to my daughter in that tone!" Sauce flew in spatters as she brandished her wooden spoon. "Stupid and frivolous," she muttered, pointing the spoon toward Enid's chest. "*You* obviously didn't take the time to get to know Sophie when she lived here."

Enid blinked, much like a chastised dog when sprayed with water; a pattern of red dots stained the front of her white sweater. A moment of shock, but just a moment, before the scent of elements filled the room, pungent and disturbing.

Oh, God. "*Mum* . . . put the spoon down." When that didn't work, Sophie repeated more gently, "*Please* put the spoon down. You're getting sauce everywhere." She stepped between the two women, handing Enid a clean dish towel, aware now that Dylan hadn't been entirely forthcoming. "Why must we stay put? What about the Guardians?"

With her weapon still in hand, Francine asked, "Who are the Guardians?"

"Enid . . ." Porter warned again.

"I misspoke," Enid said. The tension in the room gradually receded as she accepted the towel. She dabbed the front of her sweater and kept her gaze to the floor. "I assumed you were in Dylan's confidence. You must ask him your questions."

A door slammed shut from the hallway, putting a halt to the conversation. A scamper of paws on wood was the only warning before a large white dog came bounding into the room.

The dog's tail wacked against the wall in an excited rhythm as he waited to be addressed.

Sophie stared, dumbstruck for a moment until she found her voice. "Tucker? Is that you?" In response, Tucker tapped his paws and then nudged her hand. She rewarded him with a long stroke down his back.

Enid backed against the wall. "It cannot be," she countered in a low voice laden with fear.

Very odd, Sophie thought, *from a woman who had, in all likelihood, just come close to changing into a wolf.*

Dylan entered the kitchen, his features harsh and unreadable. Dark eyes scanned the occupants of the room, only to settle back on her. "Where's Joshua?"

"Luc brought him into town. Joshua wanted to take a look around and meet everyone again properly." Her chest tightened, but not due to his surly tone. "Is something wrong?"

"Why must you always assume something is wrong? I was just inquiring about my son."

Taken aback, Sophie tilted her head toward Tucker. "Oh, I don't know . . . maybe because I never know what to expect when I'm around you."

"Maybe you should be around me more often then," he replied with sexual undertones that sent her cheeks aflame.

Feeling unnerved, Sophie began to understand that *she* was the source of his irritation, for reasons not appropriate in present company—or in *any* company, for that matter.

Acting oblivious to the undercurrents, Francine shimmied around the counter to assess their familiar visitor. "If that's Tucker, then Matthew must be nearby."

"He *was*," Dylan confirmed. "But he chose not to stay."

"He left without saying hello?" Francine frowned, clearly confused. "Do you know where he went? Is he staying nearby?"

Dylan sighed as if calling to the gods for patience. "Your Matthew doesn't answer to me, Francine. I have no idea where he went or where he's staying. All I know is he wanted my wife to have that . . ." His head nodded toward the dog.

"He did?" Sophie exclaimed, too pleased to listen to her misgivings, at least for the moment. "I hope that's okay with you, Tuck?" As if he understood, he jumped toward her. Instinctively, she caught his paws, forcing him to balance on his hindquarters. Still, he managed to reach a large wet tongue across her cheek. "Okay," she laughed, getting thoroughly slimed. "I missed you too."

An odd sound came from Porter's direction.

As an afterthought, she turned to Dylan, well aware how intrusive Tucker could be. "You don't mind if he stays here . . . do you?"

"This is your home, Sophie. If it's your wish to keep the . . . *er* . . . animal, and if you can control it, then do so."

"Thank you." She settled the dog back on the ground. "Did you hear that, Tuck? You can stay." He wiggled his rear end. "Are you hungry?"

Another wiggle and a soft "*Woof.*"

"Do you want a treat?" She knew her tone had gone soft and silly, but she didn't care who heard or what they thought—because she *had* missed this dog. Tucker tapped his paws with adoration in his eyes. "You do? My boy wants a treat?"

Another "*Woof.*"

"Bugger me blind," Porter choked out, "if I'm not seeing a hound from hell do an arse jigger in our kitchen."

"Your hell has no relevance here, Porter," Enid responded gravely, "for that is a creature from the Otherworld."

A slight hesitation before Francine asked, "What is an Otherworld?"

"I'll explain later, Mum." Sophie cut a piece of crust off a loaf of bread on the counter, dipped it into her sauce and fed it to Tucker, who inhaled it in a loud gulp. She remained silent through the hushed banter, thankful her mother had the good sense to follow suit.

Interestingly enough, Enid's initial reaction to Tucker began to make sense. According to what Sophie knew of Celtic beliefs, a hound from the Otherworld served their gods, an animal that crossed between worlds, human and *Other*.

In Celtic lore, the Otherworld was the place of magical beings, the land of faery, and the home of their deities. Not necessarily a nice, happy place either. However, it was easy for Sophie to understand how time, humanity, and different faiths, had led to the misinterpretation of the old Celtic faery tales. At one time, those stories were told to frighten children from wandering too far from home.

"'Tis blasphemy to feed it that concoction," Enid muttered in a strangled voice.

A soft vibration hummed against Sophie's hip, followed by a menacing growl. Startled, she looked down. Tucker assumed an aggressive stance, teeth bared in Enid's direction. The woman had, after all, threatened his food supply.

"Heel," Sophie ordered softly, placing her hand on his neck until he resumed a sitting position. Regardless of what Tucker was, or where he came from, she was keeping him. And he needed to behave.

"It obeys you?" This from Porter.

"I earned his loyalty," Sophie said. Again, through food, but she kept that secret to herself. "*His* name is Tucker." She ruffled Tuck's pointed ears, a silent reward for listening. "He just needs some time to adjust to his new home, that's all."

"You agree this is your home then," Dylan said, his voice a low timbre of approval.

An immediate denial lodged in her throat. Old instincts were difficult to ignore. Even so, she had come to accept that her son belonged here, despite what dangers lingered beyond these stone walls, or even within. And with that acceptance came a fundamental shift of her attitude. Moreover, Joshua had made it painfully obvious that he was going to live with his father, with or without her, whether she liked it or not.

Denial was no longer an option.

Fully aware of their audience, she admitted, "I think you're right. It's time to move forward. To learn from our past mistakes and stop working against each other, for our son, and for the others who depend on you."

And perhaps mend other broken promises as well, but that was a different conversation for a more private setting.

Dylan watched her with open desire, his gaze like twin pools of obsidian heat. "Are your words genuine, wife?"

She crossed her arms, meeting his glare with a promise of her own. "I have done many things, but I've always been honest about my intentions." She nodded to Porter, and then Enid, including them both in this pledge of sorts. "I know you don't trust me, and for good reason, but I would like the opportunity to prove you wrong. Everything I did, every choice I made up until this point, was to keep my child safe. I understand Joshua needs to be with his father now . . . and others like him. And, *yes*, I wish to stay as well.

"However," she continued, turning back to Dylan, assessing his reaction to her next request, "I want to know what else you've been keeping from me. If you really want my cooperation . . . I need to know what dangers threaten our son."

A muscle moved on the side of his jaw. "What makes you think—?"

"Enid has been overly talkative in your absence," Porter interrupted before his leader dug himself further into a lie. "Your wife knows the Guardians are"—his eyes flicked to Sophie—"a pressing concern."

"I am sorry, *Penteulu*," Enid implored, wringing her hands. "I did not know I needed to guard my words." When Dylan crossed the room and slammed open the kitchen window, taking in several deep breaths, excuses rambled off her tongue. "I fear this human will weaken us. With her sweet words and soft eyes, I fear she will be the end of us yet."

"Silence!" Dylan cut the air with a sharp swipe. Enid winced as though she'd been struck. "You are blind and bitter, Enid. My wife," he began, then amended his words, "my *mate* stands before us with a hound from the Otherworld docile at her feet, and still you shoot her with your poisoned barbs. Leave us. Now. Before I make a decision I'll later regret."

A cool breeze from the open window spilled through the kitchen. As if defeated, Enid left the room with her head lowered. Dylan stood solemn for a long while afterward, saddened but resolute. Francine made excuses to leave, something about taking a nap or some other nonsense. Porter gave her a respectful nod as she passed.

Determined to end this secrecy, Sophie closed the distance between her and Dylan until she stood directly behind him. "I'm not running anymore." His back stiffened but he didn't acknowledge her otherwise. Hesitantly, she placed a hand on his arm, even more concerned as she felt his hardened muscles coil with tension. "Whatever it is, you can tell me."

He looked down at her hand and something ominous moved behind his eyes. Sophie sensed it wasn't his wolf but rather a human reaction, more sinister and less honest, as if his conscience battled a moral dilemma. The human mind, she knew from experience, found ways to justify wrong over right, lies over truth.

"Porter," he said finally, "go to my office and return with the banner."

"Before you go," Sophie added her own request, "I need you to talk to whoever's guarding the property."

Porter paused by the door; his eerie blue gaze flicked to Dylan before answering. "For what purpose?"

She sighed. These men really did underestimate humans. At least he'd had the decency not to deny that there were guards. "Did my dear mother look tired to you?"

"You think she'll be going in search of Tucker's owner?" An amused grin tugged at Porter's lips; the effect on his otherwise austere features was quite disturbing. "Let her try. The gates are secure. She'll not be getting far."

Sophie sent him a look that erased his amusement. "Just inform the guards my mother's going for a walk and not to disturb her. She'll return when she's ready."

DYLAN WATCHED SOPHIE WITH A FEELING OF DREAD, expecting her calm façade to crumble at any moment. Her hair was fastened somehow behind her head but tendrils had escaped to trail in soft waves around her face, backlit by the open window behind her.

An incessant yearning coiled within his chest, like viewing a precious gift he could not possess. He wanted to demand that she trust him, but Sophie was not a woman whose spirit could be contained by his will alone.

She stood in the center of his kitchen with her hip braced against the island as she leaned over and studied the workings of the banner. "What does it mean?"

"It's the royal banner of the Guardians, represented by the horned snake." He intended to keep his answers honest but blunt.

"I assumed that's who the markings belonged to," she said with an impatient wave. "But what does it mean that it was left on your land?"

"It means that the Guardians are watching us."

"What do you think they want?"

"I'm hoping they simply want assurances of my loyalty."

With her chin lowered, she sent him a look that implied his optimism didn't fool her. "When was the last time they asked for assurances of your loyalty?"

A soft chuckle of appreciation came from the shadows. Dylan held his tongue at the interruption. Apparently, Porter's dislike of his wife was wearing off.

"The American war of independence made the Guardians a wee bit nervous," Porter said.

A wee bit nervous? Dylan shot him a livid glare.

He returned with an annoying grin. "I'll be running a perimeter check of our grounds now, if you are having no further use of me."

"Good idea," Dylan snapped. He waited until Porter's footsteps faded until he explained the man's comment. "The Guardians were afraid that I, and other leaders who had forged territories in the Americas, would follow the humans' cause with our own."

"Did you?"

"No."

"But something happened," she hedged, too observant for her own good.

"A marriage," he supplied. "An Original Guardian married a neighbor. Her name is Rosa. Her husband, Math, now controls the New Hampshire territory."

"You have a Guardian living that close?"

"Yes." He spat the word. "Math has never bothered with us, but he is loyal to the Council."

"The gathering this weekend, with the other leaders . . ." She folded the banner and handed it back to him. "It has something to do with this, doesn't it?"

He accepted the folded material. "Yes."

"I assume Rosa and Math were *not* invited."

"I only invited a select few, leaders who have severed their connections to our homeland." He paused, contemplating how much information he needed to disclose, how much would appease her curiosity without igniting a firestorm of resentment. "I'm hoping to form an alliance against the Guardians. In numbers, our strength would be unmatched."

"I see." She stood unmoving, even composed, except for the slight tremor in her voice.

"Do you understand what I'm telling you?" he asked softly.

"I believe so. You're taking steps to protect your freedom, your land, and the people who depend upon you."

He frowned at her phrasing but chose not to argue against its truth. "Yes."

As if sensing his mistress's distress, Tucker gave a soft whine from the pillowed bed in the corner that Sophie had prepared. The hound padded over and stood by her side, its massive head not far from her shoulder. She rested her hand on his neck, whispering words of a soothing nature.

Dylan allowed her this time to absorb the enormity of their situation, prepared to accept her anger.

"Okay," she said finally, looking up with grim determination. "What can I do to help?"

Dylan's mouth dropped before he tempered his surprise. "Will I ever understand you, woman? I expected anger and instead you offer assistance?"

"Freedom is a cause I'm willing to sacrifice a great deal for." She spoke with quiet conviction. "Everything except the life of our son, but I believe I've already proven that."

The comparison of Sophie's plight with his people's did not set well with his conscience. He wanted to argue that she'd never known real danger, or that her freedom had never been taken from her.

Regrettably, she had the scars to prove otherwise, and guards, even now, who had been ordered to keep her contained to Rhuddin Village.

Therefore, he saw no other course but to offer a harsh reminder instead. "Joshua is a part of me and a part of my world." His voice rose, tempered by his frustration. "He needs to learn to live with his own kind."

"I know." Fire entered her gaze as if lit by a power within, not magical but human. A selfless love so intense it stole his breath, one that proved she would give up everything for what she loved most, even her own freedom.

My people are indeed blind, Dylan thought.

With her shoulders back and her hand resting on the great hound, she looked very much like a pagan warrior queen, not in her appearance but in her conviction. Her strength came from her devotion to her child, he knew, powerful in any race, human or other.

"I will protect Joshua," he vowed, "but I will also teach him how to protect himself."

"Then teach him," she said. "He's been given every self-defense course I could find, and Matthew helped with lessons, but the more Joshua knows, the better. I'll not stand in your way; believe me, especially on this. I want our son to be strong."

Her response made him pause, as he was not accustomed to an agreeable mind-set. And given that the expected storm had passed, darker instincts quickly rose to the surface. Without question, he wanted her to accept that she belonged with him, in his heart—*and* in his bed. But to see potential for something more, for a partner in his life, for a mate to stand by his side of her own volition, was like adding more temptation to a man who had already lost his soul to this particular enchantress.

The silence became uncomfortable, and his need was such that he no longer trusted himself in her presence. How had he thought to stay away from her at night? "I will go in search of Joshua then."

She nodded with obvious relief, as if she had sensed an elemental shift in his mood and knew to be frightened. "Dinner will be ready around five." She checked her watch. "That gives you about two hours."

"Sophie . . ."

"Yes?" She tilted her head to one side, waiting.

The words he'd been about to say froze on his tongue, expressions of gratitude—and other assertions he knew full well she wasn't ready to hear. The admission to her mother that he had overheard was the one band that held his sanity, along with her quick rise to pleasure under his hands.

His patience deserved a bloody award.

She prompted, "Is there something else I should know?"

"There are no more secrets between us now," he answered with honesty. "Well . . . nothing of abnormal importance."

"Then why do you look so agitated?"

He ran a hand through his hair. *Agitated?* He almost laughed. She had no idea the level of his agitation. "My patience has ended, Sophie. I know I promised to give you your distance, and not come to you at night, but I can't wait much longer . . . I need my wife."

Then he strode out the door, not trusting his response were she to deny their vows yet again.

Twenty

A SHARP WIND CUT THROUGH THEIR MAKESHIFT ARENA. Dylan had gathered Joshua, along with Luc, and traveled to a secluded field not far from the house. The scent of wet earth and untamed energy hung heavy in the air, drawing out friendly yet uninvited visitors.

His attempt at privacy, it seemed, had been pointless.

Malsum came first, and then another, and soon a crowd of onlookers formed a circle around Joshua as he engaged in defensive maneuvers with Luc. No weapons were used.

Dylan stood with his son, joining in when necessary to demonstrate correct positioning. Pride settled in his chest, unavoidable, for Joshua listened well and adjusted quickly, the only reason the others had been allowed to remain and watch.

His son proved himself a worthy opponent, as Luc had streaks of mud down his back and a look of feral anticipation in his eyes. Not too worthy, however, for Joshua also wore layers of caked mud that covered him from chest to sneakers.

He still had much to learn.

"That's enough for today," Dylan said, ignoring a collective groan from the gathered crowd.

"I'm good for another round," Joshua taunted. "Unless . . . Uncle Luc's too tired."

A bark of laughter came from Luc. "Tomorrow we'll use swords, boy." His brother was clearly enjoying himself more than he should. "Then we'll see how you fare with a weight to balance in those gangly arms of yours."

"It's almost time for dinner," Dylan reminded them. "Let's get you cleaned up before your mother sees you."

Joshua nodded, persuaded by the lure of food. The others followed, falling behind with murmured praises. Laughter and well-meaning shouts of advice were handed out. It was a pleasant walk, the air filled with promise, as if Joshua's competence had bolstered a much-needed seed of hope.

Thanks to Sophie, for she'd had the good sense to prepare their child. Taliesin, Dylan assumed, had helped, but she had allowed the instruction. Her intentions had not been to garner respect, he knew, but she had succeeded this day regardless.

A savory scent overwhelmed his senses as he entered the house, ripe with garlic, roasted tomatoes and baking bread. He closed his eyes briefly. For the first time in sixteen years it felt good to come home.

A few of the guards, those loyal to Enid, had already made their excuses to eat in town, and yet they had returned to the house with the rest. And lingered still. Dylan had chosen not to demand their presence at dinner, trusting his wife to earn their loyalty.

As he turned the corner, he heard Sophie say, "Oh, good . . . you're all here. Grab a plate and something to drink. Pizza night is informal, so help yourself. There are snacks on the tables, and more pizzas on the way out."

"Wait 'til you try my mom's pizza," Joshua bragged. "It's the best."

"Is that my son under all that mud?" Sophie chided with good nature, pointing toward the back stairs. "Go get cleaned up. I have a bacon and onion coming out next. I'll save it for you."

Tucker stood silent by her side, glaring at all the intruders. Sophie ruffled his ears absently with no inkling of the powerful image she presented with the great hound by her side. There were several hushed whispers and pointed stares amongst the guards.

Dylan bit back a smile, for not one left to eat in the village.

AFTER CHECKING ON HER MOTHER, WHO HAD BEEN ODDLY silent following her walk, Sophie sat for a while with Joshua in his new room. Dylan had taken her aside after dinner and explained that tomorrow night would be their son's first attempt at a transition. Joshua had been told before her, and could barely contain his excitement, whereas she felt quite nauseated about the whole idea.

However, she did not allow her son to see her misgivings. She had made that mistake earlier in the day and would not make it again. Joshua was . . . *happy* here with his father and in his new home. She refused to allow her own fears to poison his joy.

Smoothing out a spare blanket by the foot of his bed, she said, "Tucker's going to stay with you tonight."

Joshua let out a loud yawn. "Cool."

Tucker hovered over her shoulder until she finished, then stretched out on his makeshift bed and rested his chin on crossed paws. An intruder would have to step over him to get to Joshua, a comforting thought as she wished them both a good night and closed the door.

A light at the end of the hallway immediately drew her attention. The door to Dylan's study stood slightly ajar. A nervous sort of flutter settled low in her belly. She felt breathless and antsy—because of him and his hot stares and angry admissions . . .

My patience has ended . . . I need my wife.

Our son isn't the only thing I lost when you left me.

The very thought that he'd been celibate for all this time made her skin feel tight, the air a little too thick.

She wore a terry cloth robe with a plain cotton nightgown underneath; her toes peeked out from beneath the hem. Otherwise, she was respectably covered. She had taken a shower before checking on Joshua. The scent of raspberry soap lingered on her skin. She should *not* go to Dylan now, knowing how this night would end if she did. Yet she continued forward as if that meager light were a bonfire on a winter's night, a beacon of heat when she'd been frozen for too long.

She knocked softly before entering.

"Who is it?" Dylan responded with a sharp reprimand that fell into silence when she walked into the room.

He sat in an overstuffed armchair, naked above the waist, wearing jeans and holding a tumbler filled with amber liquid. At first glance he seemed relaxed, legs spread wide, the corded muscles of his stomach rising and falling with even breaths, but her senses told her to be cautious as he emptied his glass with a single swallow.

"Is this a bad time?" she asked, surprised to see him drinking.

No answer, just a pointed scowl.

His disheveled appearance gave her pause. "Are you drunk?"

A sardonic laugh fell from his mouth. "If only I had that balm to escape to. No, my metabolism is too active to achieve true oblivion, but for a minute"—he shrugged without apology—"there is a form of peace."

Provoked, she moved to take a step forward but he stopped her with a warning.

"Be advised, Sophie . . . if you come farther into this room, I will assume you're doing so as my wife. There will be no going back. Your denial of our vows will cease, as will your absence from my bed."

She froze midstride. Again, instinct and self-preservation made her cautious. To be Dylan's wife meant to relinquish her choices. And yet the choices she'd made against him had caused her the greatest regret.

Unaware of her intent, Dylan sat before her like a hardened warrior, demanding and cynical, with golden skin and obsidian eyes that challenged her to make it right. Her compulsion for him was insanity, beyond human attraction. But this was not a human world she had fallen into.

No, it was magical, and dangerous, and she did not want to be the prodigal wife anymore, who hindered and didn't help—who denied her own feelings. What she wanted more than anything—other than her son's safety—was her husband.

The way he watched her, as if she were the most forbidden pleasure in over a thousand years of living, made her defiance seem petty in comparison.

She set her foot down.

The room shifted, muddled her equilibrium. There was movement, soft colors, a rush of air and heat, and then a loud noise that made her jump. The door had been slammed shut behind her, followed by a soft click, locked.

Dylan moved so fast, she blinked to right her balance. His hands were inside her robe, circling around her waist, lifting her, pushing her against the hard wood of the closed door. She felt light in his arms, molded, feminine. Cold air sent chills over her skin as her robe was dislodged and fell to the floor.

His lips descended to the base of her neck. "Sophie . . . I . . ." His voice was hoarse. What he'd begun to say dissolved on a broken breath.

A vibrating heat surrounded her, warmed her, held her. He was trembling, she realized. This powerful man, who had the welfare of a weakened race resting on his shoulders, was shaking, for *her*—because he needed *her*.

Her dark journey, begun on a narrow path wrought with poisoned vines and jagged roots, had reached a glorious field filled with light and truth. She had circled back to the very place she'd once fled, only to prove that she'd been running in the wrong direction all this time.

She had been blinded by fear, broken trust and the ignorance of youth.

If only . . .

"Dylan," she began, wanting to free her conscience, "when I left you, if I had known then what I know now . . ."

"No talking." He spoke through shallow breaths. "We . . ." He paused. "We have talked enough."

"I'm sorry," she whispered anyway, needing him to hear this confession to free the burden in her heart. "Can you ever forgive me?"

A shudder wracked his body; the full weight of his head dropped to her shoulder and his lips pressed a soft kiss just under her ear, then another, and another.

He cleared his throat. His voice remained a rasping whisper. "I forgave you the moment you returned home with our son by your own choosing, when you came back to me. And"—he paused, took another breath—"you are not the only one who made misjudgments. If fault is to be carried, then some of it must rest on my shoulders as well."

His thick thighs levered between hers, wedged her legs open; her pelvis rested against his hard length. She gasped, wrapping her arms around his neck for support. Her nightgown gathered around her waist, the thin cotton of her underwear a sad shield against the heat and hardness that beckoned unhindered contact.

His lips moved over hers. He tasted of whisky and temptation. It was a wild kiss, inelegant and desperate. He claimed her lips again and again, biting, caressing. His tongue tangled with hers; his hands tightened around her body as if he could meld them together in this storm of broken wills and neglected passion.

She clutched his shoulders; frantic movements of baser instincts overrode dignity. Her skin was on fire. She squirmed against the hard bulge trapped between their bodies.

Bracing her weight against the door, she reached down to stroke him, to soothe him.

"No." He caught her wrist with a growl.

"But—"

"*No,*" he said again through clenched teeth. "Not this first time."

"Then what am I supposed to do?"

Her question triggered a response from his wolf, or perhaps the wolf had been there all along but he could no longer contain its presence. Streaks of gold and green bled into his black gaze as he unbuttoned his fly and lowered his jeans. His hard length sprang out, dark and heavy.

She pulled her bunched nightgown over her head. He yanked at her underwear until it ripped off; the thin cotton drifted to the floor, forgotten.

He stood motionless, like the Great Oak that beheld their ceremonies, silent and looming, his eerie gold eyes devouring her nakedness with blatant hunger. Then, slowly, as if he were testing dream from reality, he reached out and ran his thumb over her bared nipple.

"Different," he choked out. "Beautiful." Meaning her body, she gathered. Carrying his son had left its mark. She did not mind the changes and, it seemed, neither did he.

He pinched gently, rolled the sensitive skin between thumb and forefinger. A wave of heat shot to her innermost core. She tried to remain still through his exploration, but when his head dipped and he took her nipple into his mouth, she could no longer control her response.

She cried out, letting her head fall back against the door, squeezing her eyes shut because the sensations he caused were too intense.

His hand reached up and gripped her by the back of her neck. He forced her to look at him, forced her to see the anguish on his face, the price her absence had caused. They slid to the floor, too impatient to find a bed or even a chair. The small braided rug was abrasive against her back, a meager cushion to buffer his heavy weight covering hers. Not that it mattered. Her surroundings faded under his onslaught, her body softened, prepared.

His hands separated her legs; he fell between them, jeans tangled around his knees, rasping against her inner thighs. He braced his arms on either side of her head and looked down. "I can't stop . . . I want to pleasure you first but I . . ."

"It's okay." She felt the first touch of his swollen length push against her opening. They both gasped in raw awareness. She wrapped her legs around his waist for a better angle.

A rasping sound, more animal than human, erupted from his throat. "I'll not last long this first time."

"Shh . . ." she soothed. Untangling her arms, she ran her hands along the corded muscles of his biceps, over his shoulders and along his neck. She curled her fingers in his shortened hair, remembering it was much longer the last time she'd been beneath him. His gaze was unfocused, his features strained. She sensed him holding back, afraid. But of what? "Come inside me . . . *please*."

He swore under his breath as he succumbed to her plea, thrusting forward. Shoved into the carpet, she moaned as her body stretched to accept him, panting by the time his full length was embedded.

His back felt like caged tension under her palms. His hands roamed lower, dug into her bottom to hold her in place. And then he began to move, hard and unrestrained.

She was lost in complete sensation, her eyes closed. Her lungs filled with his scent, an alluring mixture of forest and man, with the barest hint of musk, *of wolf.* His chiseled stomach, with its trail of soft hair, rasped against hers as he withdrew and reentered. Skin against skin and a glorious fulfillment she'd almost forgotten, except in dark dreams on lonely nights.

Each thrust brought her closer to climax. She arched instinctively, selfishly, adjusting his angle for her own satisfaction.

"Sophie . . ." Dylan tensed and gave one final thrust, his head thrown back with a guttural shout. Hot pulses filled her, sending her over that shining edge of completion.

It felt so right she almost wept. It was more than just physical fulfillment, but rather a joining of hearts—a broken marriage made whole.

When the room shifted back to reality, he collapsed on top of her, dragging in deep breaths. Minutes passed while Sophie stroked his back. After a while he stirred, planted kisses in her hair. "Did I hurt you?"

She smiled at his concern. "No."

"There's a chance . . . of another child . . ."

His voice was so wistful it pained her as she disclosed, "It's very unlikely. I'm on birth control."

He stiffened above her. "For how long?"

"A few weeks." She sighed, aware that other assumptions poisoned his thoughts. "There have been no other men, Dylan. It was just a precaution I took when the idea of calling you first came to mind." She'd been aware, even then, of her weakness toward this man.

A shudder racked his body. "Thank you for telling me," he said softly. "I couldn't ask. I couldn't bear the answer had there been others." He paused then, obviously wanting to say more, but taking the time to choose his words carefully. "Our children are rare gifts. Conception should never be hindered."

But he didn't demand that she stop. Progress, she now understood, came within those small concessions. "Give me some time. Give *us* some time."

"Consider it given." Cool air whispered over her naked skin as he stood. She watched him drag his jeans over his hips with an arrogant grin. Silently, he held out his hand and she allowed him to help her up. The muscles in her legs gave a twinge of protest. He must have sensed her unease because he scooped her into his arms as if she weighed nothing at all.

"I have to get my clothes," she protested, slapping at his shoulder; he was carrying her into the hallway *naked*, for the love of God. "My underwear at least."

"Porter cleans my study every morning. He will gather them." Was that a teasing note in his voice?

"Dylan . . ."

"Fine." He bent her forward so she could reach her discarded garments, and then proceeded to carry her to his bedroom, kicking the door open with his foot. "I don't want your mind clouded with any distractions."

His good humor was addictive. She laughed, feeling reckless. "Why not?"

He dropped her on his bed. She bounced a few times, the burgundy comforter soft against her bare skin. She leaned back on her elbows, allowing him full view. His eyes darkened and his voice lost that teasing edge. "Because I'm not even close to being finished with you yet."

Twenty-one

DYLAN AWOKE WITH A START. HE WAS HALF CONVINCED that last night had been a cruel dream, a manifestation of what he wanted most but couldn't have, until he felt the small weight of her body curled against his. Half turning, he rose to his elbow to watch her, to confirm with his own eyes that she was actually there.

Sophie slept on her side, with her back snuggled against him and her hands curled under a pillow. She had cocooned herself in a mass of blankets, leaving him none. He almost laughed aloud with joy, having forgotten she was a blanket thief.

Anxiety skittered like seeds on the wind; it was in those forgotten moments, in a simple act, that he knew she was indeed real, breathing softly, and curled in his bed.

Her hair spread around her, tousled in sleepy disarray. Unraveling the comforter, he scooped her into his arms until her skin met his. Warmth filled his heart with a sense of rightness, as if a vital piece had finally been restored.

A contented sound fell from her lips, and then a yawn.

She stretched like a kitten, arching her back and pushing her hair away from her face.

Moisture gathered in his eyes and he blinked it away, making a silent vow to the gods . . .

Tell your Guardians to fear this day, for I have been given a second chance and will not lose her again. Whoever comes to us with ill intent, whoever brings danger to my wife and son . . . will die. This I promise you, with every breath I have taken, and every breath I willingly give up for them . . . From this day forth, I will not live a life without them in it!

A slight frown creased her forehead as if she sensed his turmoil. Her eyelids lifted once and then fell. "What time is it?"

"Early. The sun has yet to rise." He had relearned her body through the night, every blessed and beautiful inch, noting all the changes time had stolen from him. Curves had replaced the slenderness of youth; her breasts were fuller, her nipples darker, larger, and quicker to respond.

Taunted by the direction of his thoughts, he ran his palm down her side, over her hip and then her leg, wincing when he felt the jagged resistance of healed scars that one of his own had given her. How close he had already come to losing his wife and son.

Siân had feared him for good reason. He now knew why her bags had been packed, why she'd agreed to leave so readily. Acid churned in his stomach, anger and vulnerability a venomous cocktail that didn't sit well.

Needing reassurance, Dylan dropped a kiss on the soft skin just under Sophie's ear. "Do you regret last night?"

"No," she whispered.

Relieved, he nestled closer, spreading his fingers across her stomach and molding her to his length. Her bottom wiggled against him and he swore under his breath. He had used her well through the night, he knew, and yet . . . "Can you handle me again?"

"I'm not sure." A husky laugh fell from her lips. "But I'm willing to try."

A soft growl rolled from his throat. He pulled her leg over his, exposing her so he could assess for himself. Gently, he parted her opening, inhaling a ragged breath when he found heat and gathering moisture.

He readied her by stroking her flesh, circling her swollen nub with teasing touches and gentle pressure, until she turned her head into the pillow to muffle her cries.

Only then did he ease inside her opening, gritting his teeth against the pulses of her orgasm. His control was still limited, his need still raw. "Tell me if I hurt you."

"Just move." A muffled plea as her head rocked from side to side, restless.

Sweat gathered on his brow as he slowly thrust forward, grinding his fingers into her hip to keep her in place. As her wet sheath closed around him, he almost came; one night did not fix sixteen years of neglect. But it helped. He rode her into a second climax, managing to hold back his own release until hers began again. His vision blurred. Burying his face in her hair, he surrendered to the carnal fulfillment only his mate could provide.

They lay in comfortable silence for a while afterward, locked in a trembling embrace, as if neither wanted to end this moment of enchantment, of hope and second chances. But soon, the first light of dawn edged through the window, sending orange hues throughout the room, chasing away the shadows of pleasure with the responsibilities of the day.

Resigned, Dylan placed a kiss near her temple and rolled onto his back. The cool morning air did little to bolster his resolve. "If I asked you to wear the Serpent, would you do so?"

She tensed by his side, her voice cautious. "That depends on the reason you're asking."

"The weapon is your best defense against a Guardian, against anyone of our kind. I would like you to wear it, if only for my own peace of mind."

"It scares me," she admitted. "I had a nightmare the night I received it . . . of a horned snake. It seemed so real. There's something creepy about it, something . . . *unnatural*."

He agreed, yet, "There will be powerful leaders in our territory tomorrow, perhaps even sooner. Taliesin—"

She rose to her elbow and turned to face him, brown eyes searching his face. "He said something you haven't told me, didn't he? What did he say?"

Dylan sighed, wishing their reunion had happened sooner, during a more peaceful time. "He confirmed that the Guardians' arrival is a real threat we need to prepare for."

"How does he know this?"

"Taliesin has powers beyond ours. I don't know how he sees what he does, but I believe his warning is real."

To his surprise, she flopped back down and snuggled against him. Her hand rested on his chest, palm down, and absently slid lower to stroke his stomach. "Fine, I'll wear the thing if you think I should. But I hope you have a big box of Band-Aids."

Distracted and once again aroused, he slapped his hand over hers to still her motions. "The bloodletting should only be the once."

"Why?"

"I believe the Serpent needed to mark you as its new master."

"Oh, that makes me feel *soooo* much better."

"I can show you how to use it," he offered.

"That would be helpful," she said with a sarcastic edge. "Do you have time this morning?"

She was truly afraid, he realized, but committed to learning the weapon regardless, because he had asked her to.

"Of course." He hugged her against his chest, possessive. "You have changed, *wife*." He seemed to be telling her that often, but it was with admiration of the woman she'd become that had him repeating the words. "Sixteen years ago you would have argued with me."

"Sixteen years ago my husband was keeping secrets. I've learned to adapt to my surroundings. I understand the need for protection, even if I don't like its source."

His breath lodged in his throat. "Say it again."

Sending him a mischievous smile, she twisted her hand out from under his. Warm flesh slid lower as she shifted positions, womanly soft and completely beguiling. There were teasing kisses where her hand had once been, down his stomach, her breath hot against his skin as she repeated, "I understand the need for protection, even if I don't like its—"

"Don't taunt me, Sophie," he growled, half crazed by the path her mouth led. "Not on this matter . . . *Say it again!*"

"Husband," she complied just before closing her mouth over his hard flesh.

He jerked under the gentle heat. *Sweet Mother* . . . The feel of her lips around him, suckling . . .

"Sophie . . ." He groaned, tangling his hands in her hair. "You don't have to do this—"

"Do you want me to stop?" A husky torment as she ran her tongue down his length, turning his cock to stone-on-fire.

"No." *Fuck no,* his wolf added, prowling to the surface of his control, less polite and dangerously pleased. Two beings with one voice joined in need: *Claim us, our mate, as we have claimed you.*

It was his last coherent thought as his wife drove him into sensual ecstasy. And perhaps took a piece of his soul in the process, like a persuasive faery carrying the gift of a thousand wishes—*for a price.* The last was debatable, but as she brought him to his version of Tír na nÓg, a favored paradise of the Irish Celts, he was well aware that comeuppance had already been taken; Sophie had acquired full possession of his heart.

A RHYTHMIC POUNDING ECHOED ACROSS THE COURTYARD as Sophie marched toward the kitchen, her boot heels clicking on the cobblestone pavers in a steady rhythm. Tucker trotted by her side, keeping in cadence with her strides. The late morning sun was just about to peak over the rampart of

Rhuddin Hall, outlining the massive building in shades of orange and gold. The Serpent whip hung low around her waist, hidden under a long white cotton blouse.

She had spent the last hour with Dylan, learning how to wield the weapon, using a tree limb as a target. Its weight, though no heavier than any other of her weapons, made her anxious, now that she knew its potential for causing damage.

The tree would not live to bud another spring.

The Serpent's metallic fangs acted as anchors, deadly hooks that grabbed its target, securing the flexible sword for a fatal cut. No human, or wolf, could survive a well-landed strike.

Not a pleasant image to carry in her mind as she made her way through the gardens toward the kitchen entrance. "Good morning, George," she said in passing.

The gardener leaned against his shovel, openedmouthed as he eyed the hound trooping by her side. "Er . . ." He cleared his throat, recovering enough to tip his dirt-encrusted hat. "Good mornin' to you as well." It was the kindest reply the man had ever given her.

Progress, Sophie thought as she scooted around a pile of compost. Tucker had been her constant shadow from the moment she'd stepped out of Dylan's bedroom. Even now, several hours later, the dog crowded against her leg, poking her palm with his wet nose.

She spared him a quick glance. "Those sad blue eyes aren't going to work on me . . . I'm still not happy with you."

Tucker made a low noise in the back of his throat, sounding suspiciously annoyed. *Good.* He had stubbornly refused to follow Joshua when Dylan had taken him to a meeting of the guards.

She wasn't pleased, but knowing Dylan was there helped ease her worry somewhat, dire warnings of Guardians notwithstanding. Her agreeing to accept their marriage had, in many ways, relieved an enormous burden. She wasn't alone anymore, and it felt good to have someone else to rely on, trusting Dylan to do everything in his power to keep their son safe.

The kitchen was hot, filled with the scent of baking bread, and occupied by Enid and her two daughters, Lydia and Sulwen. Dylan had warned her beforehand of their arrival. He had also shared a rare moment of his past, and the reason why Enid had earned his leniency.

So it was with greater understanding, and compassion, that Sophie greeted her, "Hello, Enid. I was told you wanted to see me."

Enid wiped her hands on her apron and approached with hesitation, while the two younger women continued to work behind the counter with their heads down, acting busy. "I want to offer you an apology. As you proposed yesterday, I would like to start anew."

Sophie understood how hard it must have been for this proud woman to show humility. "I will accept your apology, if it's genuine."

"You have my word that it is."

Truth, whispered through Sophie's thoughts in a serpentine voice. She froze. The scent of apple blossoms and pollen clung to the back of her throat. She recognized that voice, with its ancient accent and eerie enticements.

You will know lies from truth . . . You will be able to protect those you love most . . .

Unnerved, Sophie pulled at the neck of her blouse and tried to concentrate on her purpose at hand. "Dylan informed me you wish to return to your former position."

Enid bobbed her head. "He has left the decision up to you, but I started early because . . ." She acted nervous, even submissive, her gaze darting to Tucker and then back to the floor. "Because there is much to be done before the gathering. My daughters have agreed to work on Mondays, as you instructed, for my day's break."

"Do you have a menu planned?"

"Of course."

Sophie walked over to Enid's daughters. Lydia was stocky like her mother, whereas Sulwen was taller, willowy. "Do you want to work here?" she asked them. "Or is there something else you'd rather be doing?"

The two women exchanged surprised glances.

"We're here because we want to be," Sulwen answered.

Lydia added, "It's good to have a purpose." Her eyes were the most remarkable color of lavender in bloom. "But it's also quite nice to be asked if we want it."

"Then the job is still yours," Sophie said, "with my gratitude."

"Thank you for giving our mother another chance." A slight smile turned Lydia's lips. "I know she can be . . . um . . . *grating* to one's nerves."

"Lydia," Enid gasped. "That is *not* true."

"Yes, Mother," Sulwen added. "It is . . . but we still love you." Biting her bottom lip, she turned to Sophie; her voice sheepish. "I would ask one more favor of you, and understand if you're not willing . . ."

"Why don't you ask me and find out," Sophie said.

Sulwen nodded as if gaining courage, sneaking a glance toward her mother. "I enjoy living in town. Our cottage is beautiful . . ." She sighed. "But our mum misses Rhuddin Hall."

"Sulwen, *hush*," Enid implored.

"Will you speak with Dylan?" she continued with determination. "He may be more . . . *willing* to forgive her punishment if the request comes from you."

"What about you and Lydia?" Sophie wasn't sure she wanted to persuade Dylan to change his original decision, especially when it concerned internal matters of his home. Nonetheless, it was the first time any person from his household had asked her for help. "Do you wish to return?"

Encouraged, Enid nodded. "Yes."

"No," both daughters replied in unison.

"What?" Enid turned on them, clearly astonished. "What are you talking about? Of course you want to return."

Sulwen placed a gentle hand on her mother's arm. "It's not like we'll be living across the country. And we'll be working together *every* day."

"It's time, Mum," Lydia said softly. "We want to stay in the village."

"But the Guardians—"

"Have reason to fear us." Lydia turned lavender eyes on Sophie. "Because your Goddess has chosen to favor our leader."

RHUDDIN HALL LACKED THE USUAL BUZZ OF VOICES SINCE many of the villagers kept to their homes. Dylan led his son through the kitchen, noting Sulwen's shy smiles when Joshua inquired about dinner.

Enid greeted him with a nod, her expression humble. Well, perhaps not *entirely* humble, but maybe at peace with her situation. For the time being, at least.

"Sophie accepted my apology," she volunteered before he asked. "She is upstairs with her mother." A pause. "I was thinking of asking Francine if she would like to help in the kitchen, but didn't want to offend. Do you have an opinion on the matter?"

Dylan's eyebrows rose in surprise, anxious to hear Sophie's version of events if it had prompted Enid to entertain a human working alongside her. "I think the gesture would be welcomed," he said.

"Then I will ask."

"Good." He turned to the sound of feminine laughter, and found Sulwen, with her adoring gaze filled with mischief and promise, hand-spooning cookie dough into his son's mouth. Lydia glared at her sister with open disgust.

Dylan cleared his throat. "Joshua, follow me, if you would. I have a gift for you."

Ignoring his son's guilty flush, Dylan motioned for him to continue down the hallway, and away from treats of more than one variety. Silently, he made a mental note to make time for a certain conversation. Every unmated female in Rhuddin Village may well vie for Joshua's attention, simply for being his son. But once he shifted . . .

Dylan shook his head, unprepared for this aspect of parenthood.

The pungent scent of lemon oil and vinegar, Enid's staple cleaners, lingered in the great hall. He paused under the carved entry, holding out his arm for Joshua to enter. Enthusiasm brightened his son's features, and yet a feeling of impending disaster lingered.

He had more to lose, Dylan realized, with his wife and son back home and the approaching gathering hovering around his family like a poisonous fog of uncertainty.

Not to mention the Guardians. Their silence was at odds with their normal behavior. Shouldn't they have contacted him by now? Made demands?

The meeting of the guards had gone well this morning. Their defense was as sound as their limited numbers could provide. Dylan had faith in their skill, trusted their honor without question. Unfortunately, their numbers, or lack of, were just cause for concern. The weak, the people who needed protection, outnumbered the strong. His territory was massive, blessedly abundant, and consisted of far more terrain than sixty-two men and women could cover at one time, regardless if they ran as a wolf. Nonetheless, they had planned well, plotted the most vulnerable areas that needed protection. And, Goddess willing, the gathering would prove productive.

But was it enough?

"I don't need a gift," Joshua said, interrupting his father's troubled thoughts.

"You will receive one regardless." Dylan walked over to the mantel on the far wall where his father's sword was displayed; copper, iron and glass forged together in unrivaled craftsmanship. "This belonged to your grandfather, *my* father." He lifted the weapon off its mount along with the iron chain that would secure it around his son's waist.

"*That's* for me?" Surprise mingled with awe.

"This weapon is for your protection. I want you to wear it at all times when not in my presence."

"You're really giving that to me? It's mine, like, to keep . . . *forever*?"

Dylan repressed a smile at his eagerness, remembering his own at a younger age of thirteen, a few months before his father was killed—a few months before Merin, heavy with her third child, had lost her sanity along with her mate. "It's yours until your first born comes of age, then it is my wish, as it was my father's, that it goes to him. *Or* her."

"Wow. Yeah. Of course, I'll do that." His voice lowered, turned serious. "I promise."

"It's Celt-forged, not Roman," Dylan explained. "Made by our kind. It's also several inches longer than other weaponry of my father's time." He pointed to the curved end, another anomaly. "It was designed with a distinct purpose, to separate your enemy's head from his or her body. As you know, if you listened to your uncle this afternoon, staking a shifter is pointless."

He nodded emphatically. "I listened."

Dylan gently handed the sword over. "It must never fall into human hands. The differences will be noted and questioned."

"I understand." He stared down at the sword as if searching for an appropriate reply. "Thanks, Dad."

Such a modern phrase, but given with heartfelt sincerity. Dylan felt his throat thicken and repeated the same direction his father had given him. "Wear it well, my son. Use this weapon to protect your family . . . Use this weapon to protect the innocent who cannot protect themselves."

"I will," Joshua vowed.

Twenty-two

ABERDOVEY, WALES

STANDING ON THE NORTH SHORE OF HIS HOMELAND, Taliesin looked out upon the moon-kissed ocean. His flight had been long and depleting, since he had been confined within a body of metal for over eight hours. Angry winds whipped his long coat around his legs; even the gods were displeased with his mortal choice of travel, when they had given him the power to live beyond human entrapments, to soar in *any* form.

Not that he gave two fucks what *they* thought about his fondness for humanity.

As if in divine answer to his blasphemy, he tasted salt on his tongue and the coppery hint of blood-soaked earth, powerful elements that clung to the back of his throat like an overdone birthday cake. Tempting?

Oh, yes . . . the power was always tempting, and just as sickening in the aftermath. His so-called "gift" had its own set of fucked-up consequences; it was those he loved most who paid the price for his unnatural existence.

An image of Francine weaved through his mind, fiery and full of life, laughing with the pure joy of the untainted. Heart-burdened, he buried that image away, unable to stomach her fate—a fate rearranged by his own actions, because *he* had chosen to help Sophie.

And Siân, poor Siân . . . May her next life be filled with an armful of healthy children. A mere sixteen years had passed since Siân had scarred Sophie in a stupid act of madness and jealousy. Despite her actions, Siân's life did not deserve to end under Math's cruel hand, an unjust fate for misunderstood wrongs.

A turbulent wave crashed upon the shore, pushing an approaching figure closer to the dunes. Thankful for the distraction, he watched the cloaked woman weave her way toward him. She paused by his side, hesitant, an unusual behavior for this formidable ally.

"Merin," he acknowledged with a slight nod, knowing she would not speak until he did.

"Sin," she returned with a low curtsy.

"Get up," he snapped, annoyed. "Humility doesn't suit you."

A flash of long golden hair escaped her hood as she rose to his side. She was the mature image of her daughter, though more confident . . . *sensual*. Merin understood the power of her allure, whereas Elen didn't care.

"When you stand just so," Merin said, tucking the fallen strand back under her hood, "I wonder if you are contemplating our future . . . or our demise."

"I fear they may be one and the same."

She stilled. "So then it is done?"

"Your banner was planted," he confirmed. "*And* found. Your warning was successful."

Merin exhaled slowly, her breath a whisper on the wind wrought with possibilities. "Have you seen them?"

It was a common question whenever they met, one he answered freely. "Yes."

"How are my children?"

"Powerful."

A satisfied smile turned her lips, reminding him of a mother cat watching her kittens devour their first rodent. Merin had been ruthless in her quest to make her offspring strong, so ruthless that even they did not know her true heart.

"Do they suspect it was I who left the banner?" she asked.

"They assume that it's a warning from the Guardians, just as they assume that you are one of them."

"I *am* a Guardian," Merin professed bitterly. "And must remain one until the timing is right."

Taliesin snorted. "I would not do your bidding if you were one of *them*."

She laughed outright, a musical sound that resonated across the beach, skittering on the waves like a fleeting caress. "As if you have ever done my bidding. You listen when it suits you."

"Did I not kill Madron for you?" He would have done so without Merin's request, having no stomach for a man who raped children. However, it was in her best interest for him to appear aloof, persuaded on occasion by boredom or fancy, rather than affection. Those he cared about had a tendency to live short lives. Consequently, Madron's death had been the last time he had wielded the Serpent against a Guardian. He had allowed Elen to watch the execution; innocence was a virtue she could not afford, even as a child.

"Madron needed to die." Merin shrugged without remorse. "He had tired of Leri and wanted my Elen."

"Stupid man," he mused openly, knowing he had granted her too many leniencies over the years. But it was easy to do, if one knew the sacrifices she had made, if one knew the secrets she had kept. "How have the Guardians never suspected the truth about you, Merin?" He shook his head. "How have they not realized that everything you've done has been to protect your children?"

"The Guardians are too distracted with their own needs," she pointed out. "Whereas you see too much."

"You'll get no argument from me there," he said dryly.

Hugging her cloak around her chest, Merin stared into the distance. "Will you tell me about my grandson?"

"If you wish." His thoughts roamed an ocean away. In his mind's eye he saw Dylan and Joshua, walking toward the Great Oak on Katahdin. The others followed a short distance away, with hundreds more in the forest, waiting, hopeful. A slight ache tugged at his heart, for Sophie looked none too pleased. He missed them still.

Not allowing Merin to know his dangerous attachment to her offspring, he schooled his voice and guarded his words. "Sophie has returned to Dylan by her own choosing. Your son and grandson have been reunited." He paused, dropping his voice to a mere whisper, fearing the wind would carry his news to unwelcomed ears. "Joshua is going to run as a wolf tonight."

Merin closed her eyes briefly in a rare show of emotion. As if called by her tempestuous spirit, a gust of wind thrashed her hood, revealing the prominent features of a Celt, fierce and proud. Laughing, she lifted her chin and spread her arms wide; she absorbed the power of the ocean, letting the salt air wash over her. Her hood fell back and long golden strands flew around her face, a wild beauty magnificent to behold.

"The Council meets tonight," she said, composed once again with a plotting light in her silver-blue gaze. "When the others learn Dylan has sired a shifter, they will demand control of his territory. I suspect they will go to Castell Avon in the White Mountains, with Math and Rosa Alban's co-operation. Until now, they'd assumed Rosa was the last shifter born."

"Don't concern yourself with Math and Rosa."

"I will concern myself with whoever brings danger near my children! Math is *Gwarchodwyr Unfed*, loyal to the Council, as is Rosa's aunt. Not to mention," she continued on a familiar rant, "the White Mountains of New Hampshire are close to Dylan's territory." Agitated by worry, she began to pace. "Rosa is weak. She agreed to marry Math with no resistance." She turned abruptly to glare at Taliesin. "Do you know what the Council has planned for her this coming Beltane, *with* Math's approval I might add?"

"I know what they have planned," he reminded her.

She made a disgusted sound low in her throat. "Three hundred years married to that vile creature is more misery than any woman should endure in silence, even one as meek as Rosa."

Inwardly, Taliesin shared her sentiment of Math, but not of his young wife. "You of all women should never misinterpret silence as meekness. Rosa is strong enough to endure what is to come." He purposely veered the conversation back to Dylan, the only topic that would distract her sharp mind. "And you've warned your children, Merin. Because of the banner, they now know the Guardians are coming. You have given them time to prepare."

"Yes, but is it enough?"

"Dylan has organized a gathering with all the leaders not loyal to the Council." Taliesin wanted to offer more reassurance but feared changing the course of events even further than he already had.

"This is good news." Merin calmed, turned thoughtful. "Let's hope the others listen. Or the Council will destroy us all in their quest for power. They think this is about land, about ownership of the earth that belongs to no one. They've forgotten that our gift is given—*not* taken."

Taliesin reached down and enclosed her small hands within his. Her skin was cold with fear, provoking him to share a private assumption, an idea conceived by a simple question from her son. "Dylan asked me why I thought Joshua was chosen over all the others."

She pulled her hands from his grasp and tucked them into her cloak. "What did you tell him?"

"Nothing of significance," Taliesin said, keeping his real response to himself out of respect. "But I've come to realize Ceridwen may have a personal bias toward women who are ruthless when it comes to protecting their children."

Like the goddess Herself, he thought bitterly, *my mother.* His story was not much different from Dylan's, the very reason, he supposed, he felt compelled to help this family.

"I hate it when you talk in riddles," she said, sounding much like her son. "What are you insinuating?"

He spoke plainly. "I believe your children are powerful because of you. I believe Joshua will shift tonight because of Sophie." He shrugged. "I believe Ceridwen favors mothers who make wrong decisions but with a pure heart."

Merin's brow furrowed with annoyance. "How have my decisions been wrong when my children still live?"

"Exactly," he said, knowing Sophie had the very same mind-set; two different women with the same tenacious objective. Was it a coincidence that their children were rewarded?

He thought not. "I know your heart weeps for them, Merin. One day your children will know the truth."

"Perhaps," she said quietly, "but will they ever forgive me for what I have done?"

Twenty-three

THE WHITE SHAPE OF A CRESCENT MOON HUNG LOW IN the darkened sky. Sophie remembered this path well, on a different night with a different agenda. No guards blocked her way this time, just Elen and Luc, and Joshua up ahead with his father. Tucker trotted by her side, with his tail wagging as if they were going on an afternoon jaunt.

Only immediate family had been invited to watch Joshua's first attempt at a transition, everyone except Sophie's mother. Dylan had convinced her that Joshua needed minimal distraction. There were guards stationed in the woods, she knew, but Dylan had promised they would not interfere.

The rich scent of earth filled her lungs, her steps cushioned by a carpet of moss as they approached the familiar clearing. Over the last few days, spring had settled fully within the Katahdin area, as rain and warmth had melted away any lingering patches of snow. Energy pricked along her skin, or perhaps that was just nerves. "Always the oak tree," she muttered under her breath.

"It is sacred to us," Elen said, reaching out her arm to lace through Sophie's.

Sophie stilled for a moment, surprised by the gesture, but soon took comfort in the contact as they walked arm in arm down the path. "Does it hurt?" she asked, trying hard to keep her voice neutral. "Does it hurt when you shift?"

"I have no personal experience," Elen said. "I cannot shift. But I am told that it does, followed by an equal amount of pleasure. And Dylan will teach Joshua to manage the pain."

Sophie gave a sharp nod. "Thank you for being honest." Although in that instance a small lie might have been preferable.

Elen pressed further. "Joshua needs to attempt a transition. The longer he resists, the more the need will grow, and the more painful the transition will be."

Sophie waved away her warning. "I'm not arguing with you. I just don't like the thought of him in pain. I would take it onto myself if I could."

"To become a worthy man, your son needs to overcome his own challenges without his mother's help."

"I know," she said with a sigh. But sometimes knowing what was best didn't necessarily make it any easier to handle. "I'm sorry for ranting. I'm just worried."

"Do not apologize for loving my nephew."

The tree stood alone in the center of the clearing. Thick roots formed a massive knot that reached out like octopus arms toward the shadowed forest. Dylan guided Joshua to stand under its woven branches as Luc hovered around the outskirts, watching the darkness.

With wide eyes, Joshua looked toward his father. "What do I have to do?"

Stepping away from Elen, Sophie fisted her hands by her sides until her nails dug into her palms. She wanted to scream, *Nothing. You don't have to do anything.* But because of the longing in her child's voice, because of the pain she knew he tried to hide, she remained silent.

Dylan stood in front of their son and placed a hand on his shoulders. "Reach out, like you did in my truck, and draw from the power that nature offers."

Joshua frowned with concentration. "Should I think about a wolf?"

"Your wolf will know what to do," Dylan said. "It will take over . . . once you give it the power."

"I've never done that."

"I know." When Joshua scrunched his eyes closed, a gentle smile touched Dylan's lips. "You might want to take your clothes off first."

"Can't I just go down to my boxers?" He inclined his head toward Sophie and Elen.

"If you want." Dylan stripped without hesitation, although he kept his briefs on.

Following his father's lead, Joshua removed his clothing down to his boxers. "What if it doesn't work?"

"Then it doesn't work," Dylan said simply. "But I believe it will."

"Okay." Joshua took a deep breath and let it out. "Let's do this."

Closing his eyes, Dylan opened his arms and reached to the sky. Pine branches whispered behind him, brushed by a wind that didn't exist. Joshua mimicked his father's actions, tentative at first, and then more aggressive, more confident.

Oh, God, Sophie thought. *This is really happening.*

The forest shivered as a flurry of pine needles floated to the ground, slowly, like falling through water, suspended by an unseen energy.

"Can you feel that?" Elen moaned. "He's powerful."

"Yes," Luc hissed from the shadows.

Sophie let out a startled gasp, for she too felt pressure build around her. The presence of elements clung to her skin, making her eyes water and her throat burn. She tasted metal in the air. Tucker paced around the outer edge of the clearing, whining in a high-pitched sound that warned of danger.

This was different from before.

Something was wrong. "Stop!"

Her cry went unheard, or ignored.

A strangled sound welled up from Joshua as he wrapped

his arms around his stomach and crumpled to the ground, curling into a fetal position.

"*Stop,*" Sophie screamed again and lunged forward, but Elen held her back. "Let me go! *Something's wrong*—"

Uncaring who or what she hit, Sophie kicked out at the nearest solid object. Elen sucked in her breath and loosened her hold. Another set of arms circled in, large and unmoving. Not Dylan's, because he knelt by their son, stroking Joshua's back and whispering to him with words she couldn't hear.

"Calm yourself," Luc growled softly, close to her ear. "This is normal."

"No." Sophie started to shake her head and then couldn't seem to stop. "This is *not* normal." She could barely breathe, barely think to speak.

Luc's arms continued to hold her. "It is normal for us, though more intense than expected. Prepare yourself. Your son *is* going to shift."

"Oh, God . . ." *Oh, God . . . help him.* She wanted to turn away but refused, even as fur began to emerge over his precious face. A strangled moan fell from his lips as bones began to break and re-form.

"Oh, sweet Goddess . . ." Elen dropped to her knees, whispering her own prayer.

Darkness swam before Sophie's eyes and she lost her balance. Luc tightened his arms, shoving her face into his chest, forcing her to look away. Enveloped by strength, warm but unyielding, she ceased her struggles. Large hands moved from her back and gently covered her ears, muting the sounds of her child's animal-like screams.

Seconds, minutes, maybe even a lifetime later, a hovering stillness settled over the clearing, a cooling mist of translucent lightness, as if a healing fog had lifted from the earth to soothe the succession of one of its own.

A deafening howl pierced the silence, followed by a softer, wolfish cry. Another canine voice joined in— *Tucker's.* Sophie recognized his boisterous bark.

Luc gently removed his arms and steadied her. She

looked up and found the dark eyes of her son searching through the mist, no longer the young man that she knew, but still her son asking for acceptance.

A sob fell from her lips. She didn't require words to know her child's needs. Stumbling forward, she dropped by his side and buried her face in the thick fur at his nape. "I love you, sweetheart. No matter what, I'll always love you."

A golden wolf made his way toward her, a silent presence in the hovering fog, watching. At some point while Luc had shielded her, Dylan had transformed along with their son. A pair of briefs remained tangled around his shanks.

Pulling away, Joshua took a step forward, crumpled to the ground, then stood again on unsteady legs. He took another step, stronger this time, more balanced.

His struggle gripped her heart. A desperate question fell unbidden from her lips . . . "He can change back, *right*?" Oh, God . . . what if he was stuck forever as a wolf? She turned to Luc and Elen, the ones who could answer. "Please tell me he can change back."

The ground shivered beneath her as Joshua lowered his head. He was trying to change, *for her*, because he had sensed her fear. Dylan brushed between them, pushing Sophie away with a growl of warning.

"Joshua can change back," Elen reassured her. "But he needs to run first. He needs to learn this new form."

"Okay." Sophie felt soft fur brush her arm, followed by a heavy weight crowding against her. *Her son*. The familiar gesture gave her strength. "Go. Run with your father. Do what you have to do."

As acknowledgment, Dylan gave her a low bow.

"Go," she said again. "I will be at Rhuddin Hall when you return."

With one final nod, he nudged Joshua toward the woods.

Elen gave an impatient sigh as the two wolves disappeared. "You can go too," she said to Luc. "I know you want to."

Silver eyes flashed in the darkness. Luc paced in front of

Sophie, back and forth, agitated with indecision. "Will you stay with Elen? Will you listen to her?"

"I would greatly appreciate the company," Sophie said quietly.

"Just go, Luc," Elen urged with happiness in her voice. "Run with our nephew."

"Protect her," Luc ordered, tugging his shirt over his head. He was down to his jeans before he hit the first line of trees.

Elen laughed and opened her arms, turning in a circle. "This is a joyous night." She stumbled to a stop, pulling Sophie into a hug. "I'm calling everyone to Rhuddin Hall. We must celebrate."

"How long before they return?" Sophie asked, too worried to share in Elen's excitement.

"A few hours at least."

A tingle of awareness tightened along Sophie's spine as they made their journey back to Rhuddin Hall. As they approached the outer gate, just before the first line of trees opened to gravel, humans and wolves stepped onto the trail. It was as if the forest bled a hundred magical beings, kissed by moonlight and disguised by shadows.

Sophie froze; her hand fell to her side, ready to reach for her gun if necessary—or the Serpent. She carried both, hidden under the folds of her loose jacket. There were more humans than wolves, three to one at least, but somehow those odds didn't ease her concern.

A twinge of pain lanced through her head, a brief pounding behind her eyes before a now-familiar voice intruded in her thoughts. *Be at peace, Sophie Marie Thibodeau,* came its whisper, *for all you love is safe this night.*

"They're friendly," Elen reassured her.

Flexing her hands, Sophie made a conscious effort to mentally push at the unwanted voice. A hiss resonated through her mind, then the presence retreated.

With a sigh, some of her tension eased. "Dylan promised me the guards would stay hidden."

"Not all of Dylan's people are guards," Elen explained patiently. "These are our friends, families who live in the village."

Okay. *Fine.* Sophie could handle that. She even let her hands fall to her sides. These were the men and women that Dylan protected . . . the ones who had sought sanctuary from the Guardians. "What do they want?"

"They've been waiting to hear about Joshua." Elen turned toward the gathering crowd. "Dylan's son runs as a wolf," she announced. "And you are all invited to Rhuddin Hall to celebrate this blessed night."

Collective whispers hummed through the group, chanting the same word, *"Dewisedig."* Slowly, the mass of bodies parted, forming two rows on either side of Sophie and Elen. Wolves bowed their heads while humans began to kneel.

"Um." Sophie leaned over to Elen. "What's going on? Why do they keep saying that word?"

"They're honoring you," she explained. *"Dewisedig* comes from our old tongue. It is a name I have not heard in a very long time. It means *chosen human."*

"Oh." Sophie chewed on that for a moment. "What if I don't want to be chosen?"

She gave a delicate shrug, an elegant way of saying, *Deal with it.* "You have given birth to the first shifter in over three hundred years. It is a blessing to our people that you cannot begin to comprehend."

BACK AT RHUDDIN HALL, LAUGHTER AND MUSIC HUMMED through the main floor as Sophie snuck upstairs to check on her mother, knocking softly.

"Come in," Francine said. "Oh, Sophie, *finally* . . . You're back. How is Joshua?"

"He's fine," Sophie quickly reassured her. "He's still with his father."

"So, it happened?"

She nodded silently.

With brown eyes filled with concern, Francine assessed her daughter, opening her arms. "Come here, sweetheart."

Without hesitation, she fell into her mother's waiting embrace. This was exactly what she'd needed, a little support from the one person who accepted her without conditions. "It was so hard, Mum, watching him go through that . . . and not being able to help."

"I can only imagine," Francine said, tucking back a strand of Sophie's hair. "Honestly, I'm glad I wasn't there to see it, but I'm proud of you. And I'm proud of how you're trying to work things out with Joshua's father."

She hiccupped. "Thanks."

"Shh," her mother soothed. "Do you know when they're supposed to return?"

"Elen assures me they'll be back any time now. And not to worry because everything is fine."

"Do you believe her?"

"Yes."

"Then take peace in that."

"You're right." Feeling recharged, Sophie absorbed one last hug before she pulled away. "Thank you . . . for not listening to me when I wanted you to stay behind."

"I love you, Sophie Marie, with all my heart; I will stand by your side until my very last breath. Don't ever doubt that. Now go clean your face and march downstairs and celebrate with everyone else. I'll be down soon."

Listening to her mother's sound advice, she changed into dress slacks with a fitted rose-colored jacket. The Serpent made an unattractive bulge underneath, but it was the most formal outfit she'd brought with her and would have to do. She even applied some makeup before returning to the merriment below.

Platters of food had been placed on the dining hall table, roasted meats and breads filled with stew, along with cakes and wine on side tables. Humans and wolves filled the house, more than Sophie had ever seen together at one time.

Enid barked orders to anyone who walked through the kitchen, pushing edible treats toward those who had hands. Those who did not had their own table positioned against the wall, about two feet high. Tucker and two other wolves seemed to be enjoying their own personal buffet.

Porter nodded at her as she passed through the outer hallway. He wore a black button-down shirt, rolled up to the elbows. He stood with his shoulders back, his sharp blue eyes scanning the area. "Will you take a walk with me around the gardens?" When she hesitated, he added, "You're looking like a dose of fresh air might do you some good."

She stared at his offered arm, wondering why she had the sudden urge to smile. Maybe the people in Rhuddin Village weren't the only ones making progress.

"Oh, hell . . . Why not?" She wrapped her arm through his, not surprised by the coiled muscles underneath the thin black material, having felt them once before on a less celebratory occasion.

The night air washed over her like a soothing balm, fresh and uncluttered with voices. Porter led her down a cobblestone path, his posture tense as Tucker's soft padded steps followed.

"Do you want to pet him?" she teased, amazed that she felt at ease enough to do so.

"Hardly."

"Where are we going?" They had arrived at a secluded section of the courtyard, with arbors and pergolas built overhead, tangled with rose canes and ivy branches. The night sky was shrouded, as was the interior to anything that might dwell above, such as cameras or satellites in the sky. A tall hedge of evergreens formed a dense wall.

It was a private garden with a distinct purpose, she realized, designed for a race to walk as their other selves and remain undiscovered to an outside world.

"Dylan wanted to see you alone," Porter said. "Before the crowd descends."

A massive wolf prowled under the canopy first, his black

fur blending with the night. A brown wolf, lighter in color and smaller in size, followed.

"Joshua?" she whispered. "Oh, thank God. Are you all right?"

"He's fine, Sophie." Dylan stepped forward from behind a cluster of pine trees, having changed back into his human form. They must have stopped by the oak tree before returning, as he wore the same clothes he had on before shifting, carrying the others' in his hands. "Our son learns well and adjusts quickly." He paused while his voice clogged with emotion, with reverence. "This night was a gift I never thought possible."

"I'm glad for you both," she said with sincerity. If this ability made Joshua stronger, better able to defend himself around others of his kind, she would learn to be thankful. "But why have you changed back and Joshua hasn't?"

"I would like our people to witness his transformation, but I wanted your agreement beforehand."

"You're asking me?" She frowned. "Why?"

"Because I know how difficult this is for you to accept. But it would mean a great deal to them. *And* to me."

"And what if I disagree?"

His shoulders sagged with acceptance. "Then Luc will help Joshua shift right now before we go into the house."

"I see." Not caring who watched, Sophie closed the distance between them. She trailed her arms around Dylan's neck, smiling at his bewildered expression, and pulled him down to meet her mouth. "If our son is okay with a demonstration," she whispered against her husband's lips, "you have my blessing to invite them out to watch."

"You are the most perplexing woman," he said, then tightened his arms around her waist and claimed her mouth with a possessive kiss. When she began to respond in earnest, he set her back down, shaking his head. His voice lowered to a harsh whisper, letting her know she wasn't the only one affected. "Will I ever understand you?"

"Respect my opinion, Dylan, keep me informed, and you may find I can be the most cooperative wife."

A bark of laughter fell from his mouth. "I will remember that, Sophie."

Porter cleared his throat. "If you two are quite finished now," he said dryly, "I will go inside and invite the others out."

Dylan reached down and took Sophie's hand within his. They stood united as their guests filed down the darkened path with expectant faces, some filled with hope, others with doubt. Wolves bled from the woods, joining the gathering of magic born. Voices murmured in hushed anticipation. All eyes fell to Joshua.

Luc sauntered forward, all black fur and coiled muscle; he was the beast of legend in flesh and fur. Still shrouded by the canopy of gardens, Luc led Joshua by example, shifting to his human form. His transition was smooth, like a dance of two forms blending into one, and then forming into another. The scent of elements filled the air, of spring and earth and promise, more prominent as Joshua bowed his head and began his journey back to human.

She held her breath to the sound of breaking bone and muffled moans. Having witnessed this once before didn't ease her torment, however her reaction to her child's pain became easier to hide. As she stood unmoving, Dylan found her hand and brought it to his mouth, uncurling her fist to place a kiss inside her palm.

A quiet calm settled around the moonlit garden. Luc stood proud as he watched his nephew complete the transformation. Joshua unfolded into a standing position, naked and keeping his head down. Before long, he cleared his throat and tested his voice.

"Ah, Mom," he said, holding out his arm. "Would you throw me my jeans?"

A great burden of worry eased from Sophie's chest, made verbal by an uncontrollable sigh of relief. "Sure." She looked around and found the blue material bunched by her feet where Dylan must have dropped it. She scooped up the jeans and tossed them in Joshua's direction. Although she wanted to go to him, she kept her distance, allowing her son to be seen as a man who didn't need a hovering mother.

"And just so you know," he added, catching the pants with one hand and pulling them back on with swift movements, "I can hear and see *everything* when I'm a wolf. I'm really happy you and Dad are getting along so well, but *jeez* . . . can you keep it behind closed doors next time?"

Twenty-four

THE GAIETY OF THE NIGHT DWINDLED INTO A SOMBER morning, wrought with drizzling rain and unsettled skies as villagers returned to their homes and prepared for the gathering. Dylan had yet to spend time alone with Sophie, having devoted the last few hours to Luc and the guards reviewing security before the other leaders' arrival.

After a quick search of his home, he found his wife in their bedroom, staring out the window. She sat in a large wingback chair, watching the courtyard below.

She looked up when he approached and offered a brief smile. "You just missed Joshua. He and Malsum are doing more exercises with the sword you gave him. You should be able to catch up with them in the courtyard."

Dylan walked over to the side of the chair and covered her hand with his. "It's you I've come to see. Did you manage to sleep any?"

"Some. More than you, I think." Her gaze dropped to her lap and her voice softened. "I missed you last night."

Her shy admission made his body respond with uncomfortable vigor. "No more than I missed you," he assured her, adjusting his stance. "I was needed—"

"You don't have to explain," she interrupted with a frown. "I understand your responsibilities will keep you occupied, especially now."

In an effort to expel a burden of emotion, Dylan shook his head, wondering if he would ever get used to having— how had she phrased it?—a *cooperative* wife. He stroked her cold fingers until she relaxed. "There are no words to express what last night meant to me," he whispered. "I'd never allowed myself to hope that I would run with our son."

She tugged her hand out of his grasp, only to rest it on the side of his face. "Make him strong, Dylan. Teach him how to defend himself against these Guardians."

"I will," he vowed. It was a promise he had given before, and would give as many times as needed, knowing he would honor his word by making Joshua the strongest warrior of their kind. And still, for her, it may never be enough, because danger would always darken their lives.

Her hand fell to her lap and plucked at the folds of her pants, a nervous gesture that betrayed her worry. "When do you expect the leaders to begin arriving?"

"This evening, after sunset." He allowed his gaze to travel down her body, appreciative of how the plain T-shirt and sweatpants hugged her curves. He frowned, noting the slight bulge against her hip. "I will ask that you not run tomorrow morning, as I am sensing this thing you do is a daily routine."

"It keeps me in shape," she informed him with only a hint of annoyance in her voice. "But I'll stop until you tell me it's safe to start again."

"You're wearing your gun," he pointed out. "And not the Serpent."

"It's in the box. I did wear it while running, along with my gun, which, I will admit, was a bit cumbersome." She gave an unrepentant shrug. "I'm used to my gun. It's instinctive for me to carry it."

Frustration tightened his chest but he kept his voice calm. "There is a reason I trained you to use the Serpent," he explained. "In battle against a shifter, the only thing your gun will do is anger your enemy."

"I shoot with hollow-point bullets," she challenged.

Her confidence in her weapon of choice only fueled his fear. "To kill a shifter, their heart or head must be completely severed from their body. If not, we will shift and regenerate in the process. Even when unconscious, even when we are shredded, exposed or limbless, our beasts will rise and suck the very life that surrounds us to survive."

She frowned, seeming more confused than concerned. Would he ever understand this woman?

"But Joshua's wolf remained dormant," she questioned. "And you said it was because his environment was constantly changing . . . because he felt threatened."

"Yes, that's true." He gentled his voice but pressed his point. "But only until an initial shift occurs, and when that happens our wolves are not hindered by anything, and are often difficult to control. You must change your strategy of protection."

She nodded without comment.

Not entirely confident that he had convinced her, he added for insurance, "The only person your gun will harm is you, or others of our kind who cannot shift to heal." He gave a bitter laugh. "And that will only serve the Guardians' ultimate goal—"

"Okay," she interrupted. "I get it. It will be an adjustment for me, but I will try."

It was as much of a concession as he was going to get, he realized. "I want you to wear the Serpent, even while in our home."

Her eyes scanned his features, too shrewd for his comfort. "You don't trust these leaders who are coming."

"I trust their hatred of the Guardians more than I trust them, especially Isabeau."

"Tell me about her."

He hesitated only briefly, having faith in his wife not to cower from the truth, no matter how horrific it may be. It was deceit that Sophie never handled well. "Isabeau's territory encompasses much of Minnesota. Her family served as slaves in the household of Rhun, one of the more . . . *disturbed* Guardians. She escaped, but her parents and siblings didn't survive."

"You've experienced things I'll never understand." She held up her hand in a helpless gesture and then let it fall back to her lap. "I can't begin to fathom that kind of brutality."

"You bear scars that prove otherwise," he said, unable to keep the edge of anger from his voice. "You have tasted the scorn of our race."

"Please," she scoffed. "What Siân did to me was trivial compared to some of the stories the villagers shared with me last night, and now this about Isabeau's family. I finally understand why your people resent my presence. They wanted their leader to be with another shifter. They wanted a union their enemies would fear."

"Our people have begun to acknowledge your rightful place in my life." To press his point, he added, "If they are sharing their stories, you have begun to earn their respect. Not an easy accomplishment."

"I'm sure Joshua's little demonstration helped."

"Of course." The hound, he admitted silently, didn't hurt either. Noting its absence, he scanned the room. "Where's Tucker?"

She gave a rueful smile. "With Enid and my mother in the kitchen, judging their offerings, I'm sure."

"I will ask that you retrieve him before our guests arrive, and keep him with you upstairs at all times."

"You don't want me with you during the gathering?"

"I'd prefer that the leaders didn't know my family," he said cautiously, still unsure how far to push her current cooperative attitude. "You are a vulnerability I don't want exposed."

She regarded him with an expression he knew not to like. "You fear I'm too weak."

"You misunderstand me." He leaned forward and lifted her chin, waiting for her soft brown eyes to meet his. "It is my own weakness I must not expose. If any of the leaders saw me with you, they would know."

She frowned. "Know what?"

"How I feel," he said candidly. "That I would do anything to keep you safe . . . give up anything for you. The vulnerability is mine, Sophie, not yours."

Her posture relaxed, melted into the chair as if her bones had turned to liquid. She took his hand from her face and enclosed it in both of hers, her expression open and unguarded, causing his throat to tighten even before she whispered, "I love you, Dylan."

He wavered on his feet. Eavesdropping on her earlier confession to Francine had not compared to hearing it directly, given freely and without hesitation. He dropped to his knees in front of her, wedging his body between her thighs until the chair pressed against his stomach. He let his head fall into her lap and inhaled a ragged breath.

He had never been one to openly profess his feelings, more suited to action than love poems or pretty sonnets. He dropped a kiss inside her thigh, then another. Annoyed by the cloth that covered her skin, he reached up and snagged the elastic material from around her waist, making sure to include her undergarments, and tugged downward.

Her hand tightened on his shoulder and pushed. "What are you doing?"

"Showing you how much I love you in return," he informed her, untangling the garments away from her ankles with determined purpose. Next, he tackled the running shirt that holstered her gun, frowning when the garment proved too snug to yank off. "Remove this," he ordered.

She sent a nervous glance toward the door. "What if someone comes in here?"

"Everyone in Rhuddin Hall knows not to disturb us in our bedroom when the door is closed, even your mother."

"Let me take a shower first," she pleaded, though he sensed submission in her voice.

"No."

Watching him through a heavy-lidded gaze, Sophie leaned forward and rolled the shirt over her head, and then gingerly placed the wrapped gun on the floor next to the chair. Another garment followed—a sports bra, he believed it was called. Finally, she sat before him blessedly naked.

He devoured the sight of her. The lingering scent of her earlier run only fueled his hunger. He leaned forward and nuzzled the exposed skin of her belly, then licked a trail from her navel to the soft curls above her sex; her stomach muscles contracted against his tongue.

Still kneeling, Dylan ripped open his jeans just enough to free his shaft, now painfully engorged. His skin crawled with heat, her pleasure and soft gasps the sweetest of tortures. Leaning back on his haunches, he snaked his arms around her waist and pulled her closer to his face, until her bottom rested on the edge of the chair and he had full access to her most private core.

"Oh, God," she whispered as he pulled her legs over his shoulders. He had a fleeting vision of her hands clutching the arms of the chair for support before he closed his eyes, greedy with anticipation.

She tasted like home and fulfillment. He nuzzled her flesh until he found the nub of her sex, circling his tongue in fast strokes until she cried out his name in husky abandon, her legs shaking against his shoulders as each pulse of pleasure claimed her body.

He almost spilled his seed on the cushions of the chair.

Before she had time to recover, he flipped her over with a growl. He entered her from behind, biting back a harsh shout as her exquisite heat wrapped around him. It was a primal mating, more animal than human. He heard the sounds coming from his mouth, yet had no control to stop them.

He came in a blind fury of pounding need.

Still panting, he collapsed on top of her, only then aware that Sophie had joined him with a second release by the pulses that continued to lick at his shaft. "Did I hurt you?"

"No!" A soft laugh shook her shoulders. "Would you please stop asking me that? You were incredible."

"I lost control," he admitted, easing some of his weight off her back.

She eyed him over her shoulder, a devious smile turning her lips. "I'm sure you'll do much better next time."

"Is that a challenge, wife?" He gathered her in his arms and carried her to the bed.

AN HOUR LATER, AFTER THEY HAD BOTH SHOWERED, Dylan leaned against the headboard and watched Sophie tug a sweater over her head, savoring this last moment with her before returning to his duties. She paced the room, full of restless energy despite the sensual workout he had just given her.

He patted the empty spot beside him. "Come here."

"No."

"If you can still argue with me, woman, then I've not tired you enough." Another pat. "Come here."

She stopped her pacing only to glare. "Stop trying to distract me."

He sighed, resigned, and more than a tad disappointed. "You're not going to give up on this, are you?"

"If you don't want me by your side during the gathering, I understand. Just let me do something else less visible." She waved her hand around the bedroom. "Give me something—*anything*—useful to do."

"I consider the past hour very useful to my mental well-being."

"Don't do that," she said softly. "I want to help. Sitting here and doing nothing will drive me insane."

He lowered his voice to a sensual whisper. "You were *not* doing nothing, I assure you."

"You're patronizing me."

"I'm not." Sobering to her anger, he ran his hands over his face. "I need you to be safe, Sophie. That's all. I will not be able to concentrate if I'm worried about you or your whereabouts."

Unfortunately, her restless attitude came as no surprise; he remembered all too well her dislike of confined spaces, and her response. Experience had taught him not to ignore her request. Therefore, he tried to think of a responsibility that would keep her relatively safe and guarded but with a purpose she would respect. "We have eight children being kept in a secluded safe house in the village. Their parents are with them. Elen is there as well, and several guards have been assigned to the area around the building. Would you be willing to join them?" At her narrowed expression, he added, "As another protector."

A worried frown creased her forehead. "How will their parents feel about me being there?"

"Allowing my family to join theirs would be considered a great honor, a further promise to keep them safe."

"Okay," she agreed. "Then I'll go."

"I want Joshua and your mother to join you," he said, warming to the idea.

"That's fine."

"Will you promise to wear the Serpent?" He remained quiet until she nodded her consent. "Then tell your mother we leave in one hour, while I go find our son."

THAT AFTERNOON, SOPHIE FOLLOWED DYLAN UP THE front steps of a quaint covered porch, with Joshua, her mother and Tucker just a few paces behind. The safe house was an ordinary blue cottage located on the edge of town, blending amongst scattered homes of similar design. A woman swung on a porch swing, reading a book, her long jean-clad legs dangling over the side.

"Sarah," Dylan greeted with a nod. "My family is going to stay with the children during the gathering."

Her eyes briefly landed on Tucker with no outward reaction. "Understood," she said with a tone of authority that proved her relaxed position was pretense. Sophie assumed this Sarah, with her cropped red hair, was yet another member of her husband's guard.

Dylan opened the door, nodding toward Francine and Joshua to enter the cottage, holding Sophie behind with a gentle arm around her waist. He leaned down and dropped a kiss next to her temple. "If you see anything suspicious, send Sarah to get me."

"I will," she promised.

"I have to return to Rhuddin Hall." Concern laced his voice.

"We'll be fine," she reassured him with a smile.

"Remember, our local cell towers have been disabled. Your phone is useless until the gathering is over."

"Porter already told me."

"Sarah will show you to the others." He claimed her lips for one last gentle kiss. "This will be over soon." And with a final nod in Sarah's direction, he strode down the stairs toward his truck. On the drive over, he had given her and Joshua instructions on the safest route back to Rhuddin Hall from their current location, a secret passage she hadn't been aware of.

His vigilance heightened her concern, *and* her annoyance upon discovering that he had only moved her to an even more protected location to wait out the gathering. But if staying confined with the children was what he needed from her, then so be it. While she had always loved Dylan, she hadn't truly trusted him.

That needed to change. If he was willing to respect her decisions, then she needed to return the gesture. Furthermore, guarding the children was an important responsibility she didn't accept lightly.

As soon as Dylan's truck disappeared, Sarah sent a sidelong glare in Sophie's direction, not hiding her displeasure. "Follow me."

The occupants of the house, Sophie soon discovered, were stowed away in the basement. She paused at the bottom of the stairs as her eyesight adjusted to the dim lighting. Sarah silently resumed her post while Sophie's family spilled around her.

"This room is depressing," Francine muttered, and Joshua returned with a grunt of agreement.

"It's safe," Sophie reminded them. "That's all that matters."

There were metal doors on the far wall, locked from within in the event of a necessary escape. Overstuffed chairs and a padded carpet had been added for comfort, with a meager kitchen and a paneled single door she assumed was a bathroom. Still, it smelled stuffy, a combination of must and too many breathing bodies in a closed space. The adults in the room sat with subdued expressions.

Elen stood alone in the corner of the room while the others huddled in a group away from her. A genuine smile of gratitude brightened her face as she walked over to greet them. "I'm *really* glad you've decided to join us."

Sophie gave her a hug, not sure why she extended such a personal greeting, only sensing that Elen needed it. "How long have you been here?"

Elen returned the hug with a grateful squeeze. "Since this morning."

Twenty-five

As Dylan had instructed, the leaders' arrivals began after sunset, their guards few but powerful. Some came from the woods, led by Luc and then released toward Rhuddin Hall under Porter's guidance. Three of the leaders arrived in nondescript vehicles and were directed through the side entrance like villagers on a routine visit.

No disputes had yet to arise, Dylan mused with some suspicion. But the night was still young. For now, at least, all leaders and their companions appeared cooperative and prepared to listen, if not entirely thrilled.

Inwardly, he remained grateful his wife had agreed to go to the safe house. Her cooperation allowed him to focus his energy on the matter at hand as Porter escorted the visitors to their temporary quarters. For the most part, Luc kept to the forest with the other guards and watched for unwelcomed intruders, a monumental task considering the size of their territory.

All those he cared about were safe and accounted for, Dylan reminded himself. Nonetheless, he felt restless and ready to have this meeting concluded, relieved when the last leader finally arrived.

"Madoc," Dylan greeted from the open door, biting back a smile as the massive man unfolded from a rented Prius, unaccompanied. "Don't tell me you drove all the way from Montana in that thing?"

"Hell, no," Madoc called back. "Only since Portland."

"Did you come alone?"

"I do better alone," he said, with the assurance of a man who had survived much worse than a gathering of wolves. "As I'm sure you remember."

"I remember our journey all too well."

Madoc was *the* notorious black knight turned pirate, his brooding features and brutal acts recounted—and distorted—by many storytellers and enemies alike. He was also the man insane enough to embark on an unknown journey without the consent of kings. He had captained the ship that had brought Dylan, Luc, and Elen to this land. Thankfully, Elen had been long removed from Merin's influence by that time and helped soothe Luc on the voyage; the wolf had not taken well to sea travel.

Madoc whacked his forehead on the doorframe in the process of squeezing out of the small vehicle. "Damn . . . I feel like a fat woman trying to get out of a well-tied corset."

"You've helped with that a few times, have you?" Dylan goaded.

"Indeed," he chuckled, stretching as he stood with a loud groan. "Goddess knows I'd take one now. If you ask me, all these modern women look like starved boys."

Dylan walked down the front entry. The light rain felt soothing as he held out his hand. "Thank you for coming."

"This assembly is long overdue, old friend." Madoc returned the greeting with a firm shake as his dark gaze spanned the forest and moved on to Katahdin. "Your territory is"—his nostrils flared as he inhaled the powerful scent of untamed nature—"abundant."

"So is yours," Dylan pointed out.

"I know." Not a threat, or a boast, just a simple acknowledgment that they shared the same concern.

* * *

SOPHIE CHECKED HER WATCH. ALMOST MIDNIGHT. AND the children had yet to settle down. Eighteen hours confined in a basement had confused their routines and tried the patience of every adult in the room, except for Francine. Her mother snored softly in one of the overstuffed chairs, blissfully unaware, whereas the children were ready to climb the walls. For kicks and giggles, Sophie inwardly decided she might join them.

A squeal of delight came from Ella, a young girl with long golden braids, as Joshua agreed to give her yet another piggyback ride.

"One last time, Pixie Girl," Joshua teased. "But only if you promise to take a nap afterward."

Ella rocked forward, kicking her pudgy legs into his sides. "Promise."

Ella's mother sent Sophie an apologetic shrug. It was the first unguarded gesture of the evening, and Sophie smiled in return. The villagers had graciously welcomed Joshua around their children, but they had kept a guarded distance from Sophie and Elen. At first, she'd assumed Tucker made them nervous, but more often than not, their worried gazes turned to Elen.

As if sensing her restlessness, a petite woman with a mass of tangled brown hair approached, holding out her hand in greeting. "My name is Gwenfair." She went on to explain, "Dylan told me you might be interested in teaching at our school. If that is indeed the case, I would appreciate your help."

Grateful for the distraction, Sophie shook the woman's hand. "I would like that."

"Wonderful." She smiled to show crooked teeth that added to the natural warmth of her features. "I fully intend to continue their education, even if we have to do it behind guarded walls. We can meet in a few days to discuss our curriculum."

"How many children do you normally teach?"

"Eight. But don't let that small number fool you. They're all highly inquisitive and bore easily," she warned with good humor. "The oldest is twelve years, and the youngest is four."

Scanning the room, Sophie recounted the heads of all the children. "Why are there only seven here now?"

After a slight hesitation, Gwenfair supplied, "Taran chose not to bring her daughter."

Sophie blinked in surprise. "I hadn't realized Taran had a child." She made a mental note to have a conversation with Dylan when all this was over, and learn the names and family history of every person who lived in Rhuddin Village. Hopefully he had begun to trust her enough to release that information. "How old is her daughter?"

"Melissa is the youngest," Gwenfair said with obvious concern. "She's four years old."

A warning chill crawled down Sophie's spine; her inner voice of reason was stronger than her distrust of Siân's family. Regardless of their unpleasant history, or whatever demotion Luc had enforced on Taran, not choosing the safest place for her daughter didn't make sense, not for any parent.

A twinge of pain lanced through her head, a warning sign she'd learned to recognize, just before an unwelcome voice not her own flooded her thoughts.

Your instincts are correct, Sophie Marie Thibodeau. The serpentine cadence weaved through her mind, an unnatural resonance that made her skin crawl with dread. *The mother and daughter are in danger.*

"Do you smell that?" Gwenfair darted glances around the room as if looking for an unknown visitor. "It smells like—"

"Apple blossoms," Elen interrupted, placing a tentative hand on Sophie's shoulder, only to pull back with a hiss. "It smells like apple blossoms and power—*old* power."

With flared nostrils, Gwenfair's chest rose and fell with several slow breaths. "Yes," she hummed with pleasure.

"I've smelled that scent once before," Elen whispered breathlessly, "when I was much younger." Her eyes fell to

Sophie's waist, covered by her sweater. "Are you wearing the Serpent?"

"I promised Dylan I would." Sophie stood, and immediately wavered as blood rushed to her head. Her vision blurred. "I think I need some fresh air. I'm going to go check on Sarah."

The mother and daughter are in danger, the Serpent repeated.

Leave me alone, Sophie answered back with silent force, making a conscious effort to close her mind, pushing against the unseen tormentor. It had worked once before, so why not again?

A serpentine laugh whispered back, not entirely displeased with her effort to expel it. *You are strong, Sophie Marie Thibodeau, but I am stronger . . .*

Dylan opted to meet in the sheltered gardens of Rhuddin Hall. A place without walls was a more practical location if a quarrel were to ensue, a likely possibility with eight dominant shifters within striking distance of one another. As the leaders arrived, each in their human form, a heavy fog settled around their unruly circle, blessing their dangerous union with a mantle of obscurity.

"Madoc, Ryder, Drystan, Daron, Isabeau." He addressed them each with a nod, followed by the two representatives sent by Nia and Kalem. "As you know, I've asked you here to unite with me against a shared enemy." He tossed the banner in the center of their circle, bright blue and gold, colors that heralded the most vile cruelties of their past. "Our time of peace has ended."

Voices rose in unison, each one adamant to be heard above the others. Arguments filled with uncertainty. In response, elements churned, pulled forth by eight powerful beings in one location. A gust of wind brushed through the forest. The fog lifted briefly to form a dense cloud mere yards above their heads. Snow began to fall, then turned to sleet, like a lover's bite, teasing and wanting. Their combined power was pure, potent and addictive. And Dylan's wolf wanted to play.

Holding her hand up for silence, Isabeau stepped forward, wearing jeans and sneakers, her hair tucked underneath the hood of a sweatshirt labeled Gap across her chest. Earlier that day, upon her arrival, Dylan had noticed her hair had been dyed kohl black, probably the only color that concealed a red so pure it attracted unnecessary attention. He saw no evidence of the broken girl who had stumbled upon his camp all those years ago.

Currently, she stood with her arms crossed and her lips pursed in feigned boredom, and looked no older than eighteen, a guise that suited her well. She had killed men thrice her size before they knew to be frightened.

"You speak as if we're already at war with the Guardians," Isabeau said. "I will fight, with pleasure, if they come, but I have not seen evidence of them in my territory."

"Has all that hair dye made you daft, woman?" Madoc blurted with his usual candor. "'Tis their bloody banner lying at your feet."

"It may be a warning," she returned through clenched teeth, her voice too sweet, "but I don't believe it was a Guardian who placed it. It's not their way." And she would know, having lost her entire family to the Guardian Rhun. "It's not in their best interest to give warnings."

"I share Isabeau's view on this matter," Drystan argued. "I have not seen evidence of the Guardians, and neither have the others. I don't know who's playing with you, Dylan . . . but I don't believe the Guardians have any intentions of leaving Europe. So why should we chance their interest if it is not yet here?"

Daran grunted with agreement. "Having Math among us is enough. I, for one, don't want to entice any others."

"None of us do," Drystan added, urged by the support. "Math has lived among us for almost three centuries now and has left us alone."

"Math likes his privacy," Madoc muttered with a sneer. "And we all know why. He doesn't want the Council close any more than we do. They'd put a halt to his little . . . dalliances."

"*Please,*" Isabeau scoffed. "As if the Council cares."

"Regardless of who placed the banner in my territory, or for what purpose," Dylan interrupted, displeased with their trepidation, "I believe it's only a matter of time before more Guardians arrive." He inhaled the scent of his forest, letting his wolf rise to the surface, a tenuous challenge necessary for his next disclosure. "I have a son." That earned a murmur of surprise and a generous slap on the back from Madoc. "He was born fifteen years ago. My mate is human. Our son can run as both a man and wolf."

Agitated by this new information, Isabeau began to pace. "If the Guardians learn you've fathered a shifter with a human mate—"

Dylan interrupted, "I'm fully aware of the danger that threatens my family, Isabeau. When the Guardians come, and they will eventually come . . . Do you truly think they'll remain satisfied not to claim it all? Do you truly think they'll not move on to your lands? Have you lived so long in peace that you've forgotten their ways?"

Isabeau winced as if slapped. "Now you insult me." She turned and glared at Dylan, her hands fisted against her sides in outrage. "I will *never* forget!"

"Then join me," Dylan challenged. "I will not welcome war, but if it comes to my home, I will fight, just as I will fight for anyone who stands with me."

Twenty-six

THE SERPENT REFUSED TO RETREAT.

Sophie pressed her palms against her temples. The pounding sharpened, became stronger. *Angry.* Outwardly, she heard whispers of concern. She felt Tucker's nose against her arm, heard his soft whine, as if he too felt the Serpent's displeasure.

The voice became more vehement and annoyed by her resistance. *See for yourself,* it chanted with dangerous intensity. *The mother is betraying you.*

A shaft of white light, too pure to be of this world, blinded her into darkness. The pain subsided to a dull ache, replaced by an awful sense of unbalance. The room weaved and the floor rose. There was carpet under her palms, damp and abrasive.

Had she fallen?

Reality shifted into nothingness, a void between truth and delusion. Blurred shapes began to appear, flooding her mind like flashes in a photo booth, monochrome and flat. Soon there was sound, garbled and then pure, as if a higher consciousness was tuning a frequency specific to her mental reception. Serpentine images weaved through her thoughts, slit like a leaf and framed by a crested oblong shape.

Was she seeing through the creature's own eyes?

FLASHES OF THE GREAT OAK SWAM BEFORE HER, THEN A *stream and a cluster of white birches. The images came fast, making her dizzy. A field appeared, matted in the center by a struggle. It was nighttime but she could see clearly; her new eyes preferred the darkness. There was a dead tree in the distance, with a birdlike image carved on its trunk. Dark shapes formed, of blood, so much blood, from a broken woman with long red hair, and other bodies fallen on the ground. There was also a child, limp and unconscious, held carelessly in the arms of a hooded figure too large to be female. He was not alone. There were other shadowed figures, watching and not helping.*

Smiling, he lifted his arms high above the ground and let the child roll . . .

"No," Sophie screamed, reaching out, *but her voice went unheard and her arms remained empty, like mist on an ocean of tears. Flashes of inconceivable cruelty lanced through her mind, a mental rape she couldn't fight back.*

The child landed by the man's feet with a sickening thump and remained motionless. The woman's screams pierced through the valley, so anguished that angels should have fallen from the sky to answer her call. She tried to cushion the child's fall with her own body, even as her legs crumpled in broken disarray. Vile laughter followed her attempt, inhuman and without remorse.

"Tell me where she is, Taran, sister of Siân," *the man taunted in the singsong voice of the disturbed.* "Tell me where to find Elen ap Merin. Tell me where to find your leader's sister . . . who keeps the forest alive in winter."

"There's a clinic," Taran *sobbed, answering too quickly, inching toward her daughter even as the words fell from her mouth.* "Just north of the grain fields. Elen is always there."

"You dare lie to me? I know she is not at this . . . this clinic." *He sneered the last word as if it were the vilest institution, a building that housed vermin that should be exterminated, not aided. A booted foot lifted, and with shining eyes aglow with malicious joy, he kicked the child, once, and then again . . .*

"Stop!" Taran curled her broken body around the child, absorbing most of the blows. "Please," she sobbed, "please stop."

"Tell me where Elen is . . . or your little Drwgddyddwg *will die for your weakness."*

"In the village." The hunched figure wept tears of betrayal for choosing her child over others. "There's a blue house . . ."

THE BASEMENT CAME BACK IN A RUSH OF SOUND AND color. Gasps of horror and pitiful cries from frightened children echoed throughout the room. Tucker's wet nose nudged her cheek. She tried to sit up but the abrupt motion made her heave.

"Oh, dear Lord," her mother exclaimed from someplace near. "Sophie, what is wrong with you?"

"Mom?" This from Joshua. Fear clogged his voice, unaccustomed to any weakness from his mother. "Are you okay?"

"Sophie," another familiar voice repeated her name, professional and persistent. "Sophie, can you hear me?"

"I can hear you." Her throat felt raw as she spoke, as if she'd been screaming the entire time. She attempted to nod but her reflexes balked. She blinked once, tried again. Elen's face came slowly into focus.

"Taran . . ." Sophie's voice broke. She swallowed and tried again. "Taran's in trouble. She's hurt. So is her daughter. They need help!"

Elen's blue eyes held hers, heavy with concern. "How do you know this?"

She didn't hesitate to reveal her source, the vision having been too real to deny its validity. "The Serpent showed me in a vision."

Elen blinked once, her only outward show of surprise before hiding her reaction. "It *talks* to you?"

"Yes." Sophie dared her to disagree.

She didn't. "What did the Serpent show you?"

Sophie lowered her voice to a whisper. "A man in a hooded cloak hurting a child. I think it was Melissa. He called her a weird name. It sounded like *droogeth . . .* something. He wasn't alone. I saw more figures in the shadows, watching but not helping." Her hands fisted by her sides as she recounted the sickening scene. "Taran was there. She's hurt. So are others on the ground." She stood slowly, gaining her balance.

Elen reached out to steady her, her expression one of horror but not disbelief. "He wanted information from Taran. Do you have any idea what that might be? Did you see or hear anything that might—"

"You," Sophie warned. "The man is after you. He said something about you keeping the forest alive in winter. I know it doesn't make sense, but it was *so* real. Taran told them where to find us. They know where we are."

"It makes more sense than you know." Her voice had gone quiet, deadened with acceptance.

"The Guardians are here." The announcement came from a male who had obviously overheard, a father of one of the children.

"It's because of *her*," another parent accused, a mother this time, pointing her finger at Elen.

"I knew she wasn't natural." A hushed accusation. "I knew she was one of *them*."

"What are we going to do?" This from Ella's mother. Sensing her mother's fear, Ella began to cry.

Panicked voices rose in unison, flooding the small room with verbal chaos.

Elen seemed to shrink into herself. "I should not have come here," she told them. "I will leave."

"We *all* have to leave," Sophie announced, not sure what had transpired between these people and Elen. Whatever it was, it ended now. She took a step forward, testing her balance, and then another, gaining their attention. "I'm going outside to speak with Sarah." Tucker sauntered by her side in silent support, followed by Joshua and her mother. A hush settled in the room. The parents didn't look pleased but they listened. "Stay here and remain silent while I discuss a plan with the guards. I won't be long." As soon as she stepped onto the porch, Sarah rose from the shadows, frowning with obvious annoyance.

"You shouldn't be out here," the guard hissed.

"I have reason to believe the Guardians are here." Pressed for time, she reinforced her story by lifting her sweatshirt. The Serpent lay coiled neatly around her waist. Sarah straightened, nodding for Sophie to continue. "The Serpent showed me in a vision. They know where the safe house is. We need to evacuate the children."

Without hesitation, Sarah turned toward the woods, issuing a sharp whistle. Malsum and four other guards came forward, bathed in moonlight while they listened to a brief explanation from their female comrade. As several doubt-filled eyes landed on Sophie, she lifted her chin, not caring if they thought her insane.

She recounted her vision, adding details with useful location markers, "I saw a man, in a field by a cluster of white birches. There was a dead tree in the distance, with a bird carved on its trunk. They have Taran and her daughter. Taran told them where we are."

"Taran wouldn't betray us," one of the guards murmured.

"The man was beating a child I believe was Taran's daughter," Sophie countered. "There were shadows on the ground. Shapes that weren't moving. I'm not sure if it was your guards or not. I just know it felt too real to be ignored and we need to get a message to Dylan."

"I know the field you speak of. It borders our land." Malsum had silenced the other guards with a displeased glare. "Sarah, you will leave now and apprise Dylan of his mate's warning. Use Yellow Moss Trail." He turned to one of the other male guards. "Michael, you do the same, but follow East Branch south and warn the others before circling back. Whoever gets there first, tell Dylan we're returning to Rhuddin Hall on foot and that we'll follow the back Arwel passage."

Sarah and Michael dispersed in the directions they were ordered, while the remaining three guards looked to Malsum for further instruction. Their grave stance grounded Sophie's conviction that danger was imminent. Her stomach tightened with unease.

And she wanted Dylan with her; she wanted to be back at Rhuddin Hall, with her family safe and under his direct protection. In just a few days she had unknowingly embraced a side of herself she hadn't acknowledged for such a long time, a softer side.

Unfortunately, Dylan wasn't there. She was. And there were children who needed to be evacuated to another safe house. A calm determination settled over her, a focus built from sixteen years of preparation for an attack. That time had come, though not as she'd predicted. No matter. She may not be as strong as Malsum or the other remaining men watching her with apprehension, but she knew how to run, and she knew how to hide, and she most definitely knew how to keep those she cared about safe.

And, if needed, she also knew how to fight.

"I think we should separate into four groups." She spoke directly to Malsum, trusting him, at the very least, to listen without contempt. "Let the others find a secure place with the children, a place that no one will suspect, and stay hidden. Without sharing their destination," she added. "We can continue to Rhuddin Hall."

She assumed he would balk at such a noncombative

suggestion, and was pleasantly surprised when he gave a sharp nod for the others to begin. "The plan is sound," he said. "Do as Dylan's mate has instructed. We'll ring the church bell when it's safe to come out. Dylan's family will stay with me."

"Call me Sophie," she added after his second referral to her as "Dylan's mate."

"Sophie," Malsum returned, "go gather your family."

"What about Taran and her daughter? We need to find Luc and tell him what's happened, about the Guardians . . ."

"I trust Luc is already aware of the situation," he said. "If Taran and her daughter are alive, he will bring them to Elen."

"Okay." His conviction eased her conscience. Moreover, Sophie had learned a bit about Malsum after his lesson with Joshua. He was second in command under Luc in Dylan's guard, a shifter and the chosen warrior of his father's people. His heritage was Abanaki and Celt. His wolf, she now knew, came from his Celt ancestors, but his human side was just as prevalent. His skin flaunted the rich tones of his native heritage, golden brown and smooth. His eyes were soft brown, but beneath the kindness was an unmistakable strength of will. Of honor.

Sophie trusted his judgment.

The removal of the children and their parents took less than a minute. They were led out the back door of the basement, camouflaged by cedar hedges and cottages not built in rows, but rather like a maze with hidden backyards. As she checked the basement one last time, she couldn't help but ponder over how much her life had changed in just a few short days. Trust, it seemed, was a powerful persuader to an even greater emotion. These people were not only Dylan's, but somehow they had become hers as well.

"Everyone is cleared from the basement," she announced, returning to where her family huddled on the back lawn, Elen included, although her sister-in-law kept trying to leave and was unaccustomed to being told no.

After the groups dispersed in different directions with their precious cargo underfoot, Elen turned to Malsum. "I will go to the clinic and wait."

"No," Sophie repeated for the third time, shaking her head. "Somehow the Guardian knew you weren't there. They must be watching it."

She pursed her lips. "But if it's me they're after, then at the very least I must separate from you."

"No." Francine joined the argument, frowning with clear disapproval. "My daughter's right. Our family stays together. We can all squeeze into one car—"

"A vehicle is too visible," Malsum cut her off. "And the road circles away from Rhuddin Hall. If we move now it will be quicker on foot."

"Fine." Francine marched toward a cluster of low-growing trees, where the hidden passage began that Dylan had shown them earlier. She turned, clearly annoyed that the others hadn't immediately followed. "Let's move, people." She snapped her fingers, motivating them into motion, even Malsum.

"ENOUGH OF THIS BULLSHIT," RYDER SPOKE UP FOR THE first time. "I, like Dylan, feel the Guardians are restless. Once they learn a shifter has been born from this land, they will come. Frankly, I'm surprised they haven't sooner. It's time to band together. I will join your alliance, Dylan."

"Count me in as well," Madoc announced, glaring at the remaining leaders in disgust when they didn't immediately voice their support.

"Thank you," Dylan returned with a nod.

"This is not a decision to make lightly," Isabeau said gravely. "I will consider what you've shared this night . . ." Her voice trailed off, suddenly distracted. Her head cocked toward the forest.

Dylan also heard the movement of sound, too focused to be random. Sarah emerged within seconds, running as a wolf in their direction. "She's one of mine," he informed the others before they reacted with force, his gut tightening with dread.

When Sarah reached their circle, she shifted. Panting, eyes wild, she turned to Dylan. "We've moved the children from the safe house. Your wife . . ." She swallowed, took a ragged breath. "Your wife believes she had a vision. She believes the Guardians are here."

"Where is she?" Dylan grabbed Sarah by the arms and shook, too desperate to hide his reaction. "Where are my wife and son?"

"They're on their way here. Malsum and Elen are with them. They took the back Arwel passage."

Twenty-seven

THE NIGHT SKY WEPT SHARDS OF ICE THAT TURNED TO
rain, acting like a troubled soul, sleeping one moment and
screaming the next. "Is this weather normal?" Sophie asked
Malsum.

"Define 'normal,'" he whispered back with a hint of humor in his voice.

"Point taken."

The trail widened once they moved beyond the under-
growth that concealed the opening. Buds had begun to form,
but many branches remained bare, their leaves not open
enough to offer protection from the steady drizzle of rain.
Moss covered rocks and roots, while puddles formed in the
dip of the trail. The pungent scent of wet pine filled the air.
Sophie concentrated on her footing, bracing her steps on the
slippery ground. Her clothes clung to her skin, pasted by
rain and sweat, as Malsum quickened their pace.

She felt naked without her gun, antsy and out of her element, even with the Serpent circled around her waist.

While they traveled deeper into the forest, the storm
lifted; moonlight brightened the path and shadows played

games with her vision. She remained close to Joshua, walking just a few paces behind. Elen stayed at the rear while Malsum bullied his way in front of Francine. Tucker crowded against Sophie's side, almost pushing her off the trail.

Something moved in the trees up ahead, a glimmer of light to darkness in her peripheral vision. An animal perhaps? Or something worse? She turned her head. Nothing.

"Did you see that?" she whispered, just as Malsum came to a halt, holding out his arm in a silent gesture for silence. He too stared into the shadows. Unnerved, she followed his line of sight, but all she saw were rows and rows of forty-foot pines, standing tall like giant soldiers, branchless except for the very tops.

Her hand inched toward her waist.

"We're not alone." Malsum turned to Joshua. "Rhuddin Hall is less than a mile in that direction." He tilted his head to the right. "How fast can you run?"

"As a wolf," Joshua said, "very fast."

"Then shift and make haste!"

"I'm not going to leave you here—"

"Do as he says," Sophie ordered, relying on Malsum's instincts.

Joshua shook his head. "No."

"Joshua . . ."

"No!" His eyes narrowed with stubborn intensity, dark as ebony granite and just as inflexible. "I'm not leaving you."

She wanted to shake him, to yell at him. *Now* wasn't the time for one of his obstinate moments. However, she remained silent while an enemy might be watching, even listening. Her eyes shot daggers of disapproval. He lifted his chin in response. Fear made her beg, *"Please . . ."*

Tucker tensed by her side, his focus pinned on a patch of evergreens in the distance. A low growl vibrated from his chest.

"It's too late," Malsum hissed needlessly. Sophie already knew their visitors had arrived. He pulled out a circular object that had been hooked to the side of his jeans, wire wound into a ball the size of a large man's fist with handles on either end. A garrote, she realized, maybe even forged by hand; Malsum held it with deadly confidence.

The hooded figure of her vision stepped onto the trail, then another, and another. The man, the vile man whose very presence leaked malevolence, was the only one who wore a cloak, resembling a demented druid of times long dead. His followers wore normal street clothes, carrying various sized backpacks and gear, like any other human on a hike through the Appalachian Trail. Except they weren't. She could see it in their eyes, feel it in the way they watched Elen with heavy-lidded focus, as if she were the next target of their own private game.

And they were enjoying the hunt. Openly, men began to shrug off their gear and retrieve their own weapons of choice, swords mostly, a few carved knives and other curved objects of destruction.

Malsum swore under his breath in a language that sounded decisively native. "Stay behind me."

Sophie intended to do exactly that, but Elen had a different mind-set. She stepped forward, her posture held high yet resolved.

"Rhun," Elen greeted with a low curtsy.

"You may stand." A pleased smile spread across his face, revealing even white teeth. "You are the very image of your mother, little Elen. At least in human form. But then you have no other, do you?"

She ignored his insult. "Why do you honor us with your presence, Rhun?" No detectible sarcasm filled her words, only calm politeness. "I would expect you to keep the company of our neighbor, Math, another *Gwarchodwyr Unfed* such as yourself. Why bother with us?"

Her lack of response to his goading seemed to annoy him. "Math and I have convened with other members of the Council. Your brother's deceit has very recently been brought to our attention." His hooded head tilted toward Tucker. "This place holds great power. The Council should have been informed."

"Not as powerful as Cymru, surely?" Elen's voice dripped innocence, a perfect ruse of confusion and obedience.

How long, Sophie wondered, had it taken for her to perfect that act? An act of stupidity, of humility in the face of loathing?

"Don't be coy, little Elen." Thin lips peeled back in a sneer. "I have been to your home. Power grows from its very walls, and I want to know why."

She gave him a blank look. "I don't know what you're talking about."

"Save your lies! Siân told us everything. You will come with us now. You will meet with the Council and be judged for your deceit. And then we will decide your fate, and the fate of your brothers."

Having heard enough, Sophie cleared her throat and stepped forward. Malsum tried to block her but she skirted away from his grasp. "Ah, that's *not* going to happen."

"Hush, Sophie," Elen hissed, waving her back. "Let me handle this."

Rhun lifted his head and scented the air with flared nostrils. "Human," he said as if choking on a piece of rotting meat. "You dare address me?" He turned to a lanky man who stood beside him. "Grwn, silence this . . . this *creature*."

Grwn stepped forward, tall and long-limbed, his tongue hanging over his bottom lip with greedy anticipation, stroking the handle of his sword like foreplay. He only made it the one step before a blur of motion disturbed the air. A familiar growl warned Sophie it was Tucker who lunged first, grabbing Grwn by the throat and twisting. A sickening crunch echoed off the packed dirt of the forest floor, followed by a gurgled wail. Another crunch. And then nothing.

Rhun stood motionless, his reaction delayed by arrogance. As did Sophie, but for other reasons, witnessing for the first time why Dylan's people feared her dog. He was—most definitely—*not* of this world.

Bile rose in her throat but she swallowed back her initial reaction. "Good boy, Tucker," she announced in front of the watching crowd of Guardians, as if in full control when she was anything but. Tucker had severed the man's spine, this Grwn who'd been ordered to attack her. His head hung off to the side disjointed, lifeless. Blood soaked into the ground, a pool of blackness poisoning the earth. Tucker paced in front of her, his canines displayed toward the intruders in further warning.

Too startled to conceal his reaction, Rhun clawed at the burnished latches of his robe and shrugged off the covering, letting the material slide to the ground in a pool of purple cloth. He shook with unrepressed fury. Nonetheless, he stood proud, arrogant, and completely naked. His body was pale but well-formed. His hair mimicked wet mud and hung below his shoulders in clumped strands. But his eyes . . . his eyes were the most disturbing color of milk white around black pupils.

The purpose of his disrobing soon registered in Sophie's mind as the scent of elements rose, not the earthy rush of wind or forest, but rather a rancid odor of rotting vegetation, like the fetid water in a vase of decayed flowers.

It was the scent of death.

"The hound protects the human," one of Rhun's men announced in hushed disbelief.

"Indeed." Rhun's eyes narrowed on Sophie with renewed interest, showing no outward sign of remorse over his lost comrade, just curiosity. With a malicious grin, he announced, "Let's see who else it protects, shall we?"

The hairs on the base of her skull stood on end, as if evil itself had just found interest in her ordinary, human soul. *That's fine,* she thought, *as long as it's my soul he's interested in and not my son's.*

Clutching the smooth metal beneath her palms, Sophie pulled the Serpent from her waist and let it uncoil to the ground. "One more step and you will lose your head." She wasn't sure if it was the Serpent that made him pause, or her threat. The Serpent, most likely.

Those awful white eyes studied the uncoiled whip, lingering on the horned details of the fanged barb, and then lifted to her face. "Who are you?"

She braced her legs apart, balancing for an assault. "The human who's going to kill you if you don't leave our territory."

"She's Dylan's mate," Elen blurted out, revealing her emotions for the first time in front of Rhun. "Their son has been gifted by the Goddess. It is Taliesin who gave her the Serpent of Cernunnos. You must not harm those the Goddess protects."

Her announcement was not received well. Rhun sliced his hand through the air as if to erase a vile presence. "Liar! You filthy little . . . *drwgddyddwg*." Visible tremors claimed his limbs. "Ceridwen protects *Her* Guardians. She protects *Her* Council. Not . . ." He leered at Joshua, spittle foaming at the edges of his mouth. "Not the bastard of a traitor and a human."

Malsum crowded by Sophie's side, obviously sensing the same thing she had: running was no longer an option. "Will you back up your threat?" he asked, keeping his gaze locked on the encroaching Guardians.

"Yes," she said simply, and as Rhun lunged toward her son with a battle cry wrought with fanatical vengeance, she didn't hesitate. The whoosh of the whip split through the air, like the roar of a bear in the middle of winter, a deadly threat that something had just awoken that should have remained undisturbed.

A brief spark of recognition, of shock, widened his milk-white eyes. Too late. A warning of death had been given and ignored. The Serpent grabbed hold with surreal accuracy and anchored around his neck. Sophie followed through, separating head from torso in one fell swoop.

And the battle began.

The others did *not* cower back as she'd hoped. They came at Sophie and her family with weapons drawn, knives and swords of varying shapes and sizes, all crafted with one purpose: to sever head from spine. Feverish anticipation shone in their eyes.

She fought for her son, for the children who cowered in homes because they feared their deaths. She fought for Melissa, and Taran, and for all those years she'd lost with Dylan because he'd been forced to contain her against this evil.

"Stay behind me," she yelled to Joshua and her mother. But her son held his sword in his hands, the one his father had given him, and was holding off one of the Guardians. She killed three others, and two more who had fixed their attentions on Joshua, while Tucker had his jaws around another's throat.

The Serpent coiled around her targets with a fluid motion that increased momentum with each kill, as if garnering strength in death. The very thought horrified her even as desperation propelled her forward.

On her right, Malsum was swarmed, though he still fought, dropping bodies around his feet with his simple but effective garrote and a lethal blur of motion. In a sudden move, Malsum faltered backward, either overcome by their zealot fury or in a strategic move to draw the Guardians away.

Clarity of purpose balanced the chaos. Sophie counted thirty-two enemies, twelve dead, eleven fully functional humans, seven wolves and two in mid-shift. Adrenaline pumped through her veins with every lash of her whip. The sounds of metal on metal rang in her ears. Faces swam before her, contorted with hatred and rage. The putrid scent of unholy elements clogged the air as more Guardians began to shift into their other forms, realizing their swords were no match for the Serpent.

Above the deafening roar, Sophie heard one voice penetrate through the others, clear as ice cracking on a frozen lake, and as jolting as if she were the one standing directly above it. She froze, horror-stricken.

Francine screamed, "Joshua . . ."

Sophie turned to see a flash of movement, and then her son yelling, "Grandma . . . no . . ."

A Guardian, still in human form, charged Joshua from behind in a rush of metal and flesh. Francine threw herself in his path, too human and too weak to offer any protection other than the shield of her own body and the power of her heart. Without thought, as if swatting an annoying insect, the Guardian grabbed her head and twisted.

Her mother crumpled to the ground and remained unmoving.

Sophie staggered in disbelief, a base reaction of utter shock. Darkness clouded her vision and blanketed her chest in a weight so heavy her lungs refused to draw air. What her heart knew, her mind refused to translate. Reality suspended, as if all justice had been drained by the dark hand of evil—and then came rushing back on a blast of color and sound. She toppled forward, unbalanced, her throat raw from a continuous scream she couldn't contain, rage and pain mixed with the sound of feral grunts and the clash of swords.

But it wasn't her anguish that stopped the battle, as it should have been. Elen moved behind the man who had just taken her mother's life. The Guardian's back was bare, sheened with sweat, his attention focused on Joshua as he raised his sword. Elen placed her hands on his exposed skin and closed her eyes, a gentle touch that jerked the man in an upright position until he stood stiff and unresponsive, his mouth ajar and his sword frozen in midair.

Without warning, the man imploded, as if turned inside out. Blood spattered the area in streams of burgundy and red. Sophie blinked, unsure if her mind had registered the impossible correctly. Or if, God willing, this was all just a nightmare and soon she would wake up to the smell of blueberry pie in the oven and her mother arguing over which fat made a better crust, Crisco or lard?

Sophie blinked again. And the forest appeared before her. A nightmare? Yes, but regrettably real. The scent of iron clung to the back of her throat. She wiped her cheek and found blood on her hands. All that remained of the Guardian was a pile of fur and pulp moving around the base of Elen's feet. The pile issued a burst of canine wails, pain-filled and disjointed, broken vocal cords that had no form. The battle ended when all eyes turned in Elen's direction, to that ungodly sound, stupefied into submission by the unfamiliar.

Elen stood in the middle of the trail, unmoving except for tremors that racked her body. She stared down at her hands. Green moss formed at her feet and then began to spread in an outward circle, consuming rocks and roots, and growing up trees. She looked up and caught Sophie's gaze, her lower lip trembling in a silent cry for help. Tears shone like a river of anguish, leaving pink streaks through spatters of her victim's blood.

"Fuck me," one of the Guardians exclaimed, stepping away from the encroaching green circle, his sword falling from his hand to be engulfed in moss. "Did you see that? Siân spoke the truth."

"Someone . . . *grab* her," another ordered.

"*You* grab her. I'm not touching her."

A grumble of voices.

"The human killed Rhun. What should we do?" A stream of foreign words ensued, angry. An argument? The name Math was repeated but the rest was spoken in their original language. And then silence. A resolution?

"We'll take the human instead."

Sophie was focused on making her way toward Elen and Joshua, striking anything in her path: trees, arms, air, it didn't matter. Still dazed by loss, it was a second too late when she realized they were referring to *her*, because *she* was the only human left. Joshua yelled, "Mom, behind you." But it was too late.

Pain pierced her vision, and then nothing.

Twenty-eight

DYLAN EYED THE DESTRUCTION BEFORE HIM THROUGH A red haze of fear and rage. His forest reeked of death. Eighteen disembodied Guardians and two of his own lay strewn across the forest floor. The putrid scent of excrement and an unblessed violation of nature clung to the air in the aftermath of a Guardian attack. The Serpent of Cernunnos lay coiled on the ground, fed and satisfied, glinting with an unnatural glow and bloodred eyes.

And Sophie, his heart and his life, was nowhere to be seen.

Terror roiled like a thunderstorm in his gut. He lifted his head to the sky and shouted his torment, his wolf clawing to the surface to add its voice.

A gentle hand rested on his shoulder. "I'm sorry I didn't heed your warning, Dylan," Isabeau said. "If your mate is responsible for any of this . . . then she is not defenseless, even for a human." Her tone held both surprise and respect. She let her hand drop and scanned the area, her soft features made harsh with the proof that Dylan had spoken the truth.

Their time of peace had ended.

The leaders remained stoic; Madoc, Ryder, Drystan,

Daron and Isabeau gathered around the outer edge of the trail, the five that had come to help Dylan save his human wife, unprepared for what they found. Isabeau bent to retrieve the Serpent, pulling back with a hiss.

"Leave it," Dylan warned, counting heads from the fallen Guardians, knowing with a deadened heart that Sophie was responsible for most of their deaths. Also knowing that even when he found her, she would never again be the same. And neither would his son. "The Serpent belongs to my wife."

Joshua knelt before his grandmother's body, his gaze unfocused and clouded with shock. His sword, the one Dylan had given him just yesterday, lay beside him on the ground covered in Guardian blood.

Dylan's hands shook as he patted him down, needing to feel a warm and breathing response. "Are you hurt?"

"No." He spoke in monotone, his voice absent of his usual whimsical humor. "They took Mom. I tried to stop them . . ."

"They won't have her for long," Dylan assured him. He refused to contemplate any other outcome, not without losing his ability to breathe. "I will find your mother."

"And Grandma . . ." He looked up with darkness in his gaze, his innocence forever lost. "My grandma's dead."

"I know." Dylan lifted his son into a desperate embrace. He inhaled several deep breaths, savoring his very alive scent. Guilt pierced his heart like a poisoned lance.

He had brought Sophie and his son into this nightmare world. *He* was responsible for the darkness that now filled his son's soul. Francine was dead because *he* had allowed her to stay. And Sophie . . .

He shook his head, expelling images that threatened his sanity.

"And they killed Malsum too," Joshua said quietly.

Madoc stepped forward and removed his jacket. The other leaders followed, shedding their outer clothing to cover Francine and Malsum, two warriors who had proven their worth with the ultimate sacrifice.

Not concealing his approach, Luc pushed his way into

the clearing. With teeth bared, he scanned the destruction; his gaze lingered on Francine's covered body and then Malsum's. Burgundy streaks marred his naked chest. Cormack followed to stand by his side, his gait slowed by an injured leg, his fur blackened with blood, his left eye swollen shut. Michael was the last guard to arrive; he had kept to his human form, but was in no better condition than his comrades, his expression solemn.

Luc moved forward and placed a hand on Joshua's shoulder, a family united in the aftermath of death. "Another war has begun this day."

No one refuted his words.

With her hands fisted by her sides, Isabeau stood over Rhun's separated head. Indigo eyes searched the crowd, found Dylan's and held.

Her lips trembled, and for a fleeting second he recognized the girl who had stumbled upon his camp with a bloodied wolf cub in her arms, caked with filth and haunted by the death of her family.

"For this alone"—she waved her hand over Rhun's torso, her voice clogged with emotion—"I am in your mate's debt. I will join your alliance."

"Count me in as well," Drystan added. "No more innocents can die without retribution."

"Agreed," Daron vowed his allegiance, followed by growls of approval from Madoc and Ryder, the two leaders who had joined Dylan's cause without proof, a deed that would not be forgotten.

Dylan acknowledged each leader's promise with a nod. "Let our alliance begin now." He turned to his brother. "Tell us what you know."

"The Guardians came from New Hampshire under Math's orders. They entered our territory from the west." Luc sneered with disgust. "We were protecting the north, and the areas around the village and Rhuddin Hall. It appears Siân requested sanctuary and informed them of Elen's . . . *gift*." His silver gaze searched for their sister, his eyes widening with concern when he realized she wasn't there. "I don't believe they had any knowledge of the gathering. They were after Elen. But Siân knows us; she gave them insight into our area, into our routine."

Dylan absorbed that information, not caring how his brother had attained it. "There was another battle?"

A sharp nod. "In Crescent field."

"How many Guardians?"

"Twelve."

"Any still alive?"

"No."

"Any more casualties of our own?"

"Taran," Luc affirmed in a low growl. "And her daughter may soon follow her mother's fate." His wolf's voice was close to the surface, a deep rumble of anger and retribution. "I have taken them to the clinic. The child needs Elen or she won't be with us for long."

"Is the clinic secure?"

Silver eyes darkened. "It is now."

Nodding, Dylan turned to Joshua. "Have you seen your aunt? Do you know where she is?"

"She was here." His voice hitched. "Something happened. Something really weird. Like . . . I don't know . . . I can't even explain it. Aunt Elen ran away when the Guardians took Mom. I fought them but I was the only one left and they had about eighteen, I think. And Tucker went with those men, like he wanted to, barking and playing like he does with Mom. I think he was trying to distract them from me—"

"Shh," Dylan soothed, keeping his voice calm when his gut churned with fury and his wolf raged for release. "I'm proud of how you've defended yourself today, son. And we'll find your mother. But first I need to know where your aunt is. There's a child who needs her care. Can you remember in what direction she went?"

Turning in a circle to assess the area, Joshua stopped and then pointed to the north. "That way, I think."

Following the scent of summer, it didn't take long to track

her journey, with Luc and the others not far behind. He found his sister crumpled on the ground less than a mile away. He stopped short, holding out his arm for the others to remain where they were.

Nature and growth expanded in a sphere around her location. An oblong ball of fur and skin moved beside her, like a wolf-sized caterpillar emerging from a cocoon yet the membrane refused to break. Her hands pressed against her ears to block out a keening sound emanating from the pile of distorted flesh.

With lethal purpose, Dylan drew his sword. A bite of power hummed across his skin as he cautiously approached. He tasted metal on his tongue. Unsure about the location of the creature's head, he slashed down the center, slicing the pile of gore into segments until the disjointed sound ceased.

The silence seemed to ease Elen. Her hands fell to her lap. "Cormack," she whispered on a broken voice. "Find Cormack."

"He's here." The announcement came from Luc.

"Bring him to me."

Awareness tightened Dylan's spine. He knew then what she had done, he knew because he'd been the one who'd planted the idea in her head. *Perhaps it's time,* he had advised her just a few days ago, *to explore your gift beyond plants.* Elen had not meant to kill the Guardian; she had meant to take his humanity, his other half, and the separation of the human and wolf forms had not gone well.

And now she intended to give that other half of humanity to Cormack.

Dylan looked to what remained of the Guardian. Softly, he said, "I don't think that's a good idea, Elen."

"It's different when I give," she snapped. Wildflowers burst around her in rainbow hues; their petals bloomed and withered in a span of seconds, singed by her anger.

Hearing his name, the wolf limped through the gathered crowd of leaders with his right foreleg hugged to his chest. As he drew closer to Elen, he paused, staring at her mantle of green in a moment of doubt.

Elen stretched out her arms. "Please . . ."

Moved by her plea, he took that final step into her circle of power. And she pounced.

"Forgive me," she said, wrapping her arms around his body. Cormack shrieked, sending a ripple of unease through the leaders. The wolf stood frozen for the barest of seconds before his knees collapsed. He rolled onto his side, gripped by seizures. Elen tightened her hold.

The scent of elements filled the air, pure and uncluttered by evil, like fresh-cut grass in summer, or laughter from a child learning how to swim. Power built to a crescendo, different from that of her brothers, or any others of their kind.

Elen's power didn't take from nature; it gave, teased, offered pleasure beyond salvation. A growl emerged from one of the leaders, Ryder perhaps, and then a muffled curse as he lost control of his wolf and began to shift. Dylan resisted the pull, awed nonetheless by the visual affirmation of his sister's ability.

Cormack began to elongate. Fur receded into skin. Bone snapped and reformed. Tears streamed down Elen's face but her hold remained steady until a man filled her arms and not a wolf.

When the transformation was complete, when he saw clarity in his sister's gaze, when he saw a human body whole and unbroken in her arms, Dylan turned to his brother.

No verbal communication was needed.

"You're going after Sophie," Luc said.

"You will stay here and handle this." It wasn't a question. "Bring Francine and Malsum to the clinic along with Elen and Cormack." He paused. "Contact Malsum's tribe. Francine will be honored according to Sophie's wishes when we return."

Luc gave a low nod, accepting his role as leader of the Katahdin territory in Dylan's absence. Not a small favor, considering . . . "Math sent the Guardians to us," he said. "I would not be surprised if they headed straight back to the White Mountains. They're too arrogant to assume we'll actually follow."

"I know." And for the first time in sixteen hundred years, Dylan walked away from his siblings, his people, and his responsibility as their protector, and followed his heart. Before leaving, he gave his son a gentle squeeze around his chest, a final promise. "Stay with Luc. I will return with your mother before morning."

"I'm coming with you," he announced. "I know the White Mountains well. Believe me, Mom made me study every stupid map in this tristate region. I know how to find my way in and out of any area."

Dylan understood in that moment Sophie's fear, understood what it meant to be a parent, understood being willing to do anything, to sacrifice anything, for the protection of a life that meant more than his own.

He shook his head. "No, son, not this time."

"They took my mother." He lifted his chin with an air of determination. "They killed my grandmother. I can't just stay here and do nothing."

"Listen to me." Dylan closed both his palms around his son's face, forcing him to meet his gaze. "I need you here to help your uncle in my absence. I need you to lead our people, to protect them." *I need you to be safe.* "Can you do that for me?"

Frustration and anger filled their embrace; anger from Joshua, frustration from Dylan. Slowly, Joshua's tension began to ease as he understood what his father was asking of him, a response of a true warrior and not a boy. With a nod, he closed his eyes and growled, "Just bring Mom home."

"I will," Dylan promised, letting his hands drop.

With an edge of anticipation, Madoc stepped forward. "Let's get going, shall we?" He snorted at Dylan's puzzled glare. "As if I would let you have all the fun without me."

"I'm coming as well," Isabeau added with more seriousness.

A brown wolf sauntered next to Isabeau, nodding his intention to join them. Ryder had been the only leader to shift, his brow furrowed as he snuck wary glances in Elen's direction.

"Aw, hell," Drystan muttered. "Let's do this."

Twenty-nine

SOPHIE TRIED TO MOVE, TO TURN, BUT FELT RESISTANCE biting into her wrists. Her head hurt. Why did her head hurt? And where was she? She tried to open her eyes but her lids felt heavy, as if she'd taken an entire bottle of sleeping pills and only had an hour's worth of sleep.

And then bits of memory poked at her subconscious. The children. Joshua. Elen. Her mother.

Her breath hitched in her throat. *Oh, God, Mum . . .*

Her heart pounded against her chest in a vicious on-slaught of awareness. Sophie recalled every horrific detail, right until that last moment when the Guardian had hit her from behind.

They must have taken her. But where?

Her legs were numb, unresponsive. That was the first sensation that pressed through her panicked haze.

They must have drugged her.

With what? And what was that god-awful smell? The scent of iron, rot and mildew coated her throat, triggered a gag. She fought against the cobwebs that muddled her thoughts with some success. Awareness came to her in flashes; a continuous drip echoed off the walls, something soft by her calf, cold air and high ceilings, dirt under her sneakers. She was in a room that echoed sound and seeped moisture, a room with a dirt floor that reeked of dampness and death. A basement?

The warmth at her leg moved. Something wet pressed against her arm, followed by a soft whine, then a tug on her sleeve. Tucker? They had allowed Tucker to follow, to stay?

Movement came from her right, a warning.

"I know you are awake." It was a man's voice, deep and refined, devoid of any discernible accent.

Adrenaline rushed through her veins and fought against the poison that inhibited her response. She tried to speak but her words came out garbled. After several attempts, she managed to say, "What did you give me?"

"You will not ask questions, human."

Willing her eyes to open, Sophie began to glimpse her surroundings through her drugged fog. Gas lanterns provided the only light. Iron restraints, polished to shine like treasured toys, hung off stone walls. Crude furniture filled the room, half tables with holes, steel chairs with vise grips for arms and legs. Something scurried through an arched doorway to an inner chamber.

The face behind the voice came into semi-focus, pallid and shrunken. Wearing a dark suit, he stood hunched over a staff carved from knotted wood, using it more for balance than anything magical. A white haze covered silver eyes, much like the Guardian Rhun, though not as stark, not as completely immersed in evil. There was intelligence in his gaze, awareness.

And anger, a deep anger that bled from his pores as he looked to Tucker, then her. "The hound protects you. Why?" When she didn't immediately respond, he slammed down his staff; the thud of wood on packed earth resonated off the walls. "Answer me, human!"

Tucker gave a deep, rumbling growl, his shoulders down, his gaze primed on the Guardian.

"I am your master," the Guardian informed Tucker, who responded with a snarl, moving forward, teeth bared in warning.

The man flinched as if betrayed. Without further comment, he backed out of the room. The door closed with a groan of heavy wood held by old hinges. The sound of scraping metal followed. Muffled voices raised in anger filtered through the door.

She was locked in, tied to a chair. Her eyes drifted closed, still drugged, still heavy. She couldn't keep them open no matter how hard she tried.

God help me, she prayed as the darkness claimed her once more.

"HUSH, PLEASE HUSH, I WILL NOT HURT YOUR MIS-tress."

The feminine voice pulled Sophie awake, soft but with a frantic edge of urgency. She became aware of Tucker's low growl and a tug at her wrists. Pain shot up her arm and she flinched.

Her senses were suddenly sharp, no longer muddled. *Good,* she thought. Whatever the hell they had given her must be wearing off.

"Call off the hound," the woman whispered from behind. "I'm here to help you."

Not questioning this stranger, not yet, not until her arms were free, Sophie swallowed, cleared her throat. "Tucker, heel."

When Tucker sauntered to her side, the woman said with quiet surprise, "So, it's true. The hound protects you."

"Where am I?"

A slight hesitation. "You're in the White Mountains, territory of the Guardian Math." Another tug, followed by a sigh. "Hold still."

With a snap of leather on metal, Sophie felt the binding give and her wrists loosen. Disabled with disuse, her arms fell to her sides, numb and powerless. She flexed her fingers, turned her wrists, grinding her teeth against the burning sensation of blood returning to her extremities.

The woman walked around to face Sophie with a swish of dark skirts. She was curved, not athletic like Siân and Taran, her chest rising and falling with rapid breaths of nervousness. She was smaller than most Guardians, at least the ones that Sophie had seen, with wolf eyes the color of purple pansies, striated with streaks of blue and burgundy. Her hair hung to her waist like burnished brass in the flickering light. She looked no older than her early twenties but that meant nothing.

"Who are you?" Sophie asked.

"My name is Rosa. My husband is Math. You met him earlier although you may not remember."

"I remember." The age difference, as much as the betrayal, took her by surprise. "Why are you helping me?"

Rosa lifted her chin. "I have a message for you to give to Dylan."

Wary, Sophie managed to keep her voice neutral. "What is your message?"

"Tell Dylan I know of the gathering. Tell him I will be in his territory sometime before Beltane, and that I am coming in peace and without my husband's knowledge. Tell him I have a proposal. Will you do this?"

She didn't ask how Rosa had known of the gathering, not wanting to indicate there had been one. "I will give Dylan your message."

"One more thing," Rosa added. "Tell him he owes me."

"For what?"

A calculating smile turned her lips. "For saving your life."

Sophie only nodded, choosing not to argue with a woman offering freedom. The price of that freedom could be negotiated when she was home with her family. Grabbing the arm of the chair for balance, she hauled herself into a standing position, working the muscles in her legs until her circulation returned. A dark stain drew her gaze to the arched doorway. The stench, she realized, emanated from the inner chamber beyond. "What's in that room?"

Rosa followed the direction of Sophie's gaze. "Siân came to Math for sanctuary." She did not refer to Math as her husband, or her mate, or with any form of affinity whatsoever.

"What are you saying?"

"Siân spent too many years with a kind leader. She forgot our ways . . ." Her voice trailed off.

Sickened, Sophie turned. "Is Siân in that room?"

"Don't—" Rosa grabbed her arm when she took a step toward the chamber. "There's naught you can do for her now. Siân's dead."

She glared down at her arm. "Dead?"

Rosa dropped her hand. "I heard she handled Math's interrogation with honor and strength."

"His interrogation? You mean torture!"

"Lower your voice," Rosa hissed, pointing to the inner chamber, silent and pleading. "Or we will both follow Siân's fate."

Sophie swallowed her reply in silence, survival instincts overpowering her conscience. Taking a deep breath and almost gagging on the stench, she gave a sharp nod for Rosa to continue.

"Let Dylan know I don't believe Siân spoke of the gathering. I know Math well." *Too well*, her tone suggested. "He would have acted differently had he known." She went on to say, "It wasn't until the end that Siân told them of Elen. And from the rumors circling our halls of what Elen did to Minka . . ." A smile of respect turned her lips. "It may have been Siân's final vengeance on us."

Perhaps it was, for Sophie had seen the way the villagers had treated Elen in the basement; they feared her, and for good reason. "I will let Dylan know."

With a nod, she unlocked the chamber door and motioned for Sophie to follow. "Come."

A man stood outside, pointing to a maze of hallways lit by torches, his face knotted with scars. A jeweled patch covered his left eye; his right eye scanned Sophie with blatant contempt. "Is it true your son is a shifter?" he asked.

His voice tagged a memory, no longer muffled but still familiar. It was the voice from outside the door when Math had visited earlier. The guard, it seemed, was more loyal to Rosa than to her husband. There was dissension in this household.

Good.

"Yes," Sophie said. Lying was pointless now.

His one eye, dark gray surrounded by scarred flesh, lifted over Sophie's shoulder to where Rosa stood. "Then you are no longer the last."

"I am the last unmated *female* shifter. It won't change the Council's plans." Tucker sauntered past Sophie and rubbed his nose inside Rosa's palm before moving toward the hallway. Rosa jumped, her wary gaze following the hound.

"What do they have planned for you?" Sophie found herself asking, even though it was none of her business.

Unsurprisingly, Rosa ignored her question. "Can you run?"

A sardonic smile tugged her lips. "Yeah, I can run."

"Take a left at every doorway. There will be a tunnel that opens behind our burial grounds. You'll be surrounded by rivers. Go north until the rivers meet. There is a shallow point where you can cross. I'll do what I can to distract Math but you must hurry." Her eyes darkened to an inhuman color of burgundy mixed with blue that reflected purple in the surrounding torchlight. A wolf resided not too far under the surface of this woman's skin. Those otherworldly eyes landed on Sophie, threatening yet desperate. "And remember our agreement."

SOPHIE EMERGED FROM THE NARROW DIRT TUNNEL AND took her first breath of clean air. Immediately, she scanned her surroundings for movement and found none, then smoothed a hand over her hair and face to remove cobwebs from her climb. It was dark, the moon a mere haze in the sky, blurred by clouds. Grave tombs stood like sentries in the night, casting shadows on the ground and concealing the secret exit.

It reminded her of the graveyards in New Orleans, rows of dank stone structures covered in mold, with the dead resting in their afterlife above ground. It was an unusual sight in a northern town, and even more unusual for a commune of immortal Celts. She could only assume the water level in this particular area must be quite high, or something other than the dead resided in those tombs.

And she didn't intend to stay and find out what. Tucker emerged like a white apparition from the narrow exit, his stance alert, silently scanning the darkness. Without pause, she listened for the sound of running water and tracked the nearest river upstream. Once she gained some distance, she began to run. Tucker kept in cadence with her strides.

Trees stood tall yet weakened, their roots exposed due to an eroded forest floor. Soon, one river merged with another, two sources of water that forked around Rosa's secluded parcel of land. Just beyond the point where the two rivers merged, there was, as Rosa had promised, a trail of exposed rocks. The water flowed in steady currents but seemed shallow enough to cross.

Pausing by the river's edge, Sophie spared a glance at the hound. "I hope you can keep up, Tuck." A disgruntled canine huff reached her ears as she plunged forward. The water seeped through her jeans and found her skin, so cold it stole her breath. Tucker kept pace through the fast-moving currents, but just as they reached the other side, he looked to the woods and issued a soft whine.

A flash of blue, too vivid to be natural, caught her eye then disappeared.

Her heart sank. Mind racing, adrenaline pumping, she scanned the darkness and found a fallen log, rotted on one side. Low brush, thick and tangled, grew along the shoreline. She began to wade toward the covering.

Tucker barked and she cringed. She dared not speak to chastise him. But then a voice, a familiar voice she would recognize in every dream, over any man, and for the rest of her life, echoed from the forest.

She almost crumpled with relief.

"Tucker," Dylan said. "Is that you? Where's Sophie? Can you bring me to Sophie?"

With a cry, Sophie crawled her way out of the water, stumbling to gain purchase on dry land, and ran toward the sound of her husband's voice. Dylan halted for a second when she came crashing through the brush, but then let out a growl and met her halfway.

"Sophie . . ." His hands were in her hair, patting her down, and then around her waist, lifting until her feet left the ground. She wrapped her legs around him, buried her face in the warmth of his neck and began to sob.

"Is Joshua okay?" She asked through broken breaths, almost unable to bear the answer.

"He's safe, my love." Dylan nuzzled her neck, then sought her lips in a desperate kiss that bared his soul as he shuddered in response. "He's home, waiting for us."

Relief made her sag in his arms, but once the tears came they wouldn't stop. "My mother . . ."

"I know. I'm sorry, Sophie. I'm so sorry." Dylan began to walk, carrying her in his arms. She told him about Math, about Siân, how Rosa had helped her escape. She gave him Rosa's message. He remained silent, listening.

"Where are we going?" she finally asked.

"Home," he said. "We're going home."

It wasn't until they cleared the trail that she realized they were not alone. Too tired to ask questions, she tucked her face in the crook of his neck and inhaled the scent of safety.

hirty

THE PAIN WAS LIKE A FISTFUL OF HEATED NEEDLES shoved under her skin, greater than anything Merin had ever done to Elen in her childhood. Power did not like to be contained. It wanted release. Unfortunately, her body was the vessel that held it. Her nerves screamed with its force.

Elen winced as she undid the latch of the iron gate Koko had designed for her, an intricate weave of faeries on lilies that offered both beauty and privacy. Following the stone path, she stumbled toward the hidden gardens behind her beautiful little house. She regulated her breaths through clenched teeth, much like modern childbirth techniques.

With a broken moan of relief, after a day full of suspicious glances and avoidance from the villagers, Elen finally allowed the power to consume her. She collapsed in a bed of anise hyssop and let its vengeful pressure bleed from her skin and into the ground. Purple flowers bloomed around her and a licorice scent filled the air like a basketful of candy, offering treats and bellyaches of a more noxious variety.

The villagers thought she was this power-hungry freak,

when in fact she was only a conductor, a mere rod of transference. She was a puppet of a merciless master, no more in control now than when it had first begun, when the gods had reached out their hands of vengeance with their unwanted gift.

Afterward, when the transference passed, she wept. If the villagers knew how much it hurt, would they be more understanding? *Doubtful,* she mused bitterly. Francine and Taran were dead because of her. And Cormack . . .

A ragged breath fell from her lips.

An ivy leaf broke ground through the hyssop, nourished by her tears, and reached for her cheek as if to console her. She ripped it from the earth until life drained from its roots. She knew when it died, because she *felt* it.

She *was* a freak. But not a power-hungry one. Never that. If possible, she would give her gift away, but her conscience wouldn't allow her to curse another soul with this burden.

Melissa is alive, she reminded herself, because of her ability to take life and transfer it to another source. Her ability had its purpose, a purpose she had just begun to learn. Still, Taran's mate had refused to see his child until Elen left the clinic, more afraid of her than a Gwarchodwyr. They had been frightened of her before, and now . . .

Even Cormack refused to see her. He had changed back to his wolf form and growled every time she approached.

She had never felt more alone.

A brush of movement caught her eye. Before she could react, warm arms enclosed her. For a moment she was hopeful, for a moment she thought it was Cormack until ebony hair cascaded around her, distinctly familiar and *brotherly.*

"Luc, what are you doing here?" She tried to push him away but he only gathered her closer.

"Tell me what I can do for you, Elen."

Shaking her head helplessly, she said, "There is nothing."

"Are you hurt?"

"No."

"You've been avoiding your family," he accused softly. "Sophie's been asking to see you."

Knowing her new sister was safe and home gave Elen some comfort. She snuggled closer to her brother's warmth. "Does she hate me?"

"Hate you?" She heard the frown in his voice, the confusion. "No, Elen, Sophie doesn't hate you. Your actions saved her son. You did what you had to do to save our nephew. You are not to blame for the actions of the Guardians. Sophie knows that."

Elen rubbed her sleeve across her face, drying her tears. Her brother thought like a warrior, not a healer. Still, his words soothed her. "I'll come to the house tomorrow morning."

"Come now," he coaxed, tightening his arms. "Or Dylan will return to get you himself. His wife is grieving. Don't make him chase after you when he should be with her."

Guilt was a powerful persuader. "Fine." She stood, bending forward to brush dirt off her slacks, a well-used trick to hide a sudden twinge of discomfort. She felt bruised internally, never before having pulled the life-force from another living animal. It had taken its toll on her body. "I'll go see them now." She hid the weariness from her voice. "Have you seen Cormack?"

A slight hesitation. "I have."

"Is he well? Every time I go near him . . ." Her voice broke, revealing her emotions.

"Cormack needs time. He needs to learn how to be a man. He doesn't know how to walk on two feet, let alone speak."

"I don't care about him being a man." She sounded like a pouty teenager but she truly didn't care. She missed Cormack. She missed her friend more than the air that she breathed.

"He does," Luc said with an odd tone to his voice. "For you, sister, he cares."

* * *

THE FOLLOWING NIGHT, WHILE HIS WIFE SLEPT IN THEIR bed, exhausted with grief, Dylan returned to the White Mountains alone. Normally, it was a four-hour drive, but on this night he didn't obey traffic rules, and it only took three. Math's home was located in Avon, New Hampshire, an hour north of the more touristy areas, and, unfortunately, closer to Maine. Dylan often sent one of his guards to Avon to pose as a vacationer, to fish and secretly gather information. In passing, the townspeople described Math as an "eccentric recluse" and "a generous man"—meaning he donated large sums of money to the local government and charities to be left undisturbed.

The Guardian's home, aptly named Castell Avon, or the River Castle, sat in a section of forest effectively surrounded by two separate rivers. Unlike the rivers in Maine, these were shallow but wide. Only one bridge allowed pedestrians access to the island. A carriage house built of stone and iron secured the entrance to the bridge, guarded by Math's men.

Dylan traveled farther north, where he had found Sophie, and crossed the river on foot. He carried an oblong pack that held his sword and a change of clothes. Once dry, he discarded his pack and wet clothes within a rotting stump. With sword in hand, he finished his journey in the shadows of trees. Castell Avon soon came into view. It sat within a section of cleared forest, as ostentatious as the Guardian who lived inside its stone walls.

Too easily, Dylan found the graveyard his wife had described with the hidden passage. A foreboding chill crawled over his skin while skirting around the rows of neglected tombs, like the hands of a dark witch bartering potions for a favor. Bodies of dead slaves, he assumed, were massed in the unmarked graves—poor souls who had suffered under the Guardian's control, only to end up rotting above ground in their afterlife.

A dull ache began to form around his joints and limbs

as his inner wolf growled, sensing danger or, more likely, the residual of misused power.

Focusing on his objective, he gained access through the concealed tunnel, wary once again that Rosa had shared this weakness of her home. Not for the first time, he questioned what Math's wife was about, what her demands would be for freeing Sophie, and how she had known of the gathering. He suspected one of the leaders had leaked her information, but did not discount the possibility of a spy among his people. Either way, he wasn't pleased and would uncover the traitor.

The air inside the castle reeked of mildew and discontent. Guards in street clothes walked the halls, eyes heavy and easily distracted, faithless and uncaring of their master's safety. Complacent.

Only a single woman noticed his approach, cleaning before dawn, pausing as she swept below the staircase. She wore modern clothes but watched him with the eyes of a slave, hooded yet sharp. She had survived a fire or something worse, unable, he assumed, to shift and heal afterward. Scars ran along her face and neck. Her hair grew in clumps, exposing bare patches of scalp with knotted flesh over destroyed follicles. She quickly looked away, too broken to shout an alarm, or too afraid of being the bringer of bad news.

Inwardly, Dylan sneered at the very idea of keeping slaves, the *Hen Was*, descendants of their kind who couldn't shift, as vile in modern day as in medieval Cymru.

The bedchambers were easy to find. Sounds, sexual and aggressive, came from a door at the end of a long corridor.

"It's locked," a feminine voice whispered.

He turned to see the slave lurking in the shadows, having followed him in silence and without detection. His initial assessment of this woman immediately changed. If she was going to raise an alarm, she would have done so by now. Yet, if her spirit was broken, she wouldn't have followed.

He shrugged. This was a minor obstacle for what he'd come to do. "A single slave and a locked door won't hold me."

"You are Dylan ap Merin."

"Yes."

A curious glint sharpened her glare. "I see death in your eyes, warrior, but also honor. Is it Math you've come to claim, or our Rosa?"

"Math." Denial, he sensed, would only delay his intent.

A contorted smile turned the unscarred side of her mouth. "Then you are correct . . . this single slave and a locked door won't keep you from your task. But I will have your word you'll not harm our mistress."

"Or what?" he challenged.

"*For* what," she corrected, holding up a stainless steel key, an oddity amongst a manufactured illusion of medieval grandeur. "Take who you've come for, warrior, and leave the others be."

"Agreed," he said, and accepted the key as the slave hurried away. The lock was new and well-oiled, turning without detectable sound, even to his ears. The visitors to this room came often and were not meant to be heard.

Dylan slid into the chamber, not overly surprised by what he found. With Rhun now gone, Math was one of the eleven remaining Original Guardians; old when he'd been gifted by the Goddess and even older now, with a rumored preference for beautiful men.

Those rumors were correct, it seemed, since it was a young man, and not Rosa, who was being thoroughly and joyfully buggered by Math.

The young man, thin and elegant, was bent over the back of a chaise longue, his eyes squeezed shut and his head thrown back in openmouthed pleasure. Math knelt at the foot of the chaise, gripping his lover's long red hair like reins, his eyes glazed and unfocused in feral joy, pounding, bare-assed, pasty and wrinkled and unaware.

Without remorse, Dylan used their distraction to his

advantage. Walking silently behind Math, he raised his sword, balanced his weight, and swung.

"For my wife," he said as the Guardian's head toppled to the side and his body remained suspended until his lover fell forward, tangled in hysteric disbelief.

With a gurgle of horror, the man scrambled to the floor, wide-eyed and knees drawn, trying to hedge backward like a spider without its web. He opened his mouth, chest rising with frantic breaths.

Dylan pressed the bloodied sword to his throat. "Make one noise to alert the guards and you will die." The man swallowed his scream. "Give the Guardians a message. I am Dylan ap Merin, leader of the Katahdin territory. Whoever comes to my territory with ill intent . . . will die. Whoever brings danger to my family . . . will die."

Dylan left without further incident. The lover did not scream nor did the slave hinder his departure. He arrived back at Rhuddin Village around seven in the morning, with his wife still abed. He settled in next to her, molding her soft body against his chest, and placed a kiss on her exposed shoulder.

She sighed, half awake, snuggling into his warmth. "Where have you been?"

"Fulfilling a promise," he whispered. "Go back to sleep, my love."

Thirty-one

THREE DAYS LATER, ON THE FIRST CLOUDLESS MORNING
since the gathering, Dylan stood next to his wife and son as
Francine's casket was lowered into the ground next to her
husband's. Dylan shook his head with reverence, wondering
if the woman had convinced her angels to harness the sun
to shine down upon her own service.

Luc had remained at home, as did most of the other
guards, but Enid, Porter, and the parents of the children
from the village had traveled to Massachusetts, Sophie's
place of birth.

The minister had long since said his blessing and left.
With Sophie's permission, some of his people dropped trea-
sures next to the grave for Francine to bring to her afterlife.
Enid gave a golden spoon, placing it gently in the roses that
covered the casket, with a blessing for Francine to "Wield
it well." That spoon, Dylan knew, had been the only treasure
Enid had carried from Cymru.

"I'm going to wait in the truck," Joshua said after the
others had returned to their cars for the journey home, leaving his parents alone.

"Okay." Sophie squeezed his hand as he passed. "We'll only stay a few more minutes."

Shaking with what he was about to do, Dylan wrapped his arms around his wife and kissed the top of her head. "Taliesin came to see me this morning."

"He did?" He heard the frown in her voice. "What did he want?"

"Your forgiveness, I think."

"Then it's me he should be visiting, not you."

"He's here, Sophie."

Her head shot up, scanning the cemetery, stopping when she found the lone figure in the distance. "Has he been here this whole time?"

"Yes." Dylan briefly closed his eyes, unable to watch her face when he made the most difficult offer of his life. "Taliesin has agreed to reopen his home where you and Joshua once lived."

"For what?"

"For you." His throat thickened, choking on the words, not sure if he could finish this but knowing he must. "And Joshua, if he wants to go. Taliesin has agreed to stay with you, to continue Joshua's training. If you wish, you can leave with him now."

"And where will you be?"

"Rhuddin Village."

"What is this about?"

"It's a choice, Sophie. A choice to leave now before the Council decides our fate." Opening his eyes, he waved his hand toward her mother's grave. "This is only the beginning. One of four lives we've lost. Others *will* follow."

Understanding hardened her features, like snow over a mountain, insurmountable to the weak of heart. But he wasn't weak, and neither was she. "And you would do this? You would allow me to leave?"

He leaned his forehead against hers. "If it will keep you alive, Sophie, I will do more than you know."

She wiped at her eyes as fresh tears began to fall.

Amazing, really, that she had any left when she'd shed enough over the last few days to fill a river in autumn, enough that his heart had bled a bit with every single one, drop for drop.

Darkness closed around him. "I'll do my best to stay away from you—"

"Stop." A watery smile turned her lips. "*Please*, just stop this right now! Thank you, Dylan, for giving me the choice." She lifted her hands and cupped his face. "Do you want to know something my mother said to me a few days before she died?"

He didn't respond, not sure that he did.

She continued anyway. "Mum told me she'd rather live her life to the fullest, around the people she loved, than fear the unknown alone."

He frowned. "What are you saying?"

"It's not the Council who's going to decide our fate. It's us, our family, and our people. *Together* we will decide our fate, while we live our lives around the people we love most. And for me, Dylan, that's you. I choose you."

Robbed of breath, he kissed her because he could do nothing else. "I won't ask you again," he warned against her mouth. It was a long while before he lifted his head, shaking with emotion in a bloody graveyard no less, with a demi-god pouting in the distance.

"So," she said, resting her face against his chest, "did our son put you up to this?"

He smiled against her hair. "He told me you wouldn't agree to it."

"That little shit." Then she laughed her first genuine laugh in three days. "Did that make it any easier for you?"

"Maybe a little," he said, though serious. "But I've learned not to predict how your mind works, *wife*. I would have honored your choice. Well," he amended, "I would have *tried* to the best of my ability."

And to prove that he may never know how her mind worked, she stood on her toes and planted another kiss on his lips. "Will you marry me again?" she asked softly. "With a minister this time. I want our family there as well. Invite the whole town if you wish." She reflected quietly for a moment. "My mum would have wanted that."

His throat tightened. He had to swallow twice before he found his voice. "Is today too soon?"

The End and the Beginning

TALIESIN WAITED IN A SHADED GLEN FOR SOPHIE AND Dylan to make their way toward him. He looked out at all the grave markers, aisles of marble and granite honoring their beloved deceased souls. They were at peace, he knew with envy, in the home of their God. Peace was something he would never know, just as heaven was a place he would never see.

With a final glance toward Francine's grave, Sophie and Dylan made their way in Taliesin's direction, hand in hand, joined in heart and in purpose, a marriage made whole by his intervention.

Taliesin heard Dylan ask, "Are you sure you want to do this?"

"I'm sure." Sophie stopped a few feet away, her eyes direct and searching. "Hello, Matthew. I wish you had joined us for the service."

Suddenly nervous, despite knowing the outcome of this day, he kicked at a clump of grass, his gaze looking to the ground. "My name is Taliesin," he said.

"I know. My husband has told me everything about you. Is that what you want me to call you?"

"My friends call me Sin," he offered.

"Are you my friend?"

"Yes." He made sure his tone carried the weight of that curse.

"Will you tell me something, Sin?"

He sighed with regret. "Of course, Sophie, but you already know the answer."

"Why did you give me the Serpent?"

"Because it wasn't Francine who was supposed to die." Whenever he changed the course of a human's fate, another always took their place.

"Was it supposed to be me?" Her voice was heavy with guilt at the thought.

"No."

A whisper of acceptance. "Joshua."

He remained silent.

Gently, Sophie placed her hand on his arm. "Do you have a place to stay?"

He shrugged. "I have many homes, Sophie."

"Will you be alone in these many homes?" she asked, ever observant as only someone with a pure heart could be.

"I'm used to being alone."

She pursed her lips at her husband's snort. "I want you to stay with us."

To his shame, because his heart rejoiced in the warmth of her embrace, of family and forgiveness, he was tempted to accept her offer. Shaking his head, he whispered, "I shouldn't."

"No, you shouldn't," Dylan agreed, but then his eyes met his wife's. After a small wordless argument, his shoulders sagged in weary acceptance. "If it will make my wife happy . . . you are welcome to stay with us. Our lake house is available."

And so will Luc's apartments soon be, when Rosa comes

to claim Dylan's debt owed to her for helping Sophie, but Taliesin kept that foresight to himself.

"I've never seen greater courage, warrior, than I've seen from you this day. I will consider your offer."

"A war has begun," Dylan said with firm censure. "A war between the very creatures created to protect you. One of these days you will have to choose a side."

"Ah, Dylan." Taliesin shook his head, using the warrior's given name as an acceptance of friendship. "Don't you realize . . . I've already chosen a side. And the side I've chosen is yours."

The warrior winced, because, unlike his wife, Dylan understood the danger that Taliesin's friendship carried.

Glossary of Terms and Characters

 = Character   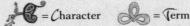 = Term

---

ANNWFN; OTHERWORLD

Homeland of the Welsh Celtic deities, similar to *sídh* of Irish mythology, where the *Tuatha Dé Danann* reside, the land of faery and magical beings.

BEDDESTYR; WALKER

Once messengers to Ceridwen in the Otherworld; four known Walkers still exist, all have lost their power to walk between worlds.

BELTANE; MAY DAY

A Celtic holiday to celebrate the beginning of summer. Ancient Celts believed that the barrier between our world and the Otherworld opened this day and that the Gods visited to bestow fertility blessings.

Bleidd; Wolf

A Guardian descendant born or trapped in wolf form who cannot change to human; human intelligence exists within the wolf.

Ceridwen; Celtic Goddess

Welsh Celtic goddess, worshiped by ancient Celts as the great sow goddess; though less recognized, Ceridwen was also revered as the goddess of wolves; known to brew potions of transformation and knowledge; master of animal transformation; birth mother of Taliesin.

Cernunnos; Celtic God

Welsh Celtic Lord of Animals; worshiped by ancient Celts as the Great Hunter; commonly depicted in Celtic artifacts with horned animals, such as the horned snake of Celtic tradition, and the stag; honored by ancient Celts as the leader of the Wild Hunt where spirits of the dead were carried to the Otherworld.

Cormack

Brother of Siân and Taran; close friend of Elen; born in wolf form without the ability to transform to human; human intelligence exists within the wolf.

COUNCIL OF CERIDWEN; GOVERNING ASSEMBLY OF ORIGINAL GUARDIANS

A self-proclaimed governing body compiled by the twelve surviving Original Guardians.

CYMRU; WALES

Homeland of the Original Guardians.

DARON

Leader of the Ontario territory; views the Original Guardians with disdain.

DEWISEDIG; CHOSEN HUMAN

A human mate of a Guardian or Guardian descendant whose offspring can transform into a wolf.

DRWGDDYDDWG; EVIL BRINGER

A derogatory description of Guardian descendants born in human form without the ability to transform into a wolf. The name was created by Original Guardians, fearful of their loss of power.

DRYSTAN

Leader of the Blue Ridge Highland territory of Virginia; views the Original Guardians with disdain.

DYLAN (AD 329–)

The alpha wolf and leader of the Katahdin territory; husband and mate of Sophie; father of Joshua; eldest brother of Luc and Elen; son of Merin.

ELEN (AD 331–)

The healer of the Katahdin territory; sister of Dylan and Luc; daughter of Merin; cannot shift into a wolf but can manipulate nature.

ENID

Mother of Sulwen and Lydia; housekeeper of Rhuddin Hall; taught Dylan how to care for Luc, who was born in wolf form.

FRANCINE

Mother of Sophie; human.

GICI NIWASKW; GREAT SPIRIT

The deity of the Abanaki people, the natives of the Katahdin region.

GWARCHODWYR; GUARDIAN

Descendants of Original Guardians who follow the command of the Council of Ceridwen.

GWARCHODWYR UNFED; GUARDIAN, FIRST IN ORDER; THE ORIGINALS

An Original Celtic warrior appointed by Ceridwen to protect her son Taliesin; taught how to draw energy from the earth to transform into wolves; served Taliesin as a child; age at a very slow rate. The oldest surviving Original Guardian was born 95 BC. There were forty-eight Original Guardians; only twelve remain to form the Council of Ceridwen.

HEN WAS; OLD SERVANT

Slaves to the Original Guardians and the Council; Guardian descendants born without the ability to transform into a wolf; age at the same slow rate of an Original Guardian.

ISABEAU

Leader of the forest region of Minnesota; family was tortured and killed in the house of Rhun while serving the Original Guardians.

JOSHUA (AD 1995–)

Son of Dylan and Sophie; the first shifter born in over 300 years.

KALEM

Leader of Alaskan territory; views the Original Guardians with disdain.

KOKO (AD 1868–AD 1946)

Luc's deceased wife and mate of choice; her works of art are displayed throughout Rhuddin Hall.

LLARA

One of four leaders who occupy the territories of Russia; views the Original Guardians with disdain.

LUC (AD 342–)

Youngest brother of Dylan and Elen; son of Merin; husband of the late Koko; banished at birth by his mother for being born in wolf form; raised by Dylan; known as the Beast of Merin.

LYDIA

Daughter of Enid; sister of Sulwen; works in the kitchen of Rhuddin Hall; cannot transform into a wolf.

THE MABINOGION

Also referred to as *The Mabinogi*; a collection of Celtic folklore from medieval Welsh manuscripts, including *The White Book of Rhydderch* and *The Red Book of Hergest*. The first translation of *The Mabinogion* into English was by Lady Charlotte Guest in the mid-nineteenth century.

MADOC

Leader of the mountain regions of Montana; captained the ship that brought Luc, Elen and Dylan to the New World; views the Original Guardians with disdain.

MADRON

An Original Guardian killed by Taliesin; had a sexual preference for preadolescent girls. His death was witnessed by Elen and Leri as children; at the time of Madron's death, Leri was his current victim.

MAELORWEN

A witch who lived in the hills when Dylan
and Elen were children; taught Elen the
medicinal uses of plants; the first
Guardian descendant born without the
ability to shift; tortured by the Guardians;
currently resides with Rosa in the White
Mountains territory of New Hampshire.

MALSUM

Second in command under Luc in Dylan's
guard.

MATH

An Original Guardian; leader of the
White Mountains territory of New
Hampshire; husband of Rosa; loyal to the
Council of Ceridwen.

MATTHEW

See Taliesin.

MELISSA

Daughter of Taran; niece of Cormack and
Siân; four years old.

MERIN

An Original Guardian;
mother of Dylan, Elen and
Luc; resides in Wales as a
member of the Council
of Ceridwen.

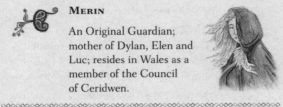

NIA

Leader of the northern New York territory;
views the Original Guardians with disdain.

PENTEULU; HEAD OF FAMILY

Leader of a territory; alpha wolf.

PORTER (AD 1682–)

Head of home security of Rhuddin Hall of
the Katahdin territory; has a tattoo of a
Celtic cross in honor of his Irish mother;
cannot transform into a wolf.

RHUDDIN; HEART OF TIMBER

The name Dylan chose for his territory,
located around Katahdin, the highest
mountain peak in Maine; the northern end
of the Appalachian Trail.

RHUN

An Original Guardian.

ROSA ALBAN (AD 1702–)

Wife of Math; leader of the White
Mountains territory of New Hampshire;
the last unmated female shifter.

SERPENT OF CERNUNNOS

A flexible sword in the shape of
Cernunnos's horned snake, forged in the
Otherworld as a gift for Taliesin. The
wearer of the Serpent is given a
heightened perception of their
surroundings and a connection to beings
of the Otherworld.

SIÂN

Dylan's ex-lover; eldest sister of Taran and
Cormack; threatened a pregnant Sophie in
the woods the night Sophie left Dylan; the
woman who gave Sophie her scars.

SIN

See Taliesin.

SOPHIE (AD 1975–)

Wife and mate of Dylan; mother of Joshua;
daughter of Francine; the first human to
give birth to a shifter in over 300 years; her
aging process has slowed since carrying
Dylan's child.

SULWEN

Daughter of Enid; sister of Lydia; works in the kitchen of Rhuddin Hall; cannot transform into a wolf.

TALIESIN; "SIN" (42 BC–)

Son of Ceridwen; possesses powers of transformation and prophecy; uses the current alias Matthew Ayres; Sophie's former employer. Taliesin spent much of the medieval ages intoxicated; therefore, it was during this time that many stories of his antics were documented by humans. Though the Original Guardians were assigned by his birth mother as protectors, Taliesin views most of them with disdain.

TARAN

Sister of Siân and Cormack; mother of Melissa; a valued member of Dylan's guard.

FROM *NEW YORK TIMES* BESTSELLING AUTHOR

Ilona Andrews

MAGIC SLAYS

➤➤ **A KATE DANIELS NOVEL** ⇐

Kate Daniels may have quit the Order of Knights of
Merciful Aid, but she's still knee-deep in paranormal
problems. Or she would be if she could get someone
to hire her. Starting her own business has been more
challenging than she thought it would be—now that
the Order is disparaging her good name. Plus, many
potential clients are afraid of getting on the bad side
of the Beast Lord, who just happens to be Kate's mate.

So when Atlanta's premier Master of the Dead calls
to ask for help with a vampire on the loose, Kate leaps
at the chance of some paying work. But it turns out
that this is not an isolated incident, and Kate needs to
get to the bottom of it—fast, or the city and everyone
dear to her may pay the ultimate price.

AVAILABLE FROM ACE
penguin.com

M828T0111